Esther Tusquets

Stranded

Translated with an afterword by
Susan E. Clark

Dalkey Archive Press

50205

Originally published by Editorial Lumen, 1980
© 1980 by Esther Tusquets

This translation © 1991 by Susan E. Clark
Afterword © 1991 by Susan E. Clark

Library of Congress Cataloging-in-Publication Data
Tusquets, Esther.
  [Varada tras el último naufragio. English]
  Stranded / Esther Tusquets ; translated with an afterword by Susan E. Clark.
  Translation of: Varada tras el último naufragio.
  I. Title.
PQ6670.U8V3713   1991   863'.64—dc20   91-15357
ISBN: 0-916583-83-X

First American edition

Partially funded by grants from The National Endowment for the Arts and The Illinois Arts Council.

Dalkey Archive Press
1817 N. 79th Avenue
Elmwood Park, IL 60635 USA

Printed on permanent/durable acid-free paper and bound in the United States of America.

When love departs,
death arrives.
—Mario Trejo

S he rests her head on the towel and the sun reaches her, as if filtered by the shady stalks of a miniature forest, the dense branches of a tiny jungle, so dark now—a rich brown with grey strands—stalks and branches flecked slightly with gold from the sun. Her hair used to be a warm mahogany, with honey reflections, and before that, even further down the tunnel of time, a yellow that with the summer sun became almost albino, so light that the inevitable comment from people who saw her for the first time was "whose daughter can this be? she looks German or English or Swedish," because even then she didn't seem to be from anywhere. The Spaniards identified her as Swiss and the Swiss as English and the English as Swedish or Danish, what does it matter—banal observations from adults, monotonously repeated ad nauseam and which make children look at them as if they're idiots, because the child hasn't learned yet that almost every word is said just to be said, that they talk just to talk. She didn't even suspect that with the years she would also end up resorting to these—or similar—clichés, the words empty of the magic

7

they once contained. The passing of time through my hair, she thinks now and smiles to herself; this time that has on some occasions paradoxically passed so slowly, has stretched, has given of itself to the point of improbability to be able to contain so many events, such intense sorrow, such fierce happiness, so that the months are remembered as years and the years expand into centuries, whereas on other occasions it has elapsed monotonously, senselessly, rapidly, in the large parentheses of boredom, large hollow parentheses that should seem interminable but are remembered later as the brevity of a few minutes, this time that now, and it's the first time Elia has had this idea, and she's surprised, seems to have become level, lost substance, flattened into an immobile present, deprived of perspective and relief, perhaps because the past has been rejected, annulled, denied, as if lived by someone else or by many other women at different levels. There's no future to expect either, since Elia is incapable of making plans for the days to come, incapable of picturing herself in the coming weeks, of seeing herself in the coming years, and it's because time, deprived of past and future, has caught her in the backwater of a static present. Elia smiles to herself, eyes and smiles crouched inside this improvised tent erected against the outside air, against the combined aggression of sun and wind: the towel, the sand, a piece of her arm, her long straight hair now so dark. The slow, incessant progression of the days through my hair, she thinks, a passing to light brown, to a mahogany now streaked with silver shadows, and later it will be grey, and later still maybe it will be white, not so different perhaps the final whiteness from that first pale yellow—that is if time keeps elapsing towards a future she doesn't see now, and doesn't remain flattened in immobility—the first pale pale yellow, she thinks, and smiles again. The photograph of a very very blond little girl, in a blouse and a plaid skirt, because the mother always dresses her like that, intentionally augmenting her foreign look ("whose daughter can this be?"), and the outfit is funny, like the disguise of an older girl, of a studious schoolgirl, and she even has, Elia thinks she remembers, a book held tightly under her arm, and little round glasses that dance on her nose, and nevertheless she is still very small, surely not even four years old; a little girl with a round serious face, tight braids, recently combed, held by a very young mother who is smiling, and who is separating her a little from herself to look at her better, and who holds her firmly, firmly in her arms, on top of the steps that lead to the uncovered porch encircling the house. Elia likes to, liked to, sometimes look at old photographs, old papers, and in the mess of the dresser's third drawer, among letters and recipes and bills and programs and catalogs, this photograph always appeared, and Elia has observed it for years with a special curiosity because she sees this little girl—so Anglo-Saxon, so serious, so blond —as a stranger, someone who wasn't she but whom she perhaps would have liked to resemble, and Elia wonders if at some moment in the past—long before time flattened and lost distinction—she could have been so funny, so pretty, so well-loved, and if it is above all possible that on a certain day she can't remember her mother held her up high in an affectionate gesture (her mother so maternal in this photograph), separating her a little to see her better, looking at her eye to eye and smiling proudly, in a very tender and almost helpless gesture, with a soft beauty, dreamy, melancholic, because the mother has always been, as far back as she can remember, a splendid and arrogant woman. Only in this photograph does there appear and survive the image of a very young woman, fragile, who smiles timidly to herself with a tender and private charm that in reality Elia has never seen. Was her mother really like that? Was she like that before, in a remote summer that everyone has forgotten? The two of them on top of the steps while her father took a picture of them on the porch of the summerhouse, a house that Elia can't remember either, and she doesn't even know if those stairs were actually, as she imagines, at the back of the house. It only evokes, or she invents, the smell of mold, of humidity mixed with salt water, huge dark bedrooms, a terrace where the clothes were hung to dry and where swallows nested, and she heard the baby chicks peeping madly at dawn or maybe it was the parents feeding them too much, an anxious uproar she hasn't forgotten. And the truth is she's not even sure her father took the picture and she fancies it is only because the father doesn't appear in the photograph, although when does she find even among the old junk and papers some indication that can attest to the real existence of an always absent father? And in this disconcerting scene in which the two of them, mother and daughter, acquire unsuspected, improbable, difficult-to-believe qualities, in this instant snapshot that is the sole testimony, disputable proof, of a past she never lived, Elia invents for herself—why shouldn't she since everything that appears in the photograph is itself pure fantasy?—a father with the camera in his hands, between the azaleas and the roses, making, with his jokes—his tender jokes from the foot of the steps—the woman who hears him from above, smile. What else could make the mother respond with that soft half-smile, that bashful and pleased expression which makes her seem even younger and at the same time so intimately maternal? A little silly nevertheless to have always gone through papers, inspecting drawers, turning over photographs, trying to redeem fragments of a past, or more than that, unravel the knot, know how it really was, how the others were, why things, people and lives developed the way they did, remote images in which only rarely does she recognize herself, letters written passionately by her or awaited with feverish anxiety, opened with trembling fingers, her heart in her mouth, read and reread and learned by heart, of which later she isn't able to evoke even the feeling or the occasion that motivated them. And Elia finds herself face to face with some initials, some phrases or names in code, which undoubtedly obeyed the hard task of preserving from foreign eyes a matter or an identity which must have been crucial during that period, which must have seemed unforgettable, and which after a few years' time, she can't even begin to decipher; the letters, poems, and diaries of her adolescence full of assumptions and symbols that make them as incomprehensible and foreign as the atmosphere of the family picture on the summerhouse's porch, although now, Elia thinks as she sunbathes on the beach, face down on the sand, that has also ended now, those landmarks of the past which I would repeatedly resort to in an attempt to understand or to explain myself better for him, and before putting the suitcases into the car with the cat and leaving the house, she checked notebooks and papers, scrambled through drawers, emptied shelves, leafed through photo albums, and methodically and without anger broke with all signs of her previous life, any indication that Elia had ever existed, everything that could evoke her or remind him of her—and she doesn't really know why she did it, the reason for this systematic, parsimonious, and tearless destruction. She wonders now if it was above all to punish Jorge with an abandonment so complete that it includes even what they lived together in the past, even what she lived (badly) before knowing him, or if it was perhaps a desolate attempt to erase herself from history—from his, from her own, from everyone's—and to leave behind her not even the slightest trace, as if I had never existed, she repeats, yes, as if I never existed, everything broken, burned, lost. And it's not exactly sadness she feels now, just as it wasn't hate or anger that she felt as she robbed the house of herself, this emptiness isn't called sadness. Elia buries her head in her crossed arms, still with her back to the sun, her back to the light, to the people on the beach, and she abandons herself to the warm sand—the sand doesn't burn yet at this time of the morning—and she gives up trying to fix what happened in her memory, trying to establish the order and the meaning of the events of the last two weeks, although it hasn't really been a question of events, and she's not even able to recall the words she knows they said, the gestures they made, that she made, and she's

11

even afraid of the clarifications and comments Miguel makes about certain incidents and conversations that are erased and confused and diluted into one sole sensation, unpleasant, viscous, like those dreams in which someone is chasing us and we want with all our strength to flee but our legs are paralyzed, beyond the control of our will, and our feet sink in a sticky paste that traps us, and our throat is unable to make any cry for help, any scream of terror, and in this viscous nightmare in which everything is confused, throughout these terrible days, Elia only remembers saying to herself "it doesn't matter what happens, because whatever happens summer will come and I'll be on the beach once again, hearing the interminable sound of the same sea, lying in the same sun, reduced perhaps to a creature no longer human, without the feelings of a person, without human memories, without human desires, capable only of the pleasant drowsiness of a lizard, submerged finally in a torpor without bad dreams," only a lizard in the sun, the first sun of the morning, which warms her back without burning it, while the sand lets her own warmth ascend slowly through the towel. Elia raises her head again and once more dense perfumed and dark branches spill between her eyes and the light, and it's better never to remember again that once, many times through the successive summers, there were two heads together on the sand, two bodies on the same towel, two mouths that looked for each other greedily and laughingly across the golden lattice window of hair, as a hand spread the oily cream on her shoulders, on her legs, on her back, in a delicious caress that she wanted never to end, better not to remember because the rest is all the same or almost the same, the same young girls with satiny tan skin, long legs, scanty shiny bikinis, who crisscross along the water's edge, who then plunge in with the sharp cries of young females sensitive to the cold or jealously excited, first stopping for a few moments at that point where the waves dissolve into foam and the foam splits, bubbles, recedes at the touch of the fine ankles, of the fragile knees of the still-unbroken fillies, so different nevertheless the sharp and excited voices of the girls who little by little get in the cold water—although not cold enough to justify so much excitement, Elia thinks as she smiles and hides her head again in her arms, at which the vision disappears—from the unpleasant and loud voices of the mature women, the young wives, the moms, who chatter together in groups as they exchange recipes, advice, boasts, and suntan lotion—what sense can suntan lotion have if there's no warm hand to spread it slowly from your neck down your back, pause at your waist, tickle your thighs, possessively and playfully grab the tip of your toes?—voices, these, that dissolve into a monotonous buzz from which Elia doesn't even try to capture isolated words (so sure is she of the inanity of what they are saying), and she establishes that a long time ago, a very long time ago—if it did happen in some past time—she doesn't shrink or scream or exhibit her body, tense, on tiptoe, while the boys observe her from the shore, and she doesn't have anything to do either with these young mothers who broadcast their huge fly buzz in the morning, as established in the world as they are on this beach, with their umbrellas, their hammocks, their creams, their children and, of course, their husbands, too possessive for a woman who possesses hardly anything, who is only a lizard in the sun, a sad smile, a waterfall of long, straight, dark hair, and it's the same children too, or very similar to the ones before, who race around and splash and play ball and cover her with sand—she's never gotten over the disgust she feels for sand on a wet body—the little children who wrinkle and dirty her towel although they seem absolutely decided not to notice, the same way they heroically and tenaciously resist the insistent calls from these women, the young wives and mothers, who have everything, who fill their mouths with possessive adjectives like sickeningly rich and oozing strawberry candy, and who repeatedly voice the names, the impossible nicknames, without any need to, just because, for the mere pleasure of leaving proof and making their property worth something, Elia says fastidiously, Elia the dispossessed, Elia the loner, she who has been exiled from the flow of time, she who lies in the sand and doesn't even hate a past she wishes to remember, a future she can assume, only parentheses—that she would like to be as long as life itself—of a lizard in the sun. The mothers (and suddenly Elia the memoryless remembers the white room in the clinic, the crucifix on the bare wall, the windows flooded with sun, the flowers, so many flowers that their fragrance makes her dizzy and they don't fit in the room and there's no space in the chapel altar and they wither lined up against the wall, the silly smiling faces, the kisses, the congratulations, everyone, doctors, nuns, nurses, and even friends, stubbornly calling her mom, a mom that should flatter her and that never-theless makes her uncomfortable, perhaps it's just that it embarrasses her, or that in spite of the interminable months of pregnancy, motherhood seems so unexpected and foreign, and she would also feel very bad and very frightened if Jorge weren't there at her side, happy, immeasurably happy, "he's a beautiful little creature, Elia, looking at him I've thought that now I've done everything I had to do in this life, that now I can die"), the mothers calling, just because, some children who've learned not to listen to them, not even hear them, while the smallest children splash on the shore with the little shovel and bucket or cry, their necks in the hands of a father who forces them into the water, and the children, terrified, latch onto the arms, the nude torsos, and try to climb up onto the shoulders and thus wiggle out of the inevitable contact with the water. Elia wonders what these fathers are doing, what they think they're achieving, and she thinks: they're teaching them fear, because perhaps for these very small chil-dren fear didn't exist or hardly existed or existed differently, but there are always adults ready to teach us fear as they pretend to predispose us to audacity, they teach us fear and they situate it if they can in the center of our lives, next to guilt. And the girls get in the water amid screams and laughter, and the boys observe them and then, when they finally can't touch bottom anymore and swim away from the shore, the boys hurry in headfirst and reach them and sail past them in an impeccable crawl (they must have seen, Elia thinks, the Tarzan movies, and probably when they stop far from the shore and laugh and whisper together and splash and attack each other, they're repeating "Me Tarzan, you Jane," but no, surely not, decides Elia the defrauded, Elia the unhappy, surely they're saying something more banal, more malicious and ugly). The little children run across the sand, climb into the boats, splash with water and sand, make a nuisance with the ball, and the group of mothers, mothers par excellence, Elia says to herself, motherhood as a way of being in the world, chatters like a diverse assembly of magpies—what do magpies discuss in their assemblies?—and the husbands, the fathers, instead of kissing greedy mouths through dense branches of the blonder or darker forest, instead of spreading creams and lotions in long interminable caresses, from the tip of the toes to the back of the neck, train the smallest ones in the ocean, or also swim in an impeccable crawl, looking askance at the young girls, perhaps as if they, so mature, were playing at being Tarzan, and some of the smaller children are afraid but it doesn't matter, they'll get over it, and all of them are, in short, occupying the exact place that corresponds to them (the exact place that has been assigned to them in the complete harmony of the universe, remembers Elia the scoffing, Elia the disbelieving, in their classes responsible for forming national spirit), to such a point that the generations succeed each other, the roles change but the scene on the beach remains almost unaltered. Only she is, it seems, and perhaps has been for a long time, a long time before she discovered and accepted it, out of place. Perhaps she's even become invisible, because the truth is the men don't look at her, the women don't pay any attention to her, and the children cross over her body with a clean jump—pouring trickles of sand and dirty water over her and her towel (finally she can apply a possessive) without presenting any signs of wanting to apologize, not even seeing her. That would be a beautiful end, thinks Elia, a pretty way to end, stretched out here, in the warm sun of the July morning, like a lazy lizard, a very old and perhaps wise lizard, so wise that it's forgotten everything, and aspires only to one day become, its scarcely vegetable existence lost, a beautiful green stone.

Pablo straightens up a few moments in the stern of the boat, and hurls himself cleanly into the water, headfirst, stays underwater only one or two seconds and surfaces with long strokes, the hard splash of a perfect style, spectacular, as if in a competition, a shining brown silhouette moving swiftly and agilely away—without once turning his head to look at them or wave—leaving a trail of foam behind him, him too—thinks Eva and she searches Elia's eyes for the wink of an accomplice, but Elia doesn't look at her, absorbed today in her own vacant staring—knowing he's being observed, sure that the two women will be attentive to or amused by his splashing until he becomes a tiny point far off, Pablo re-creating his image of a sportsman, still young, still strong, still beautiful, perhaps he too miming the gestures of a Tarzan act —a mature Tarzan—which reminds Eva of what Elia said about the excitement of the fifteen-year-old girls on the beach, the sharp ridiculous cries (Elia, always exaggerating, described them as obscene), their arms hugging their breasts, around their torsos, their waists, in a vain gesture of protection, and their bodies tense, their breath held a few moments, as if they wanted to delay the meeting with the cold water, while the boys watch them, competent, from the shore, privileged first-row spectators, or rather spectators in the wings since they too will be coming out on stage in no time, erasing their condescending winks, their pleased smiles, in order to throw themselves in headfirst (and without vacillating) after the girls, and reach them in a very short time—the girls protest against these brutes, who have flooded them with their kicks, flooded their hair, their eyes, their noses with water and foam

—and then stop and wait for the girls, until they all join together in a luminous dancing circle, moving backward and forward slowly, only the brief movement of hands extended to remain afloat, amid long dark and golden heads of hair that drift and sway like algae, short chunks of hair crowned with foam, amid screams and laughter and words that become lost in the only beam of sun of a morning at the beginning of July, almost always just as aware, all of us, of ourselves, thinks Eva. Elia's right about that, although she doesn't understand why this innocent vanity has to seem so bad to her, a narcissistic awareness of our own body, more intense in adolescence, in the first years of youth, the enthusiasm and unction we put into interpreting our own character never recuperated in adulthood, perhaps because, as Elia indicated, we begin to find it monotonous and tiresome and even annoying, and it's so difficult—she says—to keep taking ourselves seriously with the passing of the years (and it seems to Eva that, when she said these words, Elia looked at her and smiled dubiously, accusing her perhaps of being an exception, of still taking herself very seriously). Nevertheless maybe we are always in a certain way dependent on this audience that observes us from the eyes of others, and in front of which our bodies and our attitudes and our voices become a show, and it's impossible to conjecture if, were Pablo alone in the boat, like on those early mornings when he goes fishing, Elia and she too lazy to accompany him, he would hurl himself from the stern with such a swift and precise pirouette, so beautiful, and if he would take off swimming in this impeccable style, as if he were trying to break a record in the Olympic pool (and here Elia also almost always makes a scoffing expression, although today she hasn't, how strange she is, so absorbed, so with-drawn). Most likely they wouldn't take off their bikinis either with those vaporous and languid gestures, almost purring with pleasure, lying down then on the sides of the boat with the voluptuous slowness of sleeping cats, lazy, stretching, like pampered kittens, and slightly naughty, in spite of having

17

been friends, the four of them, for such a long time, and there's no room anymore for seduction or coquetry between people who know each other so well, who know everything about each other, the men as well, and not just the women, friends since youth, since college, even though Elia studied humanities and she law, but in those days their classrooms opened onto a common patio, sharing the same basement bar with its rigorous metaphysical exams, its literary movements, its conspiracies and proselytizing, Letters and Law both participating in the same movie clubs, theater groups. Elia always laughingly comments that she had noticed Eva long before they formally met, and that she remembers her exactly the way she saw her on many mornings, in the middle of the patio, next to the pond where multicolored fish agonized slowly (only Elia, thinks Eva, would think of fish suffering), heatedly giving a speech among a group of classmates, her fury so genuine and so beautiful, Elia always repeats when she tells others about those first encounters. Elia insists that when she went up to them on various mornings to listen, she can't remember any of Eva's or the others' words, she doesn't even remember what the subject of the discussion was, because what caught her attention and made her stop in the patio, approach the pond, overcoming the anguish that the fish confined in that miserable dirty water caused her, were those enormous dark eyes—excessive eyes—shining with a fury that was foreign to her, incapable, Elia, of feeling so much anger and rage (although remembering Elia's explanation now, as they remain mute today in the boat, Eva repeats to herself that that's not true, and that the other woman has her own terrible forms of cunning fury and audacity), Eva challenging and magnificent as she harangues her classmates in the patio, but what especially caught her attention and induced her to go nearer (because in those days, thinks Eva, Elia participated very little in the scuffles, in the politics of the hallways and cloisters, from laziness or indifference or that fatigue which always seems to overcome her faced with the efforts

18

she considers of a confused motivation and doubtful profit), what then would have attracted Elia on those first mornings at the university was, according to what she has said so many times, that dense voice, dark, tight, bubbling over like lava, a voice capable, and here Eva thinks it must be true, since so many other people tell her the same thing, of making people stand up, of dragging classmates to the auditorium or to the dean's office or the demonstration in the street, although it's true on the other hand that Elia has always mythified her and keeps mythifying her, because Eva remembers herself as so afraid every time the cops entered the university or they went out into the street, but she recognizes that these first memories of the other woman make her feel deeply flattered, especially now when those times are so far away. And on that first remote day or on various and successive similar days, she didn't notice, of course, an astounded Elia (sure there wasn't a reserved sneer on her face along with admiration? those airs Elia puts on so many times of a little old lady, a grandmother who's seen it all, and which she put on much more often in her youth), who observed her mingled in with the other students, a skinny girl, surely divided between her ironic smile and her surprised look, and who would ask her a short time later through a friend (in spite of her never having been involved in theater) to interpret the protagonist's role in a play she had just finished and which was already being rehearsed, although it was never put on—Eva doesn't remember now if because of someone's prohibiting it, or lack of funds, or because they closed the university. And the first memory she has of Elia is of a young girl, insignificant, whose dull blue eyes were fixed on her as she went through the audition they'd asked of her and, among the other actors who already knew their roles, she read her character's interventions with script in hand, and she hadn't even had time to read it before and she wasn't at all attracted by that pale girl but rather by the script that she was discovering, astonished, as she read it out loud in the middle of the stage, a script whose ease, whose rotund insolence—

now Eva remembers that they were on the radio, two or three days before the presentation, and Elia read a few words in her low, irretrievably shy voice and then the actors read a few scenes, and the calls from indignant listeners began, the incredible ripping of costumes, the director's fury because nobody at the station had verified what it was about before the voices sounded through the microphone and it was too late now to stop them, and at the same time the incessant phone calls had begun at their parents' houses, the conspiracy of grandmothers and aunts, what's the world coming to, and that's why, of course, the presentation had to be canceled, and Elia passive, feigning indifference, as if she had foreseen what was going to happen from the beginning and nothing really mattered, a passivity that made her even more furious than the prohibition and she yelled and protested and raved until she was hoarse, at home, at the station, at the university—a script, then, whose insolence she couldn't in the least relate to that shadow down there, in the rows of shadows, as if lost, Elia, so skinny and so grey, between the rows of seats, very strange, Eva thinks now, as she lies on her back on the hot wood of the anchored boat rocking her gently, the two women alone as on so many other occasions, while Pablo swims away amid the foam, with his figure of a mature Tarzan, of a primitive hunter, in pursuit of a legendary lobster, an impossible fish which the two women—even Elia, so inclined to fantasy— stopped believing in after the second or third summer, it's funny that Elia would retain only the image of some very black excessive eyes, a dense serious voice, the voice for Elia deprived of any meaning and even any words, whereas she, Eva, remembers in the very first place the insolence and audacity of a few sentences that passed from the paper to her mouth as she, incredulous, discovered them, and which she couldn't harmonize or fit with the character of that little insignificant girl, bashful—ugly, Elia adds when they remember together, but that's not true, she wasn't ugly, she just had a formal air about her, like a studious schoolgirl, and she could have been confused with any upper-middle-class goody-two-shoes, aspirant to the blue sash of the Daughters of Mary, eager collector of First Fridays, and one would be frozen upon reading for the first time those rotund sentences, much more corrosive perhaps, more dangerous than her own student harangues in the university patio—with whom after the rehearsals she was going to become (because they elected her unanimously for the role) closer and closer friends, in a never-interrupted relationship, because their lives have developed in a somewhat parallel fashion, although different. And now Eva sits up, looks for a cigarette and begins talking at the very point at which her reflections had brought her, as if, because they're friends, the other woman should guess what thoughts led up to it. "How strange that, being as different as we are, different in almost everything, we've been friends for years," although it's not exactly friends and she should have expressed it more precisely, something like accomplices, pals in the same flow of time, as if they had, side by side, constructed disparate but perhaps equivalent lives, and Elia looks at her unsurprised, sits up and lights her cigarette for her, as she too lights one. "I don't think we're very different, we think exactly the same about almost everything, the only difference is our style," and she laughs in that strange way Eva likes so much, a quiet, hoarse and tickling laugh, and it's true they've elaborated and gone over together a shared thought for years, and only with Elia—yes, much more even than with Pablo or with the other men—she can talk freely, easily, without the need for any preamble or the fear of misunderstanding, as if they both possessed a secret key, an old code established between them (like the gestural language with which children taking tests exchange information), keys and codes that enable them to discern the exact value, the precise scope of each word and each gesture, and Pablo, and even Jorge—who is, in any case, more like them—sometimes stare at them, disoriented and then comically offended, falsely hurt by the marginality to which she and Elia relegate them, because—

leaving a theater production, a dinner with friends, faced with any comment, banal for the men—the two women understand each other with a brief exchange, quick sentences, sometimes only words, interlaced, and they erect in very few moments an enthusiasm or a rejection or a criticism that leaves the two men behind, excluded, perhaps because, more given to long rigorous examinations, more moderate and at the same time more prolific, they don't understand what they call the women's precipitation, their female rashness that causes questionable, immoderate judgments, and which the men can't arrive at anyway in such an immediate and intuitive way. And only when she's with other people, Eva realizes completely to what point it's difficult to express oneself with precision and be correctly interpreted and understood, and she almost always feels for a few moments—hearing a piece of news, something that happened and caught them unawares—regret that Elia isn't there to elaborate a shared analysis or criticism, and she phones Elia, runs to Elia, "and it's not even that we love each other so much, it's that I've come to a point where I can go over certain experiences only with you," and Elia nods, "we've spent a lot of years going over things together . . ." and she stands up, sits on the starboard, dangling her feet in the water, shakes them, splashes, clinging to the wooden rim of the boat, her eyes half closed, her head raised to the sun, and lets herself fall in gently, almost noiselessly, in such a gentle way that she doesn't wet her hair, or hardly her shoulders, and swims away slowly, as her long dark hair sways and moves on her golden back, reaching almost to her narrow pale buttocks (not even in August would Elia get really tan): Elia, the sun's enemy, the one who escapes the tumult and hates noise, now advances through the sea, with such slow, gentle movements that they almost don't alter the blue surface, the immobile surface, as united with the water as a marine creature—never has Eva been able to fantasize her as fire or earth, always as water—because for Elia swimming in this ocean has nothing to do with exercise or sport (and Eva remembers Pablo with his Olympic crawl, with his perfect style, apt for the crowds of spectators who line up next to the Olympic pool), it's a ritual gesture, an invocation, the communion perhaps of an aquatic and sacrilegious woman. So Elia swims away, very quietly and gently, although her rushing in from the boat was so sudden that she didn't have time to follow her, only an excrescence, a prolongation of this immobile, silent ocean, which conceals, as she does, the deep calm ocean, the quiet ocean of the first days of July.

She swims away from the boat with slow strokes, feeling how the water breaks and collides against her body, always very cold here in the refuge among the rocks where it's so immobile and where it's so deep, where it acquires a darker but resplendent green, like those crystals she used to find on the beach as a girl, and to which she would attribute strange sources, mysterious underwater origins, and which turned out to be only—someone she doesn't remember explained it to her one day of her childhood—pieces of green bottles polished and rounded by the sea, the water still colder these first days of the summer than what it will be in August or even in September, and Elia feels how the sea breaks against her breasts which have become suddenly tight and hard and turgid, with the nipples slightly sore, she feels how the water then slides, divided, under her body, along her flanks and her stomach, until it disappears amid the rhythmic and brief movement of her legs and closes behind her in a newly immobile surface, and Elia swims now with her eyes half closed, bothered perhaps by the light's excessive intensity, by the midday sun, and she knows that her movement of rushing into the water today was so unpremeditated and sudden—without the long doubting and laziness and laments that precede swimming on other days, because the two women play at being indolent and anyone who heard them without knowing them could even believe they were finally going to stay in the boat, without even suspecting that in both women, so different, there exists the same passion for the sea, and that the vacillating and complaining are just another game—that Eva didn't have time to follow her, to be able to swim together in a dialogue uninterrupted by the passage from the boat into the water, both of them as talkative on the marine route as they can be on their strolls through the streets or along the beach, their talk more intimate many times here, because the ocean isolates them, protects them, encloses them in a redoubt as propitious to secrets as is sometimes the inside of a car advancing at night along the deserted highway through fields and sleeping towns, and although their conversation continues as they get in the water—barely interrupted by the brief parentheses of complaints and comments about the cold—it becomes many times even more intimate, more profound, in this solitude for two that the morning sea creates for them. But today Elia has decided suddenly, and she knows that Eva must be dubious, seeing her swim away and wondering again for the thousandth time in the last twenty-four hours what the hell is wrong with her, if the problems with Jorge are that serious, surprised above all by the fact that she, very reserved and private with others but communicative when the two of them are alone together, has been so stubbornly quiet, has remained so obstinately mute since she arrived in the town and at the house the day before yesterday, with her suitcases full of heterogeneous things and with her cat Musli—so old now that she has survived for the last two or three years in a semblance of an almost vegetable existence—and now Elia, as she glides away through the calm water, thinks that Eva has waited, through all the hours that have passed since her arrival, for her to talk, to tell her, to explain why she has come to move alone into the summer tower they've shared for so many summers, with strange baggage, full of clothes unwearable in this town, useless in summer, but without Jorge, and without saying anything at all either about Jorge's absence, because through the years both of them have had disappointments and difficulties and always, from the day they met in the university, they've told each other everything or almost everything, and maybe Eva has already guessed or is starting to sense that what's happening now is different, and maybe that's why she's renounced following her into the water and lets her swim away without attempting to reach her, resigned to waiting for her return, to waiting until Elia on her own impulse talks, and Elia wonders how she'll manage to tell her —because one day sooner or later during this summer which used to always be a foursome and now will be, it seems, a threesome, she'll have to start talking, she'll have to try explaining to them—how will she manage to tell Eva of this emptiness that has no bottom, this lethal numbness of thought, which reduces her to an almost vegetable existence, like her cat's, this profound yearning to turn into a stone, an obscure urge to become a lizard, that began a few days ago, or perhaps a few weeks, she can't specify, because time also has changed and acquired different qualities, and this too will have to be explained sooner or later to Eva, and she won't know how to do that either, because how can she tell Eva, how can she tell anyone, even Miguel, without it sounding horribly false, grotesquely affected and pedantic and literary, that time has suddenly become, in some instant during the last few days or last few weeks that she's not capable of specifying, static and immobile and flat, and that she's navigating through it—as through the sea—without altering the surface, and that's perhaps because she's actually not advancing but rather keeping quiet and immobile too, as if time had exiled her from its flow and she had been retained finally on the shore, stranded on the outside of things, at a standstill amid the remains of the shipwreck, expelled from time, vomited from time and from life which continue to glide by at her side but without picking her up, since there's no past that she can identify or remember as her own, nor is there any individual future to dream about? Because for a few days or perhaps a few weeks, days populated by noise and fury, she has thought only of this: arrive in this town with her old cat, and not feel anything anymore, only

the heat from the sand or from the wood of the boat that
ascends slowly through her skin, only this light cold caress of
the water, and it's going to be very difficult to be able to
explain to Eva, so filled with realities, so obsessed with the
truth—even though she knows on the other hand that she
won't feel like telling anyone but Eva, if she tells—this urge
of hers to become a stone or a lizard, her entire being concen-
trated on silencing memories, on banishing images, because
they explode suddenly in her empty mind with the intensity
of the sudden discharges which precede storms in the night,
images that are now intolerable, images that cause a degree of
pain she's afraid she isn't capable of bearing, such cruel and
bloodthirsty tigers the memories that are sleeping and crouch-
ing in the dark corners of her soul, and she sees, as if in a blaze,
herself standing in front of the four legendary monarchs, and
feels Jorge's arm around her waist, her shoulders, and his
mouth crawling greedily, insatiably, along her ears, her cheeks,
her throat, kissing her intimately on the lips, murmuring in
her ear consoling promises of return, establishing secret ties
of complicity between them and the mineral monarchs, and
Elia puts her hand forward and slides it along the cold,
smooth, soft stone, in a farewell she wants to be only temporary, because always, always, the two of them will come back
to this plaza, and she asks him to promise out loud, to promise
to her and to himself, to destiny, to the tetrarchs, because Elia
still believes—she's never stopped believing—in the magical
value of words, conjuring or modeling reality, Elia believes
that perhaps chimeras and dreams can acquire sudden con-
sistency and body when they are poured into words and she
also loves in Jorge, among all the other possibilities, the image
of the great Magus, the Wizard, the amazing Magician's ap-
prentice, he who can at night, when she wakes up still crying,
so horribly frightened, because she's had a bad dream, she's
dreamed perhaps that we humans are all condemned to die and
that the two of them will also have to die someday, and that
absurd nightmare, that nonsensical and grotesque nightmare

—how could something so atrocious be true?—threatens to survive when she wakes up, Jorge can then scare away the ghosts, Jorge is then above all he who can lull her to sleep in his arms, like a little girl, and swear to her a thousand times that they're both immortal, that she's never going to have to die, who could have invented such an evil, who could have continued such foolishness, and that's why Elia asks him to promise out loud, and he laughs, and calls her my little girl, my little one, my scaredy cat, my silly girl, my sheika, my silly princess, and kisses her again on the lips, the throat, the tip of the nose, the forehead, strokes her hair, and takes the hair out of her eyes, and finally, with comic seriousness, but perhaps he too, Elia fantasizes, believing in exorcisms, believing that by love's work and grace he has become omnipotent, he rests his right hand successively on the four kings' heads and promises them, promises Elia, "I swear, in the name of love, that we will always come back to this plaza," and if Elia had to tell Eva about what's happening—and she knows that sooner or later she will have to try, on some day of this same summer that is now beginning—she would have to start with a sentence as silly as "look, time stopped and flattened and became level, vomited me onto the shore, and, you know, I have the profound desire to become a stone or a lizard," because that's it or something very much like it, the desire to be a lizard getting drowsy in the sun, an eagerness to be a moss-covered rock or a piece of green glass spit from the ocean onto the beach, and then she would continue, probably tearless, because this bitterness is beyond laments and crying, "what's happening is that I'm never going back to Venice," and she knows this wouldn't justly express the magnitude of the catastrophe to others, and nevertheless Eva's questions wouldn't make much sense, and surely the possibilities for an answer would be very slight. Eva the realist, Eva the pragmatist and well-intentioned, so anxious to be useful and to help her, an Eva irritated perhaps by those vague remarks typical of an adolescent (never has Eva understood that she, so intelligent in some

27

aspects, so effective sometimes in her writing, can express herself like an idiot), and anxious to escape these morbid expansions, these metaphors that explain nothing, what she would surely qualify as a recourse to evade the truth and not establish—she'll use these words or very similar ones—what the real problems are and how she can face them and combat them, very very few possibilities of an answer are Eva's questions going to have, Eva the pragmatic, Eva the fighter, in her eagerness to get directly and as soon as possible to the bottom of the matter—have you fought with Jorge? Is what's happened between you really so serious this time? Is there another woman?—Eva will surely ask this, and yes, there certainly was a lot of noise and a lot of fury this spring, but Elia won't be capable of determining if there actually were fights or not, and it doesn't matter at all now—it never did— if there are other women in Jorge's life, it's something very different, that she won't know how to explain any other way, only with these appraisals that seem so foggy to Eva and which are nevertheless for Elia the closest thing to reality, she'll never again be able to go back to Venice, because she won't go there with Jorge, and Venice without him is un- imaginable, has no place in the world, has been erased from all maps, has lengthened the list of imaginary places, and lightning images flash through the dense stupor of Elia's mind, causing her, in their brevity, a pain, such a level of pain that she won't know how to express it when she talks to Eva or even if one day she tried to write about it, and again she has the instantaneous burning vision of the two of them standing in front of the tetrarchs' corner, about to leave in the steam- boat that will take them to the airport terminal, once again about to leave the city, the two of them standing there, caressing with their fingertips the profiles of these distant monarchs' faces about whom they really know nothing, following again the border of their robes, making or demand- ing naive ritual oaths and favorable invocations above their heads, amid kisses and laughter and murmuring—my sheika, my little witch, my silly princess—or the fleeting vision of the two of them walking hand in hand through rarely used side streets, outside the usual tourist route, narrow, humid, silent streets, interrupted and prolonged by the bridges that cross the canals, streets where their footsteps resound with a false noise and where the sun hardly ever reaches, and one day, at the end of one of these streets, they happen onto a small unknown square, full of pots and flowering azaleas, and there is a blue and white striped cloth over the marble tables, all empty because it's still very early for lunch, and sitting at the back door of the restaurant, a little blond girl plays with a cat, and how can she make Eva, or anyone, understand that that faraway day the flowering azaleas, the pale May sun (which doesn't reach the narrow side streets and bursts unexpectedly onto the little square), the tables under the blue and white cloth, the girl with the cat, make up for both of them, without a single word interceding, an instant of perfect happiness, so intense that she felt again almost dizzy, remotely sick, like the day Jorge and she met, and she leaned on Jorge because her knees were shaking, one of those moments for which Elia forced herself for years to keep on living each morning one more day, before knowing Jorge because she had a premonition of them, although she couldn't ever imagine they would be so beautiful, after meeting him because she knew they were possible and she, avaricious, accumulated them, those scarce but certain moments of harmony when we fancy we are perhaps capable of accepting this world the way it is and even of reconciling ourselves with the inevitability of death, because only on the highest peaks of love and happiness—which for Elia are reduced to one indivisible reality—death seems tolerable to us and becomes an almost friendly shadow? And Elia knows she won't be able to explain anything to Eva if she can't manage to transmit to her the sensation of that afternoon in Venice—you were happy in Venice, I know, but now, what the hell is going on with you two?—if Eva entrenches herself in her irritating simplicity, which can't be

29

completely sincere, which is more like a method, a weapon—simplicity—that Eva brandishes untiringly against what she calls, and here she coincides with Jorge, "her excess of literature," Elia won't be able to explain anything this time if the other woman insists on the same questions, because it's not a matter of having fought, or of other women existing in Jorge's life, who may very well exist, but rather of something much more terrible, infinitely more irreparable, something which has brought her to this being stranded on the shore, amid the remains of the wreck, exiled from the flow of time, something which reduces her to an obstinate longing to become a stone or a lizard, something she can't explain, just as she can't explain with precise sentences, with concrete reasons, that sensation of total emptiness which invades her as she advances slowly through an intensely blue, profoundly calm, sea, that sensation of a forever irreparable absence, which divests her even of a past, the desolate bitterness of knowing that she'll never again go back to Venice and that both of them have cunningly betrayed their oath to the tetrarchs.

From the underwater corner where he's on the watch, between the rocks where—in spite of the two women's incredulity—a lobster or a huge fish could well be hiding, Pablo sees Elia's headless silhouette, from the tip of her feet moving rhythmically, impelling the water, to the long dark hair floating around her shoulders, hiding her throat, he sees the small breasts which the ocean's pressure maintains now unusually high—the breasts of an adolescent caryatid on the bow's figurehead—the narrow-hipped flanks, the long thighs of a boy, and Pablo feels, as he ascends to the surface and breathes deep mouthfuls of air and sees Elia's head moving away amid the foam, that tender disturbance that overwhelms him so many times when he looks at her, the woman so helpless, so awkward and long-legged and skinny, an Elia who now, since she arrived the day before yesterday at the summerhouse where they'd been waiting a few days for her, with this zombielike air, as if she were returning from the kingdom of the dead or had perhaps forgotten all of a sudden—in these few days, the two or three weeks they've spent without seeing each other, talking only on the phone, and it's impossible to talk to Elia on the phone beyond setting a date or asking her how she is—her exact place among things (if she ever knew), she is even more like, more now than at any other moment during the past years, the timid and unsociable girl who would accompany Eva like a shadow, who followed her like a shadow, a shadow that seemed to extract from the other woman her corporality, breathe from her air, shine with her light, a girl who, more than twenty years old, looked hardly seventeen and who must never have possessed, even at seventeen, the splendor of youth, that magic moment, so fleeting, which gives many women a radiance they'll never find again as an adult, the opening of a flower, the first round and rotund unrepeatable ripeness of a fruit, a girl who got rattled in the presence of strangers, absurdly uncomfortable and frightened before the outside world, incapable of exceeding the framework of the strictest intimacy, of the deep and close friendship with very few friends, whom she needed, she would say, to live, incapable even of signaling to the waiter that she had ordered sole with orange and not steak with green pepper, and then quickly gulping down the bloody meat, for which she feels an atrocious disgust, and blushing as she anticipates that someone at the next table may claim the steak as his or that Eva can interrupt her impassioned speech, the heated discussion, at any moment, to look at her surprised, and tell her, as astonished as concluding, "But you ordered sole! Why are you eating that? I'm going to call the waiter right now and he'll change it," Elia afraid to bother, to be conspicuous, to be the center of everyone's looks, to create situations that she fancies are embarrassing and wouldn't be for anyone but her, without the nerve to protest when waiters make a mistake in restaurants, when someone cuts in front of her in a line, when they don't wait on her in a store, when they block her on the

31

freeway, and ashamed later for not having dared protest, or bursting sometimes into those rages shy people have, always inappropriate and excessive, always at the wrong time, which leave her much more embarrassed, much worse, with a fear it seems of not being understood or not being accepted, sliding awkwardly and clumsily between the tables in the half-light —the day they met, the day he met both women—as if her limbs obeyed a rudimentary mechanism, hardly sophisticated, or as if she suffered from an excess of legs and arms—Elia only light, only sure and harmonious when she moves, as now, through the water—staggering hurriedly, colliding with the chairs, threatening to knock down the tables and overturn glasses—intercepting the waiters' steps, responding with a gloomy voice and a forced smile to the people who greet her and whom she hardly ever manages to recognize and who will blame her later for being stuck-up and uncongenial and even impolite, and to top it off, carrying an abandoned kitten in her arms that night (a kitten she'd just found and who would become Musli the she-cat, the old cat today almost a vegetable, who sleeps all day and all night as if in an apprentice-ship to the ultimate and definitive sleep, as they look at her apprehensively and afraid, wondering what they'll feel, what Elia will feel especially, when this animal dies, whose life has spanned the years of her youth, everyone's youth), offering an almost pathetic image of confusion and helplessness, and finally sitting down, after the difficult and interminable cir-cumnavigation between waiters, dancers and tables, next to them, and the others—including Eva—haven't even noticed her presence until now, and aren't aware in the least that she's panting, blushing to her ears and tenaciously mute—on days like those, Eva's efforts to bring her out of her silence and make her take an active part in the get-together were useless —Elia smoking cigarette after cigarette—and it turned out later that she didn't like to smoke—stroking the kitten who's mewing on her knees and sticking its claws into her clothing and licking her hands, listening to the music—jazz—as if her life depended on every note (and they would find out later that Elia is deaf to any kind of music, for any music other than words), and already on that first night so many years ago, although fascinated very quickly by Eva of the beautiful eyes, of the splendorous body, Eva the passionate, Eva the locquacious, Eva the intrepid, he did notice that girl who followed her, who had ventured out to follow her, crossing—and with so much toil—the packed summer disco, who had sat, distrustful, at this table of strangers—who luckily for her didn't pay the slightest bit of attention to her—and who listened to them —to the people as well as to the music—with the utmost attention, without intervening or saying a word, but who had in her eyes, in the corner of her mouth, a hardened irony, a touch of frolicking laughter, which led one to guess, which made Pablo suppose, that the girl could be brilliant and ingenious and fun in smaller groups, in more intimate circles, and he was certain that—however much in a way they intimidated her—a part of Elia had distanced itself already, catapulted to myriads of light years away, and from there, was analyzing them and judging them, curious this division of Elia which he noticed already then, disconcerting the speed with which the shy girl of then transmuted without them even noticing into a judge who relentlessly—more rigid many times than Eva the supposed doctrinairian—made decisions and condemned them or condemned herself, Elia the helpless, yes, but at certain times Elia the relentless. And on that first night of summer, so many years ago, perhaps fifteen or sixteen, Pablo can't specify exactly now, and although he had met Eva on that very day, just a few hours before, and was already starting to feel attracted in an inevitable way (it was very hot in the closed place, the jammed place, and they went out to the plaza the two of them without waiting for their friends, intending to get some fresh air—leaving Elia abandoned among strangers, because only later, as they strolled down the Ramblas towards the sea, Eva remembered they'd forgotten her friend inside, and lamented, between laughter

33

and earnestness, the horribly bad time she must be having, sitting there among unknown people, without having the nerve perhaps to just get up and disappear—and they passed the monument to Columbus and further, on the dark pier, in front of the trembling silhouettes of the shadowed boats, he confessed to what point he felt alone and sad and trapped, and he even recited some poems from memory, poems he'd been writing for another girl throughout the winter, and Eva listened attentively and seemed capable of understanding everything, and then she laughed, although she told him his verses weren't bad at all and that he should, above all other commitments, keep writing, but she laughed anyway, and he couldn't understand what there was in his confessions or in his verses that could provoke laughter, although it was in a way a liberating laugh, banisher of ghosts, like a mouthful of fresh air in his limited and confined and strange universe, and Eva was so beautiful—yes, she was splendorous and bursting like a fruit, prodigiously warm and fruitlike, with that golden skin of women who tan easily and those very white teeth that accentuated her remotely exotic and tropical air—so beautiful on the summer night, with her back and shoulders naked, only some very thin straps, two brief and satiny straps, making a cross on her back, and the black dress fell so beautifully, dense and tight, clinging to her body, and Eva had the most beautiful and biggest and darkest eyes Pablo had ever seen in his life, and perhaps because of that—because of the depth of her eyes—the girl seemed capable of understanding every-thing, and Eva bubbled over, shone brightly, exulted, choked on laughter and words, Eva purred, Eva hummed, affectionate and mocking and happy, Eva listened to him with her head a little to one side, her shiny black hair falling on her shoulders, her mouth open, her eyes glistening, and then she burst into a warm laughter, and to him, who a few hours before was certain he'd come to the end, that desolate certainty of the irremediable one only gets when one is twenty years old, who had been dragged along by friends this Saturday night to bars

34

and discos and who had not abandoned his aura of the romantic hero crushed by the sorrow of some important and unhappy loves, it seemed suddenly, standing next to her there on the pier, that the situation could easily be reversed, that many things could be recuperated and conquered if Eva listened to him and understood him, it seemed to him that the old ghosts were backing away from the girl's audacious look, her impudent laughter, and that happiness could have been waiting for him without his discovering it around the corner, and that right there he could start a new life if he gave himself up to it without too much resistance, if he let himself be pulled along by this girl, so strange, much more vital, much happier, much much freer than all the other women Pablo had met until then, because Eva offered immediately to accompany him to his apartment and she even made a little fun of him when he, conventional and scandalized, invited her to have a few drinks somewhere, "do you think the engagement has been too short?" and was therefore absolutely unclassifiable according to the norms of those repressive dark times, impossible to line her up among the choruses of virgins or in the supposed covens of prostitutes), but even though he met both of them the same day, and his interest was overwhelmed, his attention absorbed, by Eva, by her black eyes, by her golden skin, by her contagious, crazy laughter, by the spontaneity and strength and happiness of a young animal she showed, even on that first night Elia the pale and foggy, Elia the skinny and timid, became—not because of all that, and he intuited it right away, less unusual and even a transgressor—an important part of his life, both of them in a way merged into an indivisible and unique reality, perhaps because they were such close friends when he found them, on the night of that remote summer sixteen or seventeen years ago already, and perhaps the coincidence of having met them almost at the same time helped, complementary sides, although opposite, of the same coin, Eva solar and powerful, Eva source of life, Elia lunar and perhaps secretly bewitching and playful, and when Pablo says laughingly "my women," this possessive doesn't at all include—and they know it—the different women he has frequented and possessed during his life, who have been at some moment his lovers, when he thinks silently "my women," he's referring to the two of them, even though it's true he's never gone to bed with Elia, but he has strangely assigned them an opposing and shared love, or perhaps his deep affection for Elia, this emotion he feels watching her swim across the water's surface, her body even more helpless naked, with the abandonment of an exiled water nymph—a loving and vanquished nymph—who is finally returning to her lost world, impossible to know if seriously wounded, perhaps this love is due in part to the fact that both of them—Elia and Pablo—are accomplices in an identical devotion, extinguished planets in a solar system in which Eva bestows upon them and shares with them her own light, both of them united perhaps in the pride of admiring her, in the eagerness to understand and second her, in the vague fear of losing her, in the sorrow of never feeling her—impossible to know if Elia experiences it this way or if he's only imagining—entirely familiar and theirs, Eva never wholly given to her friend or to her lover, and it's undoubtedly this dark complicity of two followers of the same religion, of high priest and priestess of a fascinating and sometimes arbitrary cult, what united them and has made them love each other through the years with that fixed and intimate, incestuous and sacrilegious love.

For a while, she doesn't know exactly how long, since time has altered its course, or has expelled her onto the shore, or, in any case, she has escaped its monotonous, homogeneous, regular succession of seconds and minutes, and before or after don't have much sense for a woman who has banished her memories and is trying to murder hope, and is not even capable of establishing the order in which the events over the last weeks took place, but the truth is she's been sitting for a long time in front of the typewriter, a blank piece of paper in the platen, and even though she can't tell if something over an hour has gone by or a good part of the July afternoon, the truth is that on the other side of the window the whitewashed houses have acquired a salmon tint, and the swallows are flying low and excitedly in an unharmonious flight that makes her uncomfortable, and the sea, which from here seems almost immobile, the surface disturbed only by the white track of foam, by the wake the barges and sailboats open at their passage and leave behind them, has been colored pink and silver at the touch of a crepuscular sun, so that the afternoon has indeed been fading on the other side of the open window, as Elia, absorbed, contemplated the houses, the birds, the church, the white lines in the blue water behind the boats, the big boat that crossed the bay and the landscape from one side to the other, and she kept repeating, "I must write, I have always been able to, I'll be lost if now I can't manage to write," but she knows that nothing that may have happened in the past has anything to do with what is happening now, and hers is a quiet and not very convincing lament, tainted with an opaque and too distant desolation, as if the words—"I must write"—were directed to the mysterious inhabitant of a remote planet, whose fate we are vaguely interested in, instead of being directed at herself, while Elia went over and over the painter's sentence, who, whenever they ask her, when Elia asks her, how she manages to have such a hard time—the painter almost always has a hard time —and continues nevertheless to work so much, to produce so much, she frowns and laughs and says, "you want to know how I do it? Look, I dry my tears and blow my nose, and I keep painting," and to Elia this seemed a laudable and marvelous formula, it seems so simple, and now Elia exhorts herself, reprimands herself, as if she were scolding without conviction an unknown child of a very distant country or planet, "go on, wipe away your tears, you too, and keep working," since it's only a question of following word for word an elementary and simple and rescuing norm, but Elia isn't crying—how to cry about something that's happening to someone else miles and miles away?—there are no tears or runny noses to dry, Elia is dry and empty, her mind a blank, waiting for something that should hurt and which in fact doesn't hurt, or maybe it's because the pain hasn't started yet, because Elia senses vaguely that they have inflicted on her a wound that can be terrible, that they've perhaps ripped out a part of herself, and that's why she doesn't dare separate her hands, take off the bandages, take the protecting helmet off her head, because, even though it doesn't hurt yet, the damage has necessarily to be terrifying, perhaps irreparable, and Elia, confused, fears that the pain, when it finally begins, will be atrocious, but maybe while the wound isn't made evident, while it's not formulated and recognized in words, while its magnitude isn't measured, while it's not exposed to the light, nothing will be irremediable yet, while she keeps ignoring the gangrened bone, the cracked cranium, the amputated limbs, while she obstinately remains standing, Elia thinks the authentic pain won't begin, the most total and true pain, and maybe this is the ultimate objective of her apathy, of her blank mind, of the inability to concentrate on anything, to evoke with the least bit of coherence and lucidity what has happened, maybe this is why for her time has stopped and flattened, a vulgar trick, an ingenuous contraption, not to escape the pain, but to postpone to whenever possible the irruption of a level of suffering she doesn't know, but of which she nevertheless had a fleeting intuition, a livid reflection, and which she fantasizes since then as intolerable, because they've ripped her open, they've extracted from her something that was very deep, very deep inside, stuck to the root, and Elia doesn't dare separate her hands, take off the poultice and the bandages, feel around the wound's edges, look at the wound and establish which organs the savage amputation has hurt or taken along with it, and now, sitting in front of the typewriter, straightening for the hundredth time the same blank sheet of paper, adjusting the margins, Elia feels only an uncertain fear of waking up, of emerging from the anesthesia and discovering that they've cut out of her something so vital and so personal that she's not going to be able to stay alive perhaps without it, fear of discovering a level of pain she doesn't know but of which she did have a remote glimpse, so frightening, that she called Miguel, her psychiatrist friend, who had never treated her before as a patient—very ironic and critical the Elia of before the shipwreck as to psychiatrists and drugs and psychoanalysts—or maybe it wasn't she who called, maybe Jorge told him, she can't remember. What she does know is that she was there, in bed, in the penumbra, feeling a suffering she intuited to be intolerable grow inside her, feeling the beginning of a disease for which there weren't going to be any remedies and they weren't even impossible remedies, it wasn't the miraculous cure of a sickness supposed to be lethal, what she was asking for or what she was expecting at the moment when she phoned Miguel or when she let Jorge phone him, this wasn't her demand, as Miguel sat on the edge of the bed and took her hand and gave her little slaps on the cheek and called her by her name, as if doubting she could hear it, and he looked at her so worriedly, however much he tried to smile and make light of the situation—nothing had really happened—and getting himself all rolled up in a confusing story, an unusual moralistic parable with a lesson, according to which a woman can make love the center of her world, and in such a case, even though she may lose love, the world will be deprived of its center, yes, but nothing worse will happen, whereas if a woman, and this of course she should never do, we mustn't let it happen to us—turns her love into a totality of which the world is the center, upon losing love, she will have lost everything entirely, and nothing will be left for her to hold onto and enable her to subsist. The psychiatrist gave her more little slaps on the cheek and on the shoulders, and spoke about a movie he'd seen in a theater or in Perpignan about two chess players, the final match of a chess tournament, Elia thinks she remembers, one of whom, maybe the American, made chess the center of his world whereas the other, possibly the Russian, made the world the center of chess, and when he lost the match, because he was the one who lost, he lost everything, chess and world, "a small masterpiece, a little jewel," Miguel had concluded, referring to the movie, and Elia had tried to understand with her intelligence idle, blocked, asleep, what the hell he had meant, what all that —she didn't half understand until several hours later—about chess and possible centers and the world and love actually meant, although she vaguely intuited that there was something she'd done wrong, couldn't have done worse, and she even sensed what it could consist of, and she would have liked to ask Miguel how this was straightened out, how this was arranged, how the hell would she manage to move Jorge out and reduce him from now on to being only the center of her world and not what he'd been for years and years, so many years, an omnipresent and total reality in whose interior the world was included and recorded, and in fact she didn't dare ask—for fear of all the answers seeming absurd and unworkable—how would she manage when the pain started, when she realized completely what she'd lost—how silly, Miguel would perhaps scold her, nothing's happened and nothing's been lost—what had been pulled out of her, ripping with it branches and roots, how would she manage to mold herself to the emptiness, in order to keep living in a world without Jorge, and she didn't even ask—and she was also afraid to ask —what became of the player who'd made the world the center of his game, and who'd lost the match and the tournament, Elia hardly said a thing, but Miguel undoubtedly guessed he hadn't been called—whether it was Jorge or herself who'd talked to him on the phone—to bring remedies, since nobody dreamed of an impossible cure, he was only asked to prescribe analgesics, something that would prolong to the edge of what was possible, that apathy, that stupor, that saving insensitivity that had mercifully invaded her at the moment of the catastrophe, that sensation that it wasn't about them but rather about different beings who lived in a different galaxy, because when Elia observed that the world was caving in on her, when Jorge with his words, full of noise and fury (and yes, words had at last had a magical power), the world of the two of them caved in and sank in an irreparable way, and hurled her into this ultimate ruin, Elia had no tears or words, she didn't even really feel any pain, only a slight anticipation of what this pain could be when it began, only emptiness and fatigue and an irresistible, uncoercible desire to sleep, and although now too, with Miguel sitting on the edge of her bed, she hardly said a thing, and there was a long silence, he must have understood what was going on and what was being asked of him, because he let out a sigh, looked at her worriedly—without daring to repeat that nothing had happened—and advised her without much faith, "go alone to the beach house, just as you both had planned, try not to be obsessed, give it time, try to work, try to write, take these pills . . .," and Elia had followed this advice, she had erased every trace of herself in the house, she had emptied it of herself, so that nothing would remain of her when Jorge returned, she had indiscriminately packed her bags, filling them with the first things her hands found, she had scooped up Musli, so old and so much a part of her that she couldn't leave the cat behind in the ruin, and she had come to this town and to this house, next to the sea, so near the sea that on stormy nights you could hear the noise of the waves, and now she's here, with a certain zombielike air, of someone recently arrived—Pablo had said this in an affectionate joke—from the kingdom of the dead, but who's going out in a boat, strolling through the town, greeting friends, even buying detective novels and magazines in the only bookstore in town, but who's incapable of crying or feeling sorry for herself, incapable of telling Eva or Pablo, such good friends, what's happening, incapable herself of understanding all of it really and of assimilating it, incapable above all of writing, shrinking in every way possible from the moment when sooner or later she'll have to face reality, and

41

that's what they're for—that's what these pills and capsules and drops and syrups and potions that Miguel prescribed are for—a complete arsenal of medication, a complicated gamut of opposing and complementary potions designed to keep her just enough on her feet, to minimally raise her spirits just a bit, to make her sleep at night and able to eat when they sit at the table, designed in short to prolong the anesthesia, the mind's torpor, the tenacious somnolence that transforms wakefulness into a light sleep, preventing her from reaching the lowest point, from really touching bottom, from crumbling into ruins, from perhaps stepping out of the nightmare and establishing with a certain lucidity that the damage has indeed been done, that that dreamed horror has really happened, in other words that Miguel, in spite of his triumphant attitude that nothing had happened and that everything has a remedy and almost everything is recoverable, in spite of his unworkable parables with a lesson, and his dissertation about chess players and small masterpieces—a little jewel—he had agreed to do for her the only thing that perhaps he could do, the only thing anyway that she accepted or permitted, to prolong more and more, to the last possible limits, that lethargic state, semi-anesthesized, that dozing that allowed her, allows her, to consider what happened as something very distant, definitely foreign, a nonsensical and asynchronous story that took place in another time and to other people on a different planet and in which nothing at all has been lost forever.

Y ou choose people weaker than yourself, like Elia and me, and then, when you want help and we don't rush to give it to you, you get mad at us," Pablo has said in an opaque voice, and although it's evident that he's joking, Eva feels slightly anxious, because she never knows with Pablo, when he's being serious, and others accuse her of a scarce or non-existent sense of humor, and possibly it's true, and now it seems to her there's a sad note in Pablo's voice, a touch of fatigue, a tenacious veil of reproach, although it's more likely that he's joking, and she would like to be able to see his face at these moments, as he finishes pronouncing these words, but the terrace is dark on this moonless night, and the man is only a grey shadow at her side, collapsed in the rocking chair, a grey shadow from which, at the level of his head, there emerges from time to time a brief spark, each time he lifts the cigarette to his lips, without this little light able to illuminate his face, so that Eva can't know for sure if Pablo has spoken just to speak, if it's an affectionate joke or if he really feels like a stranger and sad, if there are veiled or explicit reproaches in what he said or not, so that she doesn't know what answer to give, although what her husband has said—if he was in earnest—is irritating and seems unjust to her and it's not that Elia and he—besides, why put Elia in this same bag?—are weak at all, since neither their timidity, nor their vacillations, nor their susceptibilities have stopped them from making their way through life, and however much he and Elia and their closest friends have joked about what they call her "nursery school" or her "foundation," however much it's a recurrent theme in their talks, an unending topic for jokes, that excessive tendency of Eva's to give shelter, to protect under her wings, to direct and resolve other people's lives, and even to invent for them a happiness that she imposes on them against any resistance, so that the house is permanently full of friends or acquaintances, even strangers, an obligatory place for meetings and discussions of all kinds, of fun and work for the children's classmates, a tendency which has transformed her office of a feminist and labor-supporting lawyer—an office of impossible causes, of lost causes, which she nevertheless manages to win frequently—into a kind of sentimental consulting office or a switchboard of hope, and then work transcends the limits and schedules of the office, and ends up invading their entire life, and it's possible—Eva recognizes—that, in spite of never showing it, Pablo is really bored and tired, annoyed even, by the fact that his wife devotes so little attention to him and even less time, by the fact that almost never in the last years have they been able to take a trip just the two of them or be alone at home with the children, immersed in an incessant disorder, in an incessant coming and going of strange characters, Pablo fed up sometimes with poets lacking in inspiration and funds, with utopic small-time politicians, more or less leftist and frustrated, with frustrated artists, with disoriented adolescents, with drug addicts being rehabilitated, with women abandoned or thrown out or chased or raped by husbands or lovers or bosses, invariably sexist and without scruples, with neurotic women of the most diverse kinds, with permanent candidates for suicide, Eva incapable of rejecting them or even of putting limits on them—because deep down, it doesn't bother her, deep down, she likes it, she recognizes—so that they show up at the house at the most inconvenient moments and in the most unexpected circumstances to get food, take a shower or a bath, stay asleep in some corner and tell her their problems, for hours or for days, and Eva understands that all this can annoy Pablo—it's been so many years of the same thing—much less sociable, much more jealous of his intimacy, much more tired and in need of tranquility and rest when he comes home at night from the agency or they take a few days of vacation here, but the truth is that Pablo's complaints almost always have a joking character, an almost festive tone, and that she hadn't taken so seriously his insisting he wanted to spend the summer only with her and Elia and Jorge and with the children, and he surprises her now, on the dark terrace where she can't distinguish his face, this rather foreign and distant voice, perhaps resentful, and it surprises her too that he's included himself and Elia, as a joke, among the weak, in the throng of nursery schoolers or of lost children and she protests now in a vague and unconnected way, because she's not sure where jokes stop and the truth begins, and especially because she can't bear talking to people whose faces she can't see, and so her words advance haltingly, groping and trying to orient herself among the shadows, and Elia's voice surprises her—Elia so immobile

44

and so quiet, without even the fire from the matches or the red spark of the cigarette, whose existence she'd almost forgotten—the voice that Elia has used these days, lower and more monotone than ever, as if she were talking to them from another level, from another dimension unknown to them, recently expelled from the kingdom of the dead, and as if it took a tremendous effort for her to conquer inertia and laziness and be able to articulate each word, and she speaks so low that Eva can't quite get what she's saying, and then she does hear her, and Elia is talking about how much they love her, "that love they all, we all, feel, Pablo and I the first—why do you think with us two it would be different?—for you, all of us a little in love with our abbess, our Black Mass priestess, so naive, venerating you, admiring you, desiring you, fearing you, all of us whirling around you like lost children or like dogs without owners, while you govern us and shelter us with the abnegation of a very loving mother or with the perverse and innocent whims of a crazy queen." With the last words Elia has abandoned her monotonous voice, her absent tone, and taken on a theatrical and grandiloquent tone, and both of them now, Pablo and Elia, laugh like accomplices in the dark, and again she's not sure if they're establishing solidarity in a veiled reproach the reasons of which escape her, and so she opts for laughter too in an attempt to ignore what could have been a certain implicit accusation in Pablo's sentence, a certain sarcastic melancholy in Elia's tone, as if the love they undoubtedly feel for her—it seems to her—weighed on them too much today, as if it perhaps was in the way, like an annoying burden, and Eva persists in taking it as a joke, "I suppose you're not lamenting it? is it so bad a thing to love me? don't I love you too?", "a lot, a lot," they both answer at the same time, and Elia adds again theatrically, again in a parody or farcical tone, "I think we're the abbess's favorites, the foundation's two spoiled children, the only ones who sit at your table and eat from your hand, your best followers and propagandists, your most fervent disciples," and this doesn't amuse Eva at all today and the three of them become quiet on the July night, on the moonless night, dark night, the sea so immobile among the shadows, so that more than distinguishing it they sense it, important nonetheless for them to know it's there, as they sit in front of the ocean on the terrace even though they can't see it or even hear it, mute, invisible, but so present, and Eva feels a touch of uneasiness, but she doesn't feel like insisting, continuing to probe, the other two so close and she unable to discern their expression or look deeply into their eyes, so strange they are too, remote and distant tonight, even perhaps aggressive, "as if they had something against me, as if they didn't approve of what I'm doing," she thinks, and it surprises her to suddenly feel frightened and helpless, about to say, "don't let me down, I need you both very much," although she doesn't say it, made mute by an unusual timidity, a sudden embarrassment, that modesty which overcomes her sometimes and which Pablo and Elia can't even imagine, as they can't imagine that the censorship they sometimes insinuate, the disapproval she senses in them tonight, can do as much harm and leave her unsheltered to such a degree, because what she needs, in a certain way, is their unconditional love, their unchangeable affection, to be able to feel strong and sure of herself, and someone has to remain minimally adult and standing in the foundation at her side for Eva the integral, Eva the strong woman, not to find herself intolerably alone in a world of sick people and children, reduced to a ridiculous and involved woman who likes to play at being God among a chorus of adorers and false friends, and Pablo is the one who breaks the silence because he has sensed Eva's anxiety, her uneasiness, but he attributes them to a more concrete cause, a different cause, "don't worry Eva, we were kidding, you know that if you decide to bring that girl here, we'll do everything we can for her, we'll help you in any way we know how," and Elia, "don't pay any attention to us, we're like travelers on a train, remember? the ones who travel without a bed and, when night comes, get comfortable taking up all the space, and close doors and lower curtains, and whoever gets on the train has to knock on the door and protest and get a seat any way he can and bear the offended looks of the ones already comfortable, and then, as soon as he's put his luggage up, and has sat down and stretched his legs, he's the first one to look at whoever knocks and sticks his head in and ask if there's room, with a murderous look, well then, something like that happens to all of us with the foundation or with you."

She wakes up startled in the middle of the night and doesn't know what time it is, but these days it gets light very early and there's not the faintest light in the sky yet today, only dark night on the other side of the open window, she wakes with the sensation of emerging from a terribly anxious dream, or maybe only terribly sad, because she can't remember what she's dreamed, and still she keeps sobbing, awake now without even knowing why she's crying, and the tears run down her cheeks and she touches the pillow drenched in tears, awake now as she used to wake so many times thousands of years ago, in childhood, in adolescence, in the beginning of youth, and there is in the first instant of waking an anxiety that drowns her and of which she still doesn't know the cause, and then, always unexpected, brutal, absolutely implausible because it's so intolerable—that stupid faith that only what we can bear will happen to us, as if there were someone somewhere controlling the intensity of pain and the level of our resistance—the certainty that at some moment, it doesn't matter whether it's soon or later, since it has to come anyway, she'll necessarily have to die. So she woke in the middle of a dream of which she almost never remembered the actual experience—not the idea, which would have been bearable—but the experience of the inevitability of her own death, an acute premonition of what that strange, incredible thing death would be. She woke soaked in sweat, out of breath, drowning in pure anxiety and terror, and perhaps the worst was that, in the first instants, before having emerged

47

entirely from the dream—a dream she wouldn't remember anyway—Elia had told herself "don't be afraid, it's nothing, just a nightmare, it can't be true," with the hope that the bad dream would dissipate like so many others upon waking, until, just a short time later, she realized that on this occasion it was different, and it wasn't going to be at all easy for her to scare away the ghosts, drink a glass of water, read some pages in a book, light a cigarette and go back to sleep comforted, because the worst of all imaginable nightmares, the one that had less sheen, fewer probabilities of being true—the inevitability of everyone's death and her own, the inadmissible fact that men are mortal: they know they have to die and they don't want to die and finally they do die—turned out to be true, and there was no one during her lonely childhood and her difficult adolescence and the first years of youth capable of calming this fear of hers, no one with whom she could even share it, and Elia remained paralyzed with terror at night, as she could never be during the day, in a state of wakefulness— all of her alert, all her defenses prepared—surrounded by people—it didn't matter that they talked incessantly about death, in those talks death was always little more than a word, related to the existence of a god, to immortality, to the different answers different cultures gave, it was never present as a reality, and naming it that way was the same as warding it off, reduced to one more topic of conversation or of controversy—to the possibility, the years of childhood gone, of going out into the street or telephoning a friend, no, death was only certain when she woke in the middle of the night, after a nightmare she could never remember, and there were first some anxious moments, thought still suspended, in which it seemed possible that everything would turn out, like so many other times, to be nothing, and then, like a big club that left her astounded and paralyzed, drowning, the total certainty that her own death was waiting for her at some unspecified but inevitable point, death was for Elia what she had known during nights of anxiety and nightmares, that was the only complete evidence, the only sensation of death possible before really dying, because there—for some moments that must have been very brief, but in which eternities fit—Elia lived her death with an intensity that made it an experience which didn't compare to any other, and which was undoubtedly worse than all of them, and left her annihilated, unarmed, without the slightest possibility of reacting and protecting herself, until Jorge arrived, and Jorge slept for years and years at her side, and she believed it would be all her life, and in fact, it was, because what preceded Jorge's arrival was only prehistory and what follows his leaving her can't really be called life, and Elia slept night after night huddled against his chest, her head sheltered in the hollow of his shoulder, his arms wrapped around her from her back to her waist, and some of those nights—in the beginning—she woke still afraid, and woke him (and never before, although she slept accompanied, had it occurred to her to wake anyone with her fears), "tell me we don't have to die, tell me I'm not going to die, that you're not going to die," and he would hug her tighter still half asleep, he would dry her tears with kisses, he would drink her salty tears, he would cradle her, he would make fun of her, "we'll never die, never, my pretty one, my little girl, my sheika, my silly princess," but it wasn't necessary really for him to wake up or for him to lull her to sleep or for him to tell her anything, because there was, around Jorge, in the physical and concrete proximity of his body, something that chased away all anxiety and fear just by being there, and Elia lived for years—she thought it would be forever—in this magical halo, and that was when she learned that love is stronger than death, so happy with Jorge, so lavishly alive, that death lost dimension and importance, it lost the last residue of plausibility, because—Elia thinks in the big bed where she sleeps alone (although it's not the same room she shared in this house with Jorge), as she looks out at the night and expects to see the dawn soon on the other side of the windowpanes, and she keeps crying in a mechanical way now because she doesn't even realize she's still crying—it only vanishes at the height of happiness, and only when we are truly happy do we not care about having to succumb, death annihilated in a way by the joy and intensity of existing whereas it's in unhappiness, in dissatisfaction, that anxieties and fears flourish and expand, and death becomes unbearable, and these days, in this July month of abandonment and of solitude, Elia has woken again many times—in spite of the sleeping pills and tranquilizers, of that unending list of medications —startled and frightened in the middle of the night, she has woken again crying, with the tears running down her cheeks and the pillow is damp from her weeping, and she's hardly able to suffocate the sobs—and she doesn't want Eva to wake and get up and come to console her from the adjoining room —unable to determine the first instant why the hell she's crying, unable to evoke what she's dreamed, incapable of establishing the causes of her anguish, until—now also with the surprising violence of a club that makes her huddle up with pain and leaves her paralyzed afterwards—the image of Jorge appears, the bed surprisingly empty of him, Jorge's words in that terrible scene of noise and fury—"hasn't it occurred to you that we may have stopped loving each other? we aren't going to spend the rest of our lives playing at Abelard and Héloïse," and Elia doesn't understand what's happening at all—Jorge, going away from her, leaving on a trip with an unknown destination, unknown to her, and maybe he doesn't know either what his return date will be, leaving her alone in the middle of the wreck, amid the broken remains of what was her life, while time stops and expels her from its flow, because Elia can't evoke an altered past in which value and fate have changed and in which it's not known what anything means, nor is she capable of imagining for an instant what her life will be without Jorge in the future, it's possible that a future doesn't even exist for her, unimaginable anyway what her life would be without Jorge, and so she stuffs herself with antidepressants and anti-anxiety pills, in proportions and mixtures she has to hide from Miguel, swallowing pills and capsules with unction, as if she were performing a magical exorcism—she doesn't even know if it's to sleep or to try, leaving it to chance, her luck at dying—and she goes to the beach and swims some, almost all, mornings, and goes out in the boat, and sleeps in the sun and watches the clouds cross the sky, the boats on the ocean, on the other side of the window, in front of the typewriter, it too mute and drowsy, and actually—she confesses to herself, terrified, she says to herself, desolate, in the middle of the night—she's doing nothing but waiting for the miracle, appropiating the symptoms of the prodigy, and it's useless for her to repeat to herself a thousand and one times that it's a stupid illusion, that there's nothing left to wait for, that she has definitively lost the match and sooner or later she's going to have to get up from the playing table, that it's necessary to put out of its misery this clumsy, bad, dirty hope that refuses obstinately to die, the hope that makes her wait every hour of her days and nights for a phone call which won't happen, that impels her to the post office to see if a letter without an address has arrived or if the mailman who's known her for twenty years has forgotten her name, that makes her walk along the beach, by the ocean, looking for his face, following someone who moves with the same gestures through the streets—head in front, the glance straight ahead, so funny and distracted, with those enervated Pink Panther steps—or who talks with the same accent—that beautiful calm voice, often a little overprecise, sometimes fairly mocking, with that slightly foreign touch of someone who's lived in other lands—waiting for him, contrary to all reason, minute after minute, and she doesn't even know what she wants, she doesn't even know what she's waiting for—for time to go backwards, for what happened never to have happened, for things not to be what they are—looking for him still in everything and finding him in everything and discovering his face everywhere, and maybe her body is after all to blame, this free, strong and blind instinct, because in her mind

Elia knows very well what to rely on, she knows she's lost everything together and there's nothing left to wait for, nothing to propitiate, nothing to discover or prolong, and nevertheless there stubbornly exists in the deepest part of herself a deaf, blind, obtuse tendency that doesn't understand anything, there's something in her that waits unceasingly for Jorge's return, as an old faithful dog waits for his master, a docile, stupid dog incapable of understanding—or maybe only of accepting—that his owner has died or has gone on a trip with no possible return, that his owner has disappeared forever, abandoning him amid the shipwreck's remains.

The voices are now behind her, in the main street of the big town, of the small city, that stingy, tiny ocher city attached to the earth, enemy of the sea and of open spaces, enemy of the birds, whom the boys kill with stones, with shots, in the asphyxiated gardens, the miserable vegetable gardens that barely survive in the back of some houses, and however much the car is moving quickly away—because Eva understands her impatience or because she too is wishing to leave everything behind—and the voices of the aunt and uncle who came to say good-bye at the doorstep, in the street are left far behind, it seems to Clara that these hard voices, these evil voices—especially the sharp voice of the woman— have transformed into multiple steel needles that still follow her, looking for her flesh in the distance, into bands of wasps that have lost their stings along the road and arrive transfigured into clouds of gold, into poisoned arrows that don't manage to reach them either and which crumble at the limit of their flight's power on the asphalt and in the dust, useless now any poison against the two of them, and nevertheless the memory still scares her of the threatening, aggressive, ill-omened words—"you won't get anywhere, you're making a big mistake, I tell you the girl is a liar, a malicious brat who's tricked you with her lies, because who knows what she's told you about us"—of the snake woman, the wax woman, the woman without eyes—because that imposter who has claimed with incredible insolence for years to occupy her mother's place has empty and terrible sockets for eyes, even though no one notices, and she has wax for skin—only as the car gains speed, and the city's center is left behind, the girdle of miserable hovels that surround it, and they're advancing through the sterile countryside amid inhospitable piles of rocks, does Clara finally feel liberated and safe, and she even dares to glance at the woman of light, the white woman, the warm and soft woman made of feathers, who is sitting beside her, driving the car along the highway and taking her far far far away, to a different and beautiful universe which she'll never have to leave—foolishness for them to have asked her to visit them often, for her to come home when the summer's over—and she won't have to see ever again the miserable flat town, with its filthy ramshackle houses, with its alleys full of grime and dust, its stingy gardens and miserable vegetable gardens agonizing from the lack of air and sun, the town they toil and attack and harm each other in, the reptile men, the frog men, with opaque or empty eyes and heads bent to the ocher earth, all of them enemies of the sun and the sea, of the big open spaces where birds fly high and far away. Where she's going, the sharp screaming voices won't be able to follow—poisoned arrows, steel darts, enraged wasps—the voice of that imposter, who has harassed her for years and years around the gardens, around the last and most hidden corners of the house, because even the most secret refuge among the dusty thickets or in the top of the trees, even the deepest part of the wardrobes that smell like mothballs and old clothes, clothes of death, that tenacious, imperious, relentless voice has chased her there, always filling her—it has been impossible for her to get used to it—with apprehensions and fears, always causing her a secret sensation of rejection and displeasure, making her appear uncomfortable in front of the wax woman, the reptile woman in this town of reptiles, who is almost transparent, because viscera and wickedness are drawn under the green, thin, sky blue skin, the reptile woman even though she has no eyes (impossible that the others haven't realized), capable it seems of guessing her most secret thoughts, her most fragile dreams, and twisting and staining them with indelible viscosities, and for a few weeks, since the day someone drove her to the city and she found there the woman of white light, the bird woman, who listened attentively, frowning, her head slightly to one side, and then offered to take charge of her destiny, with a firm and secure voice, a slight smile, as if what she was promising were simple and natural—"you can't stay in that town, in that house, you have to come here, study, don't worry, I'm going to arrange everything"—since that day Clara has known happiness and her vain dreams have transformed into real hopes, and her vague world of ghosts has become more concrete, harder, more corporeal, and she has lived devoured by impatience, so anxious that the passing of time hurts her, such a slow passing of time, full too of apprehensions and fears, harassed without respite by her aunt, who had perhaps found out or had at least the confused intuition that something important was happening behind her back, like a premonition that she was going to fly away, that Clara was escaping—or had already escaped—her ferocious dominion, that ignoble parody of motherhood and affection, although she couldn't in fact ever guess that what was going on behind her back and everyone's was called love, and that she had finally found her lost mother, never known, permanently missed, imagined for years and years, a mother made completely of bird warmth, of very soft white feathers, whose image Clara had had a presentiment of and had invoked like a talisman against all misfortune, all dense solitude, all desolate orphanhood, against this big, flat, ugly town, against the constant and malicious vigilance of the wax woman who claims to see everything, know everything, and who doesn't even have eyes, against clumsy attempts at affection, the tender and nonetheless confused and disquieting attacks from her uncle, the frog man, so short and so dirty and so ugly, the viscous body full of scales, who has claimed to play at being her father, call him dad, and how could this being from other worlds who doesn't look at all like her, not at all, be her father, however much he follows her like a faithful little dog, and looks at her with his little bloodshot eyes, and caresses her clumsily with his damp and hard claws, and actually she knows now that she's never had a father, daughter only of the erect white woman, who has also spent perhaps all these years —as many as she's spent longing for her—looking everywhere for her lost little daughter, and now she's found her at last—Clara fantasizes, lost now the most remote contact, she recognizes and doesn't care, with reality, and she told her "don't worry about a thing, don't be afraid, leave everything in my hands and come with me," and it hardly matters that these last days, since they took her to the big city and to Eva's office, the persecution has in a way been worse, and it's unbearable living in a world of reptiles, the wax snake's words hurrying after her in the form of poisoned darts, of enraged wasps whose hive has been stepped on, the empty sockets of her eyes scrutinizing her suspiciously, spying on her malignantly, in the corners of the vegetable garden and of the house, worse too since now, for the first time in her life, Clara has a marvelous secret to safeguard, an extraordinary possession to defend, and however much she knows she's invulnerable, protected by love like a shield of gold and fire, a magic armor made from the light of the stars and ocean algae, against which the darts and wasps and snakes crash and succumb, and now nobody can hurt the girl who has been recognized as the daughter of light, and nobody can stop her or impede her flight, avoid her takeoff if the bird woman tells her "get up, leave everything and come with me" (as indeed has occurred), she has nonetheless experienced these last days a more profound dread, not that they can curb her and lock her up or keep her there by force, but rather the fear that the imposter could manage, with her obscure powers, with the look of her eyeless sockets, to penetrate her and find inside her an image that must not in any way be profaned, because if the wax woman discovered what her love is like, something would have perhaps been irrevocably degraded, fatally blemished, but now this last dread, this final fright, has also been vanquished and warded off, because the white mother, the bird woman with the snowy white plumage, has come to get her and has made her climb into the car and the begging and complaints, the almost weeping, of the frog man couldn't do a thing—how can he have claimed to assume the role of her father, this poor fellow who doesn't look at all like her?—sad frog with the rough tongue and clumsy claws, nor have the snake woman's insidious and sinister prophecies been able to do a thing, the woman with no eyes, nor have the inhabitants of this filthy city of reptiles stuck to the earth, bent over the ground, who have leaned out their windows or have interrupted their passage through the streets for a moment to watch them go by, only the arrow voices, the dart voices, the stinger voices have followed them for a stretch, and now these same voices are left far behind, everything is far behind, in a past that has to adjourn and to which she'll never have to return now, and the car moves ahead, faster and faster, as if Eva too were anxious to get away, and Clara is going there by her side, Eva is taking her with her as she promised to a more beautiful world, whose inhabitants will probably be made of light and feathers, magnificent kingdom of birds of the air, much closer to Clara, more of her race, more her people, and she'll be able to sit at last among her family, in the kingdom near the sea where her mother is queen—impossible for there to exist a more beautiful, more erect and powerful woman—the kingdom where she herself must have been born one day, many many years ago, because her sixteen years seem like so so many years to Clara, and where she perhaps lived the first months she hardly remembers, but that marked her forever as a daughter of the sun and of the sea and of the great blue-white spaces, even though those viscous, insidious, wax and mire snakes snatched her so soon from her nest, from the warm shelter made of such big white silk feathers (perhaps, she fantasizes, the snake woman with evil-minded designs stole her when she was still a little girl), and that's why she's had to live so many years in that harsh, dust-filled, miserable land, in the small, flat city, in narrow and sunless hovels, among sallow and viscous beings bent to the ground, without eyes to look at the blue sky, without wings to take flight, where she has grown up like a stranger and only the frog man with the rough tongue and hard claws, who looks nothing like the man who could have been her father, has loved her—a poor variety of love, but love in any case—although the truth is, in her fantasies, she's never imagined a father, and she thinks now she never had one, daughter only of this beautiful and resplendent mother, feather soft, sweet honey taste, who's taking her with her to her kingdom, and who, when the familiar countryside is finally left behind, abandons her stern and decided expression, the hard obstinacy of her very black eyes, and relaxes and breathes and looks at her and smiles and runs a hand through her hair, "don't be afraid, you'll see, everything will be fine, I'm sure they'll love you a lot and that you'll feel comfortable in the house," and she shivered under the soft, firm hand—it was only a brief caress, very fleeting— and notices shamefully that her eyes are filling with tears, luckily Eva has returned her gaze to the highway and isn't looking at her, and Clara's heart is beating wildly, so loud she's afraid the other woman can hear it, and it's difficult for her to breathe with this emptiness in her chest and this knot in her throat, and she thinks that if at some moment Eva kisses her, she will inevitably have to die.

E verything's going wrong this summer, Pablo thinks, with Jorge absent—and they don't even know where he is, and Elia, if she knows, hasn't wanted to tell us—with Elia sleeping a thousand hours, hardly leaving her room, and moving, when they manage to get her out, around the town and around the house like a sorrowful soul, sitting for hours and hours at her worktable, in front of the typewriter, but without anyone hearing her type (like other times), without the wastepaper basket full of wrinkled papers, papers torn in half (sometimes written almost to the end, sometimes with a few lines, because she doesn't like corrections or strike-outs), at dawn, without them filling the cloth binder—a violet, brown, purple cloth because Elia can't work it seems without these small things that she turns into magic fetishes, a pretty new binder, special paper they've brought to her from London or that someone has sent from India, and inside the binder, next to the poems, an effigy from the day of her first communion, with the Virgin of the Rocks, the drawing of a blond curly-haired girl with roses in her braids, roses a friend sent her years ago, a photograph of Jorge as a child, a little boy with light eyes, long legs, a serious expression, riding a cardboard horse—without, like other summers, the pages which have managed to reach the end, in a very tidy writing, of an expert typist or a maniac, almost always without a single mistake, because Elia is apt to repeat the entire poem in order to correct one word or change the placement of a comma, filling up the binder, and other years she has proudly shown them, with that vanity of hers just like an industrious little girl, a shy little girl who, blushing, exhibits her work at lunchtime, putting the binder on the tablecloth, untying the ribbons, showing them the little pile of tidy finished pages, that Eva and he and Jorge have always celebrated with enthusiasm, as proud as if they had written them—with a certain envy, Pablo recognizes for himself—because Elia will never permit anyone to read a single verse before it's finished, but she will show them morning after morning how the pile has grown, until it constitutes a finished book, but now, in this month of July, Elia is, as before, shut inside her room, sitting in front of the typewriter, and nevertheless no one hears any typing at all, and every morning the wicker basket is empty and inside the binder there are no written papers, only the effigy with the Virgin, the photograph, the postcard, forgotten there, because Pablo is sure she hasn't looked at them, sure even that they've lost all their power, the magic dissipated, if they're still there it's because of Elia's carelessness, that she's forgotten to tear them up or burn them or throw them out, and sometimes he has knocked on the door and entered on any pretext, suggesting they go for a stroll through town or have tea together, and Elia is indeed sitting in front of the typewriter, and there is a blank sheet of paper in the typewriter, but the woman has this absorbed and sad expression, the same as when she sunbathes in the boat, on the smooth, warm wood, or when she dives unexpectedly into the ocean and swims alone and far away, with her eyes closed, or when they walk through the whitewashed side streets and run into lifelong friends whom she doesn't seem to recognize, or has in any case no desire to greet, and Elia, sitting absorbed in front of the typewriter, looking sometimes absently out the window, is almost always startled by Pablo's presence in the room, even if he's knocked on the door before coming in, and it's as if he caught her redhanded, her face and her attitude naked in an almost immodest helplessness—that for her, so modest, it's surely uncomfortable—and it seems as if it takes a great effort for her to react, concentrate her attention, return to reality, understand his proposals, and invariably respond that, no, she doesn't feel like a cup of tea, thank you, she doesn't feel at all like going into town, and even though he and Eva have spent days exhorting each other, repeating to each other that they mustn't worry too much, that what she needs is time, that sooner or later Elia will let down her defenses and tell them, and then they can help her, and the truth is the days are going by and nothing's happening, she hasn't explained anything, and she keeps wandering around the house like a zombie, shutting herself for hours and more hours in the bedroom, without anyone hearing her type, sitting in front of a typewriter she doesn't use, so oblivious to everything that she doesn't even notice some dusks that it's going to be dark and she should therefore turn on the lights, and she remains there, in the dark, until they call her to come eat dinner, and then they don't have to insist or convince her, they don't have to argue with her as they feared, because Elia stands up, follows them to the table, eats docilely and absently what they put on her plate, and Pablo is sure that she doesn't even know what she's eating and she doesn't care one bit if she eats or doesn't eat—he would almost prefer sometimes for her to resist ingesting food, anything but this indifference—and she lines up, next to the glass, in perfect order, as if she were arranging little lead soldiers for an imaginary battle, the capsules, the ampoules, the multicolored, sugar-coated pills, on the table-cloth, with the rigidity and seriousness of a ritual, god knows what she expects from so much medication, while Eva invariably, uselessly, rails against drugs, they can see what they're doing to her, and the other woman doesn't even hear. And the truth is that the summer is going badly, and it's very different from so many other summers, with Jorge far away, without their knowing where he is or the date of his return, without his phoning or writing nor his having even gotten in touch with them, and nevertheless oppressively present, since his absence is weighing on the three of them and on the house with an unbearable force, Elia reduced to another ghost with whom it's not possible to communicate, lost in her remote world to which they don't have access or to which she stubbornly refuses to give them the key or show them the way, and nevertheless, sooner or later, she and Jorge will have to return and explain to them. And as if the situation weren't already difficult enough, annoying enough, in this summer hardly at all like other summers, Eva has the brilliant idea of bringing them this girl, Clara, and it's just like Eva to ask them their opinion beforehand, solicit their advice, try to attract them and win them over to the idea—has she ever really needed any collaboration or help from them?—and then, when they were lazy and stubborn, he because he truly doesn't feel strong or enthusiastic enough—nor does he even want to assume this kind of responsibility and take on a half-crazy girl, and it bothers him to have strangers in the house, who interrupt and ruin their intimacy à trois, and Elia, because besides being incapable sometimes of connecting with the outside world—she's always had difficulty relating to others, she's always looked for someone else as an intermediary, as a bridge between her world and the world of others, and Jorge, Pablo can't deny it, has acted for all these years as the interpreter for a deaf-mute or a Martian, and perhaps without him, Elia has been stuck, isolated in a dream from which she doesn't want to awake or show them the way, immersed in an obsessive sadness that doesn't leave her, that possesses her second after second, every hour of her days, and perhaps even of her nights (that is if the anti-anxiety pills and the sleeping pills and the tranquilizers don't at least work to chase away dreams)—besides being distracted and badly connected with the outside world, Elia, in spite of Eva's getting her agreement and support one night on the terrace, she responded yes, and had forgotten all about it and had a brief expression of astonishment when she found Clara at the breakfast table, her surprise and curiosity so fleeting—and that's new because Elia was very curious—that she didn't even give them time to materialize into questions, and Elia surely still doesn't know who this girl is who follows Eva everywhere like a little lapdog with a frightened look, that look dogs have who've been repeatedly beaten, and Pablo wonders if they have really beaten her at some point or if it's only one more fantasy, and Clara follows Eva with a devotion, with a fervor, with a tenacity that, Pablo thinks, will end up irritating her, as has happened in similar circumstances, and already on a few occasions Eva has tried to put limits on this adoration and separate herself, go alone to town or into the garden alone to arrange the plants, and then Clara watches her through the window, hidden behind the curtains and blinds, not to find out what the other woman is doing, not at all to spy on her, but just to see her even from far away a few more minutes, as if seeing her as she waters the hortensias or prunes the geraniums or goes down the street towards the market or the hairdresser meant conquering a part of the spoils, a fragment of happiness, Clara, beaten dog, a greedy collector of her god-master's gestures and words and attitudes—Clara picked up who-knows-where and given shelter—images and voices which she hoards greedily but to which perhaps she feels she doesn't have the right, and that's why she hides behind the doors, behind the shades and curtains, and blushed to the root of her hair—it's not hard for her to blush, she blushes at anything, and that makes her so mad, which increases even more her confusion and embarrassment—the day he surprised her on the watch, spying next to the window, frightened and about to cry, like a little girl caught with her fingers in the cookie jar, and such childish embarrassment, the beginning of tears, was unusual in this splendid body, because Eva hadn't warned them that the girl who she planned to incorporate into her nursery school, into her foundation of helpless and marginal people, was so pretty, with such deep dark eyes, almost as big and beautiful as Eva's, and a full red mouth, and thick perfumed hair that fell down her back, and that tight golden flesh and magnificent, aggressive breasts that she tries use-lessly to hide, hunching over, hiding behind books and binders and crossed arms, and thin legs and long thighs, incredibly good-looking girl this Clara, who looked at him from her hiding place next to the window with her eyes full of tears and blushed to the root of her hair and who couldn't manage to say a single word, nor did he say anything to her, he just looked dubiously at her and smiled, amused—aware that Clara hated him for that smile—because the house this summer seems like a refuge for the conspirators of silence, an asylum for mutes, Elia shut all the hours she can in her room, everyone feeding the fiction that she's working and knowing that she's not doing a thing, responding in monosyllables to almost everything they say to her, Clara too timid, too bashful, too frightened, too different her world maybe, the world where Eva picked her up, from the world of this house, to be able to dare separate her lips, even though she probably does speak when she and Eva are alone, and he feeling invaded by a discouragement greater than what he's used to, as if he'd become much older in a few months, with that heavy feeling that the years have passed by uselessly, youth has ended, and he hasn't lived what he really would have liked to live (he can't tell Eva this, because Eva would look at him, surprised, a little skeptical, and would ask him "what?" and he wouldn't be able to explain it to her, since he doesn't know exactly, he can't specify what he means by what he wanted to live and what life should consist of, and with Elia he could talk about it, and she would ask him the right questions and probably between the two of them they would understand, but Elia has shut herself up this summer in an impregnable world, in a tower of sadness to which she's thrown away or lost the key), because at some point along the way which he himself is incapable of specifying, although it does seem to him that it was a long time ago, Pablo took the wrong road, and only now, seeing himself so far from the foreseen goal, he has realized fully that there must have been some mistake, a detour in the road that must have been of the lowest order, minimal, in the beginning, hardly even perceptible (and he didn't perceive it), but which has been widening with time, the fissure which mediates between the reality he's been living and what his desires were, widening (probably something similar has happened to Jorge, and it's only the women who don't understand) and he feels now too—never before this summer had he confessed it to himself with such hardness—that it's certainly too late now to rectify, and he'll have to keep taking more and more steps in a direction he knows is wrong and which takes him further and further away from what could have been his destiny, so that any effort to force the gear or do more turns out inevitably to be in vain and probably counterproductive without there existing besides any possibility of going backwards or of correcting the direction, too accustomed for years to what's comfortable and easy—a certain kind of commonplace comfort, of apparent easiness—too lazy, too much of a coward or too skeptical (not everyone can, like Elia, keep asking and hoping for absolutes at age forty) to quit his secure job as a top executive and try to recuperate a position in the university or to attempt at this point the uncertain and dangerous adventure of writing.

Pablo knocks on the door, but enters the room before she's had time to answer, Pablo sits on the edge of the bed and looks at her and sucks on his pipe—a beautiful pipe, a Victorian pipe of amber and sea foam, that she gave him a long time ago when he still played at being Captain Ahab or the taciturn lone wolf of the seven seas, surprising the frequency with which men see themselves as wolves of the steppes, as warriors in need of rest, as fighting navigators in tortuous pursuit of the impossible—and the air is filling with white smoke and especially with that warm, dense, honey perfume that the tobaccos Jorge has always smoked have and which she used to like so much. Pablo smiles and looks her in the eye and asks if she was working, pure formula of courtesy this question, because they both know she hasn't written a single complete page since she arrived at the house two weeks ago now, however much she spends the dead hours sitting in front of the typewriter (almost all those that don't pass by in the boat or in bed) arranging the margins, removing papers or looking towards the sea, and Elia says no, she wasn't working, and smiles too, with the fear that the smile will be forced, rigid, pathetic, little more than making a face or a sham of a smile, even though it matters little today, Pablo himself so somber, so absorbed in thought, so forlorn, so desirous or in need of telling her his sorrows—for almost twenty years, almost an entire life, Elia thinks, she's lived, sitting dark and tame in a corner, understanding and attentive to whatever is told to her (and it's not true, as they have reproached her sometimes, that it's only a feigned attitude, that she doesn't listen to anything or that she doesn't really care about what

64

others tell her: she listens to them with real, with genuine interest, with an inexhaustible curiosity, even if afterwards she's too lazy, too selfish, to make a single expression of support, to help them in a practical way to solve the problem they outline), so she has fulfilled the role of confidante, of counselor, of comforter above all, to men and women and children and cats whom Eva maintains it seems in a permanent lack of attention or of love, because even giving them a lot there is a certain distance in her generosity that makes them feel, at one moment or another, omitted and unsatisfied (how to satisfy them if their demands are always unlimited?) and then they go to Elia, so close to Eva, almost Eva herself, for her to attend to their protests and their grief—Pablo so ready today it seems to tell her his own sorrows that he mustn't notice at all her forced smile and Elia has the comforting certainty that he won't investigate what's wrong with her today, nor will he risk some perjorative and critical appraisal of Jorge—never have the two men loved each other overmuch— that she still can't bear, Pablo will talk today only about himself, or about himself in relation to Eva the omnipresent, the woman loved by all, and this will calm her, but she also feels at the same time, Elia so bereft these days of recourses, a sensation of fatigue, of laziness, a desire to get the man out of her room with any excuse and not to listen, but even for that, she's too apathetic and passive, too tired, so she remains there, sitting in front of the typewriter, with a rigid smile that is slowly being erased from her sleeping lips, forcing herself without too much commitment to be attentive, to make convincing expressions of understanding, to make herself in some way a partner to Pablo's discontent, a discontent that he displays today in tragic tones—Pablo has her propensity for the heroic, for the theatrical, for the melodramatic—as if it were something he'd just discovered, astonished, fearful, in the most hidden part of his soul, as if dissatisfaction and discontent weren't something common to everyone—who doesn't pass the barrier of forty years frustrated and unsatisfied?—as if the deep roots of this discontent had not always existed in him, or at least for many years, although it's very possible that it's solidified now and been made dense in this terrible summer, and Elia forces herself to help him discover at what moment of his life he took the wrong road, and it's anyone's guess at what point Pablo and Elia herself and everyone took the wrong road, because men suffer and aren't happy, says Elia, and they ask each other for the moon in vain, and they feel—we all feel—frustrated to a greater or lesser degree, says Elia in her serious little voice, absorbed in thought, but inside she thinks that it's not entirely true, since she had the moon for a very long time of her life, because on a faraway day a foreigner arrived in the city, and he had skin made golden by the tropical sun, and the most ironic and melancholic eyes Elia had ever seen, and the foreigner spoke with words they'd never heard in that place, which at his arrival became somber and miserable and small, a city of dwarfs, and the foreigner came from very far away and had furrowed all the seas and had captured all the white whales and had unveiled or assumed all the secrets of the wandering Dutchman, and he brought, although they didn't know, the moon, hidden in some corner of his very light luggage, and he approached the prettiest, the most brilliant, the most audacious of the princesses, daughters of the sun, it couldn't have been otherwise, in each other's arms and around them a magic circle of light, but in the middle of the feast, the foreigner left Ismene, they parted friends, without anger, they'd never been more than friends, and besides Eva had already met Pablo at that time, and because of an incomprehensible mistake—here indeed there must have been some error—he approached Antigone, who observed him, astonished, from her corner, immersed in the cocoon of her dreams, wishing herself invisible, more awkward and embarrassed, more helpless than ever, but he—impossible to understand why—chose her among all women and gave her the moon, and they walked together for years and years—she believed it would be forever—with the moon shining in her blood, warming and illuminating her inside, living lamp in which love burned like a sacred flame, inextinguishable, and Elia thinks now that she possessed the moon for a very very long instant of her life, that someone went to get it for her in the highest part of the sky and put it in her lap, and that this marked her forever, whatever happened later, what did happen later, because even now, in this extreme desolation, in this indigence which has left her empty and exiled to the margins of time, to the shores of existence, Elia is still a privileged woman who possessed the moon, and so it's a lie—a merciful lie—what she's telling Pablo, to console him or because she doesn't really know what to say, that we all suffer and die and feel frustrated and we ask for the unattainable, and it's possible that Pablo doesn't know that the woman is partly lying to him, but he rejects her words anyway, because the suffering of many doesn't help him at all, doesn't solve anything for him, and Pablo keeps going over and over his discontent, the bad opinion he has of himself, that way of life he often feels trapped in, like caught in a trap, and it seems impossible that life, what's left of life, is reduced to this, but he doesn't have the necessary boldness to get out, escape, although maybe the worst of it is—he tells himself in moments of the most cruel lucidity—that it's not really a question of laziness, nor of cowardice, but of total insecurity about his own worth, and he shouldn't talk then of a mistake in direction or of a betrayal or a desertion of his most intimate longings, but rather of a radical incapacity for doing what he knows he would have liked to do, because if he truly—he confesses to himself and he confesses to Elia today for the first time—had believed in his own talent as a writer or a teacher, in the originality and validity of his abilities in the field of literature, there wouldn't have been anything, not the grieving memories of his childhood in a well-to-do family come down in the world, with a father permanently devoured by money problems, and a mother he remembers as grieving and who could hardly permit herself anything (Elia wonders now what she did so that the moment inevitably arrives when men tell her the sorrows of their childhood, in the double manner of rich children or of poor children, with all the nuances and variants of a similar conflict with the father, and if the same thing happens to all women, redeemers of wandering Dutchmen in their phantom boat, repose for warriors, warm refuge for steppe wolves, untiring listeners, since that's what, among many other things, they've educated us for since we were little girls, to listen attentively and understandingly to the sorrows and anxieties of males—what the hell do they tell their psychoanalyst or psychiatrist?), not even this, Pablo continues, not even the subsequent zeal he felt since he was a child to take revenge, to achieve for his family and for himself comforts and privileges that had been denied them, also the desire to really prove to his classmates, to the other kids in the neighborhood, to go ahead of them and leave them behind, with their mouths wide open in astonishment, mute with admiration (and here Pablo laughs), drooling with envy, because it's incredible, he recognizes, the number of things a person does to get revenge, to impose himself on others, to show them who we are and what we can do, to demonstrate to them and to ourselves what we're capable of, in a rancorous, inflamed, wild competition, which impels us to unsuspected successes, because the history of culture and of humanity would be different if we erased the achievements due to the dirtiest competition, to the most sordid envy, but not even that would have been enough to draw him away from his teaching position at the university, to make him abandon all attempts at writing, if he had had a minimal essential faith in his own talent, just as the longing wouldn't have been enough either, the longing to surround Eva with comforts and luxuries (so so many things that he hadn't had in his house, that his mother had never had), even to get for her a good apartment in the city, the best school for the children, books, paintings, trips, even jewels, the shared house by the sea, and here Elia interrupts Pablo's discourse, "but Eva never had suffered economic austerity, Eva didn't need any of these things at all, I'm sure she's never asked you for anything," and while he recognizes this is true, that his wife doesn't ask for or probably want or seem to need any of these things, that she didn't seem to miss them either in their first years together, when they lived with very little money, Elia thinks how curious that Pablo has persisted for years in getting things and offering them to a distracted, indifferent Eva busy with other very different problems, that she's accepted everything a little astonished, amused or sometimes enraptured, almost uncomfortable other times, never sincerely happy or interested, taking them and leaving them right away to one side, with the bewilderment and confusion that overwhelm us when we are presented with a gift we don't know what the hell to do with but we recognize as valuable, or faced with a favor we haven't asked or needed but is undoubtedly well-intentioned, because Eva hardly ever wears jewels, however much she assures that she does like them, and she has modernist brooches and pendants, Syrian or Tibetan bracelets, earrings that Pablo chose for her in the jewelry stores in Paris or the antique dealers in London, piled up or scrambled together in a dresser drawer, among underwear and the gas or light bills, and two or three fur coats hang in the closet, which she swore she loved, but which Elia—who adores furs—has never seen her wear even once, because Eva is apt to wear the same pants and the same sweater for days or weeks, leaving them on a chair next to the bed at night, and she puts them on automatically the next morning without even asking herself if she likes them or not, and which she substitutes when they get dirty or they tear for other ones almost identical, whereas she feels uncomfortable in the sumptuous silk or brocaded tunics, the elegant silk blouses that Pablo has risked buying for her a few times, and the clothes or the jewels often disappear, and it's impossible to find out if they've been given away or stolen, she even gets impatient if others insist in their questioning or in their suspicions, and nor do these exotic and costly trips that Pablo

69

sometimes proposes seduce her much, and she doesn't feel—
as does Elia, and it's another one of the little things that brings
her close to Pablo and makes them accomplices—a gratuitous
but intimate love for superfluous but very beautiful objects,
she doesn't even have—and she recognizes it laughingly and
without a trace of anger—enough good taste to appreciate
them, and she didn't understand for years why they had to buy
an apartment in the city, a house in the mountains or on the
beach, instead of renting them, and only at the insistence of
others and always reluctantly did she enter this consumptive
possessive race that devours us, but it seems, Elia thinks and
tells Pablo, as if this indifferent attitude of Eva's, that tendency
to reduce necessities and material wants to a minimum, that
easiness with which she gives away something just because
someone says she likes it, that facility with which she can use
everything if necessary, because she really seems capable of
living with almost nothing anywhere, that this would have
stimulated paradoxically in Pablo the zeal to buy and possess
and give her, so outside that order of things, his wife, that she
doesn't even usually oppose or reject them, they don't even
make her uncomfortable because she doesn't really pay attention to them and she accepts them as one more whim, one of
Pablo's manias, and he recognizes that her indifference probably does stimulate in him paradoxically that common type of
ambition, very difficult living year after year with a woman
who doesn't ask us for anything, who never needs anything,
who doesn't expect anything, it seems, from us, terribly
demanding and difficult after this apparent absence of demands
("do you remember the merchant's third daughter, the one
who asked for only one white rose, which turned out to be the
most difficult to get, much more so than the jewels and
dresses that her sisters had asked for, and made the merchant
fall under the Beast's power, and then made the Beauty and
the Beast meet?"), and it's as if the complete freedom in
which she leaves him, the unconditional support she's always
been and is still ready to give him—"because surely Eva

would prefer," says Elia, "for you to quit your job and earn a lot less money, but so that you could devote yourself to something that satisfies you more and would be more stimulating for both of you, Eva ready for whatever it takes, whatever sacrifice, so that you could write or prepare for a university position"—were working inversely like a hindrance, probably because, among all the risks, he's not capable of assuming the supreme risk of attempting a higher commitment and failing and letting her down, for Eva to know exactly, with total evidence, what the limits are of the man she chose as a partner, what his real stature is, and probably because even when it could be true that she would prefer for him other kinds of objectives and work, she would prefer it with total altruism, for Pablo's own good, in Pablo's benefit, not because she needed—as so many other women need it—the success of her mate so that she could affirm herself, so that she can feel indirectly justified and valued and endorsed, Eva always so self-sufficient, so centered in herself, so filled with herself that her goodness generously overflows towards others, and it's hard sometimes, it's very hard sometimes for him—Pablo repeats—even though he loves her very much, to live years and years and more years in the shadow of a woman who doesn't ask us for anything, who doesn't seem to need us at all, who doesn't receive and in fact hardly accepts anything, and who overwhelms us incessantly and excessively with the gifts that pour forth and overflow from her plenitude.

Clara wanders around the house like a big doll with strangely staring and disoriented eyes, like a little girl who lost her mommy and daddy among the fair booths or in the confusing spaces of some big grocery stores, like a stray cat—very similar to the Carlos You'll-Never-Amount-to-Anything Cat, who is always her opponent or her accomplice in the dialogues the girl writes, and which Eva hasn't been able to elucidate yet if it refers to an imaginary cat, to a literary artifice, or to an exterior reality that Clara transfigures and fantasizes—who one winter night leaned, skinny and cold, against the window and who we let in, Clara wanders around the house like those lost dogs who take away Elia's sleep and tranquility, Elia the exquisite, Elia the hypersensitive, who knows by the shine that burns in their eyes, by the tongue hanging out of one side of their mouth, by their way of walking—gradually more and more lame, as their paws hurt them, gradually swifter and more transported, as if they wanted to deceive the passersby, confuse the fellows who can take them away to die in the dog pound, making them think that they're going, sure-footed, towards a definite place where someone is waiting for them, when the truth is that their walking is mechanical now and without any final objective, or at least this is what Elia explains about lost dogs—so Elia knows the amount of time they've spent wandering through the city and even the home they were thrown out of, and Elia affirms sometimes that they were born in the street, on a plot of ground among the thickets, in the hallway of an abandoned house, and other times that they're garage dogs or dogs that were at a construction site until the bricklayers finished the job, or even dogs that had a master and a house but that have been pitilessly abandoned, and Elia should be the one who gives these animals shelter and who looks for an owner or puts them in a house, since she understands them so well and they make her suffer so, instead of tormenting herself in vain and doing nothing more than calling Eva for her to intervene and put them in the car that's in the street or even—it's happened a few times—take them out of the pound assuring that they're hers, identifying them from the description Elia gave her, while the other woman waits outside, incapable of bearing the spectacle of so many dogs suffering at the same time inside the cages, condemned to die, she, then, burdened with the responsibility of finding them an owner or moving them into the summerhouse or entrusting them as a last resort to the animal shelter, to Elia's displeasure, who looks at her as if she were committing a crime, and the children protest because

72

they don't want to be separated from the animal now, so that almost always, when they don't find anyone to take care of it, the dog ends up here, in the garden of the house next to the sea, where one more dog doesn't matter much, and they have a shed to protect themselves from the rain, and the neighbor gives them food and changes their water when they're not there, and notifies them in case of any offense or illness, and everything is a bother at times and problems, and this doesn't matter to Eva, but it makes her a little angry to see that Elia and the children have already forgotten about the new dog— they forget about it as soon as it's no longer a puppy or as soon as they know it's safe—and Elia begins with great application and skill to invent another pretext to get obsessed with and to suffer, and it should be Elia, so fanciful and understanding, exceptional listener to others' sorrows, valid speaker for that half of humanity that never finds adequate speakers, who listens to Clara and tries to understand her, Elia much more equipped than she to share this world of snake women and frog men and talking cats, to find out even how much is true and how much invented in these confusing tormented stories that the girl repeats or fancies, or tells her she dreams, stories in which Clara crawls through narrow tunnels full of bats, closely pursued by the woman without eyes, or she sinks slowly and irremediably into a swamp that absorbs her and sucks her and kisses her and gulps her down with rattles of fury and desire, fury and desire, as the midget people of her city without birds or sun watch her, motionless, from the bank and laugh, and their laughter turns into reptiles that come near, amphibians, through the mud, and bite her but- tocks, cling like vents to the warm hole between her legs, where they stick their rough tongues, they suck her nipples or she looks for her, for Eva, in a landscape of fog which leads her to a castle of smoke, and the merlons are smoke, the walls are smoke, smoke the drawbridge, and she penetrates into the rooms, getting lost, and there she finds her, and tries in vain to grasp her because the image escapes again and again like

73

smoke between her fingers, and Eva doesn't know if it's dreams or delirium that the girl lives awake and she can't determine either if she's asleep or if she's putting on a farce—the girl's aunt insisted it was a farce—or if it's madness pure and simple, these nights Clara moans and screams and struggles in bed, and it's impossible to wake her and she clings to Eva with so much strength that she hurts her (and the next day her arms are full of bruises) and Clara keeps crying and screaming when she has her eyes open, saying senseless things, calling her Mamma, and Elia could probably understand something in all this gibberish, this game of crazy people or children in which farce, derangement, and literature are subtly interwoven, and in which she loses (perhaps because confusion is deeply disagreeable to her, Eva an enemy—she recognizes—of all kinds of ambiguity), since Elia understands everyone, listens to everyone, even though afterwards she almost never does anything practical, anything real and positive to help people, just as she does almost nothing for the cats she opens windows to on the sly, for the dogs she gets others to pick up in the streets for her, and nevertheless that attentive, serious, truly interested listening—because Elia, who hardly hears about what's happening in the world (however much she's pretended to for years in order not to confront Jorge's disapproval, who each time, when Elia would ask with an innocent air something that everyone in the city, in the country, knew, looked at her, astonished, and scolded her later), is capable of identifying with and being moved and sharing the troubles of the first talking being you put in front of her and who tells her his sorrows—and she's almost always comforting and positive, and Eva would therefore like Elia to pay more attention to Clara, for there to be a closer communication between the two of them, and not only because Elia seems equipped to identify with any story but because there exists in this case a very special likeness. Both of them, Elia more mature, Clara crazier, possess an almost common language which should facilitate their understanding each other, and a friendship between the other two would be much better than this obsessive, absurd love that the girl has placed in her, unique center around which her universe of derangements and fantasies revolves, a love that annoys Eva to no end and even makes her regret sometimes having brought this girl to the house, Clara so dependent on her every move, on her steps through the rooms, her escapes to town or to the beach, that she surely hasn't even discovered that two other people live there—apart from the children, who only appear punctually to receive provisions in the form of enormous sandwiches or to fall, exhausted, into bed—on the border of invisibility and muteness, true, but existing anyway, and there Pablo is sucking on his discontent this summer like a sweet and sour candy he doesn't want to let go of, licking his sensitive, pampered (little-loved, he would say) man's wounds, in the corners of the house, lamenting everything he could have done and didn't do, what his life could have been, what it actually is, complaining that they attend to him badly, and don't pay enough attention to him, and in this state of mind, how was he going to take care of anyone else's anxiety, of anyone else's lack of love or dissatisfaction or fears? So that he looked for a minute at Clara the first day— true that she had already been warned that she shouldn't count on his help much—said a few innocuous and friendly words to her, commented to her and Elia "you didn't tell us she was such a very good-looking girl," and he forgot her immediately, or he directs at her every once in a while, when they're on the boat or at the table together, those looks that can appear indifferent to other people, but which Eva knows to be appreciative, evaluative, of an expert wine taster or cattle appraiser, the same looks he sometimes directs at the women who cross the streets, or in a public place, or who they meet in friends' houses, and which annoys Eva to no end, not because of envy or jealousy—she thinks—but rather because of spontaneous solidarity with individuals of her same condition, although it's more than possible—and Pablo says this laughing at her anger—that these individuals of her same condition, but so different from her, don't feel in the least vexed or offended, and accept, pleased, some looks that perhaps reduce them to the category of object, but a very valued, very coveted object at least, "what you feminists seem to ignore, or at least don't admit, is that few individuals in the world enjoy the degree of power that a beautiful seventeen-year-old woman has," Pablo says sometimes, and Eva would like to recuperate for a few instants her beauty at seventeen to be able to reply without being subject to all kinds of suspicions, that it's not true, it's almost never true, because these girls, so young and so beautiful, are disoriented and lost enough to hardly know how to take advantage of an initial superiority which partly enhances their value and partly leaves them even more defenseless, but as far as Clara goes, these looks don't flatter her or offend her nor does she hardly ever seem to notice them, absolutely unaware of the attractiveness so much flesh together can have, tight brown flesh, perfumed soft flesh, as if she hadn't realized she'd grown up and become a woman, and remained a stranger to these magnificent breasts that make her blouses and dresses explode, to these firm buttocks, to these long thighs, her body detained in that exact point—says Pablo—in which exuberance would become (and it will probably happen soon) fat, and Clara, it seems, is not aware of any of this, or she experiences it anyway as an incongruous and disagreeable reality, and not only does she not notice the occasional, very discreet looks from Pablo, but she has returned to the house sometimes with her face aflame and her chest heaving and her eyes lost in the distance, breathlessly telling unlikely and broken stories—again Eva can't determine where the real ends and where literature or fancy begins—about men who look at her, strangers who follow her, monsters who harass her, and one day she even arrived with her hair tangled, her dress torn, her arms and legs scratched, trembling from head to toe in a fit of horror that seemed impossible to lessen or contain, vomiting her disgust in unending retchings, and Eva doesn't know what to say to her, how to explain to her—as Pablo looks at them, ironically, behind the whitish, sweet-smelling pipe smoke as if he were witnessing a faraway scene that doesn't affect him in the least and in which he had decided at all costs not to intervene, and Elia still with her absorbed look, her distracted expression as if she were a Martian or everyone else had metamorphosed into insects, when actually it should be much easier for her to understand Clara than for Eva. She doesn't know how to warn her that she shouldn't go out into the street like that, half naked and with that crazed look, and to top it all off, as soon as she begins to talk, Clara looks at her astonished and confused, without wanting to understand, or understanding only that the other woman is scolding her, and then there is such desolation, such confusion on her face—"don't scold me, I'd rather die than have you scold me"—that Eva sighs and shrugs her shoulders and stops, and thinks, perhaps for the first time in her life, that she can't handle everything alone, it must be because she's getting old, or because she feels tired, or that this sinister summer is making them all (her too) sick, and it's too much for her, the effort it takes to keep managing such a big house and the children and the dogs and the cats and the children's friends and their own friends and this complicated man who is her husband, who these days is licking his wounds and sucking on his discontent and anguish, and who is blaming himself for everything he hasn't done and thinks he would have liked to have done, for the many trains he's missed, and he definitely blames her, even though he never says it, as if Eva were universally guilty for all his misfortunes and frustrations even though it can't be determined by what means or why (it must be inevitable in couples that one person makes his or her own failures and limitations fall upon the other), and it doesn't even occur to Pablo in the least that she too can need him, that she hasn't been at all in a good mood in the last months, that she too has a right to feel bad, to feel frustrated, to think, rightly or not, that she's not loved enough, nor does it occur to him that she can say to them any day—to him and to this ghostly Elia, who sleeps almost every hour of the day and looks at them in the hours that are left of wakefulness as if she didn't see them, as if she were looking through their transparent bodies at the wall behind them, probably remembering her dreams, that is if she dreams, or anticipating what to dream, gulping down in massive doses the little pills that according to Miguel, should work to make her not think so obsessively of Jorge, and of course she doesn't think, not about anything now, since she hardly does anything but sleep—and she can say to them any day, maybe even before this summer's over, even though the two of them, her husband and her best friend, haven't sensed even remotely such a possibility, "I give up, I've made it this far, and now I'm not going one step further."

Everything is full of smoke, a whitish smoke that smells like honey, that tastes like honey, a whitish mystery with a honey taste, multiple and faint threads of smoke that interweave, disperse and go up and up and up, and there's no ceiling or sky or anything, only a strange empty space where the thousand threads of smoke weave an enchanted castle, of milk and honey, no, of hashish and marijuana, and wobbling, floating, because I hardly weigh anything, I cross the drawbridge made of smoke, I manage to open the enormous thick doors of smoke, I walk through great salons of smoke, and there's nothing there, nobody anywhere, and the silence is so total that I hear my own heart beating, like in Poe's story, remember? booming between the walls of smoke, and I advance stubbornly towards the center of this smoky universe where I think a mystery reserved for the gods or the mad awaits me, and they let me enter surely because my eyes are empty and I'm almost as light as the air and I seem to arrive from very far away, and in the most hidden chamber of the palace, reserved for the gods or the mad, there you are, and you too are made of smoke, and you walk, indefatigable, around the room, from one side to the other, and I walk behind you and I grab you again and again, but again and again you escape between my fingers, and then I wake up and there's a red star in the sky." Clara speaks now in her good little girl's peaceful voice, very low not to wake the others, so that Pablo or Elia doesn't hear her from the adjoining rooms, and everything's fine now with Eva sitting on the edge of her bed, taking the hair out of her eyes, giving her sips of water to drink, taking her hand and caressing it with a repeated, automatic gesture, but very calming and soft, all of her honey and milk, thinks sleepy Clara, warm milk and honey from the most hidden and perfumed herbs of the forest, rivulets of warm and very sweet milk where, in the back of a boat cradled by the waves, there rocks a good little girl whose mamma calms her after silly dreams, bad silly dreams, in the middle of the night, and Clara wonders with a pang of anguish, if she screamed very loud, if she woke everyone in the house, frightening the other children, disturbing the sad sleeping woman, the exiled nymph, submerged in a dense, dreamless torpor, if the fat cat, the huge, shiny domestic cat jumped onto her bed and wrinkled his snout and whiskers and let out a snort of annoyance, cats masters of the house don't like stray cats one bit, skinny cats with sad eyes, who amble along the roofs and manage to slip in sometimes by mistake, because of unpardonable negligence or tolerance on the part of the owners who have left the windows open, into the padded interior, and if the Big Cat of the Castle—who knows nothing of the street or of the night, who knows nothing about the cats of the night and of the street, who doesn't even know the cat Carlos You'll-Never-Amount-to-Anything, the Cat Who Never Grew Up, the Cat Who Learned Everything in Books, not to mention the Cat Muslina or the very Queen of the Cats, who doesn't know anything about anything— had turned over and found the other side of the bed empty, and had lit a pipe or had kept sleeping, although it's very probable that he decided not to sleep and wait, awake, for the woman of light (so like the Queen of Cats whom the Carlos cat waits for, not impatiently, that Clara thinks sometimes that they're the same person, the same dream), in order to ask her, "What the hell is wrong now with that crazy girl?", because the winged and luminous woman, the woman of smoke, the woman who pours forth honey and warm milk, who provokes such a profound eagerness to fall asleep forever between her breasts, will return sooner or later to the huge lustrous domestic and conjugal cat's bed, although now she's at her side, and she strokes her hands and her forehead and asks her, she too in a low voice, "and that was all that frightened you so much, that's why you were crying so downheartedly?", and she again feels a mortal shame for her screams and her cries in the night, for the words she may have said and doesn't remember, and not remembering them pushes her into suppositions and conjectures even worse than what they really were, and now she attends to Eva's question and vacillates, in her slow and still serene voice, "no, it wasn't the dream about the castle of smoke that woke me up so badly in the middle of the night, there was something else, I think I was looking for you in a strange city, an oriental city, with narrow and steep streets, and with a lot of steps everywhere, that went up and down from one street to another, and I was very frightened because I knew something terrible had happened to you, and I was asking everyone about you and I asked for their help, but nobody paid any attention to me, they answered in meaningless sentences or they didn't listen to me, and then I wanted to go back to the castle of smoke, and in the place where the castle had been, there was now a cemetery, and the graves were so close together that I couldn't help grazing the marble of the tombstones when I passed between them, and it was damp and cold, stickylike, and then the cat Carlos came up to me and smiled mysteriously: "You see, everything in life passes or changes, first there's a void, then a castle of smoke, then a cemetery," and I felt a horrible anxiety, and from beneath the earth, the dead were talking to me, you were talking to me, even though I didn't understand the words among so many voices together, and then I saw you, they had buried you alive, in that party dress, the white and pink one you wear sometimes and that I like so much, and a swarm of black cockroaches, a legion of hairy spiders were walking on top of your body, and were looking at me, staring me straight in the eye, but you weren't looking at anything, you were crying, crying, crying with an unending grief," and again, her heart shrinks, remembering now Eva's face, so so sad, so distant and alone, so unreachable, as if in the dream they'd switched roles, because Eva's is the warm interior, the fire in the hearth, the secure and confident everyday life, and hers is anxiety and crying, she's the one who must wander through streets and rooftop terraces, huddling against windowpanes from the outside, untiringly smelling out a place to go, from roof to roof, as if she still hadn't learned that all the windows are the same, especially when someone closes them from inside and one is left outside, and why, besides, does it always rain so much when humans leave cats outside the house? stray cats, skinny cats with sad eyes, cats of the street and of the night, who arrive at the wrong time, and are very stubborn and insist on having an owner—and there's no one like her!—as if a skinny stray cat could be the same as a shiny house cat (a big fat cat like the ones sometimes seen on the other side of the window, sleeping peacefully, with tranquil breathing, without any bad dreams, without ever waking up screaming and sobbing in the middle of the night, on a velvet pillow that someone has put next to the fireplace for them, near a bowl of milk and biscuits, roof cats, stray cats, who dream, to top it all off, impossible dreams, unworthy of cats with fur on their chest and bristling moustaches—stray cats, skinny cats with sad eyes hardly have any dignity—cats who try, who want, who believe it might be possible . . . and don't ever learn that at the very instant they get ready to enter through the window, the fat shiny cat with peaceful breathing arrives, the lord of the castle, who knows nothing of the street or of the night and who jumps, maybe because of that, more agilely, and takes his place on the windowsill, and closes the window with a thud of his paw, and that's when it rains, and she knows that even if she continues her walking on rooftops, there won't ever be any more windows left ajar like this one, nor any more pillows next to the fire, nor any more owners as lovable (they love a lot even though they love badly, these skinny stray cats with sad eyes, they love a lot and very badly, maybe because they don't know how), so cheerfully and happily found, so sorrowfully and sadly lost, so cried for, because everything is rain, and the skinny stray cats with sad eyes know and fear the end, the jump towards the window that will hurl them to the street, against the asphalt soaked from the rain, because it happened one day to a stray cat, skinny with sad eyes, and it will keep happening, always, always, always, while the skinny stray cats with sad eyes keep being so innocent, so foolish, so stubborn, and a little selfish, with their crazy, innocent, slightly selfish, so childish dreams, and they don't know or don't understand that the owners sometimes don't know or understand either or can't understand a certain kind of cat, stray skinny cats with sad eyes, cats of the street and of the night, who make a mess of things, and make mistakes and love badly, who love a lot and badly, and always always always lose their pretty owners . . .

She wakes once again startled and frightened in the middle of the night, and for a few moments, as she slowly emerges from the dream as from a blind well, a marine deep, dirty with lime and algae, as she feels her wet cheeks, the damp pillow, and tries to recuperate her breathing's regular rhythm and stop the runaway beating of her heart—that sick and crazy colt—she believes that it's she herself who has been screaming, and fearful, she even brings her hands to her mouth as if she could thus suffocate the noise, but she discovers right away that it isn't she screaming, that they have not been her own laments that have awoken her in the middle of the night, because she's still mute, with no capacity yet for screams or even for words, deprived even of her voice, as if the voice also were a prodigious find, a magic gift from Jorge, as if Jorge had invented her voice for her, this total Jorge who encompassed everything and contained the world inside him and who took the world with him when he left her ("exclusive measurer of all graces," Eva mocks her when she hears her talk like this, "and what is this about finding your own voice in him? You wrote long before you met him," and Elia must recognize that yes, she had begun to write years before meeting him, and nevertheless she knows that since she's known him—how absurd critics and friends and journalists are: who do you write for? for your contemporaries or for posterity? do you write for the public at large or for a minority of middle-class people and intellectuals? what kind of reader do you think of when you write?—she knows that since the day she met him, even though she's never told anyone, she writes exclusively for him, so that Jorge reads her, so that she thus has one more way of getting close to him and surrendering herself to him, another road to arrive at him, so that Jorge is content, so that he's proud of her, Elia dependent on his approval like a little girl can be on her daddy whom she adores, or like believers in a god to whom they offer their sacrifices wondering anxiously if he will appreciate them and accept them) and now without Jorge, all that's left to her is this mute cry on dreamless nights, because Elia never cries during the day, while she's awake, she cries only at night, and nevertheless she's not able to remember afterwards how her dreams were that made her cry, deprived even of her dreams, the past and the future wiped out, mutilated, and the present reduced to a numb void, this insurmountable fatigue ("once upon a time there was a silly princess," Eva mocks her when they remember the past together, and Elia interrupts right away, "once upon a time there was an ugly, grey, stupid princess, who had nothing at all, so timid and so belittled," "so little loved," she interrupts her again, so little loved between a mother whose only maternal traits appear invariably in old photographs, never in memories or in reality, a mother who already prefigured future abandonments, and an absent father, whom she must invent perched behind the camera and playing hide and seek among the garden's rose bushes and hortensias and gardenias, "who does nothing but remain still and dream awake, invent stories for herself underneath the dining-room table or in the very back of the children's wardrobe," and around the ugly, grey, stupid princess, Elia thinks, although she doesn't say it—it's too literary, and surely Eva would make fun of her—forests and branches began growing, trees and climbing plants and vines, an impenetrable mess, gigantic spiders laboriously built their webs, pinnacles interposed their stone wall, plains burnt in an endless fire, "she did nothing but invent stories in her corner," Eva usually goes on, "but then one day Prince Charming arrived," "no," she always protests half in fun, half in seriousness at this point, "he wasn't a prince, and he wasn't even charming, right? what was he, then? a foreigner?" and here Elia becomes quiet, because he was in a certain way a foreigner, a long thin fellow who arrived from very far away and had gone down every road and had furrowed every sea, a distracted and very clumsy foreigner (clumsier even than she) who first approached Ismene, then Antigone, with that swinging walk tall thin men have whose bodies become all arms, all legs, and he had a straight, tricolored moustache (like the coat of this town's cats), behind which he perhaps hid a sad smile, and above, the most melancholic and mocking eyes they'd ever seen in their life, "so, a foreigner," Eva rectifies, "and he came from very far away, and he lifted you up onto the croup of his white horse, or on his dapple-grey cowboy's horse or on his black wandering Dutchman's horse, even though he surely had to wake you first from your one-hundred-year sleep," and before him the thick tangle of branches and leaves, the dense corrupt mess of vines and climbing ivy gave way gently, offering hardly any resistance, and the webs that the gigantic spiders had so laboriously spun opened like revolving doors at his passage, and the stone walls receded and divided up, and the fire on the calcified plains agonized, and then he took her with him, and invented colors and a voice for her so that she could play with them, like you give a little boy a gold ball and a red or multicolored balloon, and he dressed her in his love, as if it were a sumptuous tunic, and turned her into the most loved, the happiest, the most beautiful of all story princesses, "God, the things you say!" Eva usually exclaims at this point, although Elia isn't listening anymore, mute, absorbed and lost in her dreams), and now the past and future have been wiped out, because the past would hurt too much and a future without Jorge is still unimaginable, and all that remains is this mute weeping on these dreamless nights, this numb grey void, this inexplicable fatigue, which is only the fatigue of living, a dark hollowness in which everything crumbles and dies, her last possibilities of faith and hope reduced to those little bottles full of multicolored pills, because only they, she thinks, stop her from hitting bottom, from really reaching the end, and keep her floating, even though she's adrift, the mooring cables broken, the roots torn off, the kite's string lost in the wind, detoured, turning in a circle which seems to have no end and perhaps, Elia thinks tonight as she hears in the next room the now calm and quiet whispering with which Clara must be telling Eva her misfortunes or her bad dreams, it might be preferable to renounce these subterfuges and sink helplessly, maybe if she arrived at the very bottom, at the miry floor of the pool, at the cloudy abysses of algae and sand, she could hold her breath, hit the bottom with her feet, and get ready to ascend again, maybe she could even emerge alive to the surface and breathe again, begin to live, because it's necessary to overcome the ultimate limits of desolation and suffering in order to finish with them and then begin to repair oneself, maybe, Elia thinks in the night, she should stop resorting to these pills that make her stupid, that keep her in a constant doze, and let herself sink, this might be the only possibility of a cure, of salvation, but she is too tired for such an effort and besides she's very afraid, Elia always frightened, since she was a little girl but not any less now, of the unknown, what she can't evoke or imagine, and it's unknown and unthinkable to her that steel trap of pain that's watching her and waiting for her in the deepest part of the swamp, in the marine abysses, in the last confines of the ocean, in the point of no return where the kite goes crazy and escapes from gravity's dominion, it's unthinkable what her life will be in the future without Jorge, and just formulating it in her mind "I'm going to have to keep living without Jorge" leaves her terrified and aghast, paralyzed, sweating, like those beautiful felines, the wounded lioness, unexpectedly pierced and destroyed by an arrow unimaginable a few seconds earlier in the luxuriance, in the magnificent overflowing vitality of the forest, an arrow which in its steel flight has broken her spine and destroyed the world, so that the lioness, as death penetrates her and ascends, inexorably, along her back, opens her jaws in a howl that expresses something which isn't pain, which can't even be identified with fury or fright, but rather with incredulity and surprise, and raises her eyes in an ecstatic and astounded gaze, incapable of understanding or accepting that everything has abruptly ended for her, that everything has been destroyed in an instant, amid the luxuriant leaves, under the pale sun, in the middle of the jungle in spring.

He has let the women go out in the boat without him, and they haven't even asked him what's wrong, nor have they insisted like other times that he accompany them. It's possible that Elia and Clara don't even realize he's not there, and Eva shrugged her shoulders, resigned to what she considers his strangeness, his bad moods, his susceptibilities, with an expression that means more or less "I don't know what's wrong with you, but it will be over soon," and the truth is that the three women are immersed these days in their own craziness, in their untransferable obsessions and fantasies

—he too, he recognizes, is strange these days—each one shut up in herself, but capable it seems to him of allying themselves to each other by means of a bond in which Pablo, being a man, doesn't participate, the three of them moving in a pernicious and strange circle, thickly female, to which he can't have access, and this makes him ridiculously jealous, and he's fed up with the summer—that he had planned and fancied differently—bored with the town and the house, in which he feels at some moments like a stranger, someone passing through, who hasn't even been invited, and who they attend to with a distracted air, because Eva is busier than ever—or busy in a different way—nervous and unhappy, occupied with running the house as if she were participating in a contest of domestic abilities, when everyone knows she's never liked them, and that she's always done them because someone has had to, and it was taken for granted that Elia, Pablo, and Jorge weren't good for anything, but this year Eva moves around the kitchen and through the house with a mortified and heroic air that annoys him to no end, and Pablo wonders and asks her why it's necessary to arrange from top to bottom some wardrobes in which odds and ends and clothes have been accumulating for centuries but where nevertheless there's still space, or to spend hours in the kitchen when they don't care or almost don't care whether they eat superelegant dishes or a potato omelette, and they could solve everything like other times by going to the restaurant and letting the kids fix themselves a sandwich. Why wear the kids out besides with classes and homework that the school hasn't assigned and that they don't want to do and that they've never done any other summer, and Eva regrets that she hasn't been able even to start all the work she brought from the office, that everything is on her shoulders, and it's very possible that she hasn't forgiven them—Elia too, but him especially—for refusing, from the beginning, to collaborate actively in Clara's redemption, above all because the redemption has become complicated and difficult, and although she doesn't have to confess it, it's

fairly probable that Eva is up to her eyeballs with this taciturn
and timid girl who follows her everywhere like a dog, doesn't
do a thing during the entire day but follow her with puppy-
dog eyes, and when she can't follow her, escapes to the town
or the countryside or the beach, where nobody knows what
she does, but from where she returns sometimes with her hair
a mess and her dress torn, full even of bruises and scratches,
this girl, so strange and so beautiful, with a bursting adult
woman's body, a model woman, and that mentality belonging
to a nine-year-old, who flees from him—Pablo wonders if
she also flees from the boys or men who probably follow her
to the hills or along the beach, and if the bruises and scrapes
are from resistance or compliance—and shrinks in his presence, trembling and frightened, blushing to the roots of her
hair, when he finds her alone, as if she were afraid he would
throw himself on top of her right there, on the dining-room
table or against the balcony curtains, rape her, and Pablo feels
misunderstood and offended—"would you please tell that
idiot she has no reason to be afraid every time I look at her,
that I haven't eaten anyone yet?" although it is true that he's
disturbed sometimes by so much brown, tight, compact flesh
(very different from the magnificent body Eva had in other
times, delicate and golden and thin, although both of them are
very tall and dark-haired) and those somber eyes of a trapped
animal that avoid him tenaciously and which he hasn't been
able even once to see face to face, and that puppy smell,
because Clara doesn't smell like an adult woman or even like
a baby, she smells like flowering underbrush, like fruits ripen-
ing very slowly in the loft, like earth or hay wet from the rain,
and it's a shame that Eva has her—it must be part of the plan of
regeneration, the educational program—permanently under
the shower and washing her hair. It's true that he's provoked
and excited, Pablo recognizes, by her screams and weeping in
the night, those hoarse cries of a lioness in heat, and that he
always feels absurdly cheated, left out when it's Eva and not
he who gets up lazily and sighing from the bed and goes to

console her, because it's not a matter really of listening to her stories and her lies and her bad dreams, of taking her hand and turning on the light and making her drink a few sips of water, it's a matter of—although neither of them know it, or although Eva knows and doesn't admit it—ripping off that ridiculous nunlike nightgown she's drowning in, and mounting her and riding her, with energy and with infinite care, and making her scream finally with pleasure and pain, genuine pleasure, and real pain, not confusing anxieties and vain fears, the pleasure of a woman who has discovered authentic tenderness in the male, the definitive support that will enable her to leave behind her blushes without a cause, her vain fantasies, her childish fears, it's so evident what she's looking for and needs, and Pablo wonders—as he strolls through town with the newspaper in his hand and sits at a table facing the sea and asks for a double whiskey with a lot of ice—why women are so often mistaken, why they almost always set their objectives so badly, since it's not just Clara, such a novice still, who's rushed into a passionate and painful pursuit of someone who, like Eva, can't even begin to understand what's happening, what they expect of her, and so touchy and aggressive faced with demands that overwhelm her and that in short she doesn't want to understand, a waste such useless passion, so much youth and so much beauty launched into an impossible endeavor, but it's not only this silly big girl, because there's Elia, intelligent and exquisite, so keen and wise at elucidating other people's problems, bewildered nevertheless, she too, by an excessive passion, consecrated exclusively for years and years—"from the day I met him" she would recognize with her simpleton face—and it's been more than fifteen, to this pedantic, conceited, unbearable fellow, impossible to guess what women see in him, with his self-sufficient air and always talking like a professor, always with his books and papers, and organizing Elia's life as if she were retarded, protecting her and guiding her, indicating to her what she has to do, what she has to think at each juncture, in a hateful variant of enlightened

89

despotism, Elia dependent on him as on a god, surrendered and immobilized by a limitless fascination, quoting him at every step, soliciting his learned and almost always extremely boring opinions, then imposing them on others, sharing them until she exceeds them and overdoes it, asking him in a delicate voice for some things she could get or buy for herself but which only acquire value it seems if it is he who buys them for her, not only turning Jorge into the center of her universe but also insisting that everyone else, Eva and he and the others, share this stupid, excessive admiration and that they let him be right even when they know—and Elia too must know it—that he isn't, that they accommodate their four lives to the tastes and appetites and whims of Jorge, always dependent on and compelled by the fear that he'll be annoyed or angry, because Elia has turned Jorge's silences and bad moods, his slightest annoyances—just like everyone else's tantrums and annoyances—into a kind of universal cataclysm—and it is after all Elia's fault, not Jorge's—and they walk around from the moment they get up to the moment they go to bed— in the city too, but above all during the shared summers— harassed by the fear of bothering him or pulling him out of his beatitude, and now for the first time there's been a conflict between them, between the two of them, and it hasn't even been because Elia abandoned her permanent submission for a few hours or a few days, but rather because Jorge wanted it that way, playing at not loving her or at leaving her, in a stupid, cruel game that nobody believes, expressing in words and actions a dissatisfaction, an impatience, an unhappiness that many people undergo—perhaps it's the age—but that they don't dare show, but Elia has indeed believed him, sure that they've come to the end, and she moves around the house and around town, estranged and somnambulant, like an unjustly beaten domestic animal—not like a wounded wild one—like a dog whose master has kicked her out of the car and left her in the middle of the street, turned into a zombie, without talking to anyone, hardly looking at them, without even being aware of them, because even her son it seems has stopped existing for her and she spends days and more days without deciding to go get him, without even the desire to call him, surely not to write him either, maybe she doesn't remember him, stupefied by pain and anxiety, confused and made sleepy by so much medication, and she hardly even looks at him, or answers his questions, or listens to him however much she adopts the expression of listening to him like she used to, such friends the two of them for years, always, because Elia for a long time has been for him the most valid listener, much more sensitive, more doubtful, more flexible than Eva, both of them, he and Elia, allied in the shadows like two iconoclastic and fearful little children, irreverent and mischievous, sharing besides the fervor and affection for Eva —Jorge has never liked her, and Elia knows it—so friendly always Elia, so close and so warm, such a comrade, until this summer when everything's going wrong and she seems outside everything, incapable of becoming interested in anything or listening to them, precisely now when Pablo is invaded by a profound melancholy, an unhappiness that overwhelms him, as if he had suddenly acquired awareness of his limits, of his own aging—probably something similar has happened to Jorge—as if he really understood for the first time that all those things, so many, that he has wanted to do and hasn't yet, he'll never do now, that he's in short not living a waiting period but rather the one that will have to last until the end of his life, and Pablo feels bored and tired these days, asphyxiated by the monotony of this closed town, a town the railroad doesn't pass through, trains can't be heard or seen, nor do cars cross through it, separated from any other semicivilized place by sixteen kilometers of curves and bad roads, often razed, even in the summer, by a relentless wind, maddening—no wonder they're all walking around half crazy—authentic last stop on a dead-end street, where they don't understand sometimes, when things go wrong, how they could have committed the rashness of coming here, and Pablo is fed up with moving between three female ghostly figures who don't listen to him, or pay any attention to him, or look at him, or share anything with him, as if Pablo were invisible, improbable, because Elia isn't the only one reduced to this zombie condition, unable to become interested in anything that's not her sick and untransferable obsession, and that big little girl that Eva has put among them asking for their collaboration but without consulting them one bit at home, with her dazzling female body that has right now reached its fleeting and unrepeatable plenitude, and her smell of very ripe fruit, of flowering thickets, and her dark eyes of a little trapped wild animal, and those screams and cries waking the night, that silly girl who escapes from him, frightened, who blushes and shrinks every time he finds her alone, and all Pablo needs this summer is for someone to look at him as though he were Count Dracula or the Düsseldorf murderer, but it's not only Elia's apathy and Clara's fear, it's also Eva herself who's treating him this summer with unusual coolness, understanding and affection magically evaporated, caresses erased, she interpreting day after day the role of heroic and mortified housewife, a role that doesn't suit her at all, that doesn't fit, exhausted by chores she's always done without any apparent effort, surly and hostile, making them all feel, even Clara, useless and abusive and completely unnecessary.

She commented on it as soon as she discovered him—a few days ago now—walking a few meters ahead of them during their stroll, "do you realize?" and she immediately regretted saying it, better not to try sharing these things with anyone, least of all with the touchy and difficult Eva of this summer, who has adopted the air of a resigned schoolteacher faced with a class of kindergarteners, but the words were already in the air, shrunken and tremulous, as if they were agonizing with cold in the late-afternoon breeze along the ocean, but perfectly audible, and Eva has caught them in flight, even though she doesn't even look at her, she fixes her attention on the car's controls, on the people and children and dogs crossing in front of her. Eva has a slight smile, "of course I've realized, but nobody dares tell you anything," and to Elia the smile seems mocking and superior, although it's probably her excessive susceptibility as always which makes her see ridicule and arrogance where possibly there isn't any, because in this total destitution in which she's lost love and the world with it, some scraps have subsisted, some insignificant and stubbornly persistent tics, like her timidity, her fears, her susceptibility, or perhaps they bloomed again with renewed strength when Jorge disappeared, Jorge who almost always barred their passage, kept them at bay, and the truth is that Eva's smile mortifies her, although it's very probable that it has nothing of ridicule or disdain, and that it's only a smile able to become understanding, an attempt at an almost maternal smile, a smile of the only adult in this closed world of invalids and the mentally retarded, so evident these days that Eva considers herself for better or for worse the only adult and that she looks upon them as meddling and crazy little children, stupidly obsessed with love and happiness, or with the absence of love and the subsequent loss of happiness, three stubborn and obstinate and selfish and not very intelligent children (even though Eva would never even to herself formulate the description of "not very intelligent" and would replace it at the last minute with "mature") awkwardly trapped in a personal and irrelevant situation that makes them lose sight of the world, as if only their individual dissatisfaction could make the universe overflow or was enough in any case to turn everything upside down, and it's possible that Eva's right—if she is really thinking what Elia attributes to her—and that the three of them are acting like children who haven't known how or haven't been able or haven't wanted to grow up, more excusable in Clara, so young still, so long the time left to her to rectify the situation, more understandable in Pablo, who hasn't been able to make his way because he has gone down many roads but none of them was the one he wanted, the one he dreamed of in his youth, and this has made him concentrate on himself, shut up inside himself, in his own failure, turning his annoyed narcissism into the core of his life or his nonlife, but without extenuating circumstances in Elia's case, bright enough, lucid enough, strong enough—because Eva has always fantasized her as intelligent and strong—to have left behind her inventions about total love, her foolish insistence in transforming the first man in her life into a grotesque pastiche of the wandering Dutchman, steppe wolf, tired warrior, measurer of all graces, because Eva must have been thinking something like this when she smiled disdainfully or understandingly, without looking at her, and recognized, "of course I've seen him, but no one dares tell you anything," and they had in fact the same enervated gait, the head in front, the same awkward swinging like the Pink Panther, the same long thin body of a boy who's grown a lot and too quickly, and there the resemblance ended, because when they sped up and were able to see his face, there was no longer even the most remote likeness, and the meeting was reduced to one more of the multiple starts she feels every time she thinks she recognizes him, and she recognizes him everywhere, a sudden pain in the chest, an abrupt interruption of her breathing, her ears burning, as if she didn't know Jorge were thousands of miles away and couldn't have come back. And now, a few days later, strolling through town, Elia had the idea of going into the only bar, the café, where they never went together, the music too loud, the people too crammed together, too young as well for Jorge to like the place, and for years and years Elia has believed that she didn't like dark, packed places either, places with red lights, or nightlife, or street life, taking once again his tastes for both of theirs, for her own tastes (maybe because she met him when she was very young and Jorge already an older man). It's now when she discovers once again the pleasure of huddling in a corner, against the wall, in the semidarkness, with a tall cold glass in her hands, a cigarette lit, although she doesn't usually smoke, and Jorge would ask her, surprised, if he were here, "you smoke now?", isolated and protected by the noise and the tumult, by the music and the smoke, in a contradictory and strange intimacy, a little like what's produced on a night train when it passes through empty stations and sleeping towns, and it's cold outside and one invents it all, and thinks about the people for whom this decor is their habitual landscape and not a fleeting and irremovable curtain, people shut in their houses, surely in bed, whom she will never know, because the train crosses through their sleeping lives without touching them, at most they can hear the engine's whistle and think it's such and such a time and turn over and then go back to sleep, and the car's interior becomes then sometimes padded and warm, intimate as a den or maybe as a nest, the closest thing to a true home, and something similar happens to Elia in these bars where there are a lot of people but nobody knows anyone, where the presence of strangers, and the music—really too loud—and the smoke and the sparks of the cigarettes in the dark and the sliding between tables of a tall thin waiter who advances furtively and dodging obstacles with the tray full of tall cold glasses, although it might not be probable that everyone drinks, as she does, choosing, above all for the color, peppermint, or is guided by the glorious shining apotheosis of the cherry and the round slice of lemon and orange and red sugar on the rim of the glass, a "San Francisco" without alcohol, and Elia feels sometimes, in this kind of place, on the very border where invisibility begins, the permanent yearning of shy people, of those who never manage to love themselves or accept themselves. And the invisible adolescent girl of the night and of the street, the neurotic woman, pursuer in vain of moons, has decided today in favor of peppermint, in spite of the disadvantages of mixing the pills Miguel has prescribed for her with alcohol and of the unforeseeable consequences, although what are the consequences that could still frighten, that could worry Elia the somnambulist. And at some moment without her noticing it, the thread of music has stopped, and someone has sat in front of the microphone with a guitar, and sings a mushy, wet and sentimental ballad that strikes Eva and Pablo as ridiculous and banal—and on top of that, badly sung —but which Jorge might have liked and which without a doubt Clara would like, and which fills Elia's eyes with tears, about to cry awake for the first time in such a long time, as she wonders if living on dreams is really the true way, and concludes that true or not it is in any case the only thing she has managed to do in her life, insatiable devourer of dreams and longings, tenacious manipulator of experiences and realities, so badly equipped deep down for real living, and it hasn't been true after all, she recognizes now for the first time, that Prince Charming penetrated into the jungle, violated the humid and warm and sticky thickness and woke the ugly stupid princess from her hundred-year sleep. It's not true that he carried her away with him on the croup of his white horse to a world of reefs and realities—because something had to misfire, something had to go wrong from the beginning since the story has ended this way—it's all been nothing but another fantasy, one more dream lost in the depths of her sleep, because nobody perhaps came to look for her and nobody woke her to life with a kiss, and Prince Charming and his white horse belong to the absurd world of fairy tales, and it's impossible for the prince to proclaim in the last lines of the story, "hasn't it occurred to you that we may have stopped loving each other?" in front of a silly and mute princess who wouldn't understand anything, just as she didn't understand either, but now, in the café, Elia's sadness becomes more tender, almost warm, almost unbearable, and maybe it's because she's finishing, she who never drinks, and much less when the consequences are unforeseeable, her second peppermint, or maybe it's because the Argentinean boy with the beard and the guitar keeps humming silly tunes and sad longings and for the first time in a long time, something has given way inside Elia and Elia is crying, a gentle crying, without twitches or noise, because she doesn't make the least effort today to control the crying, to stop crying—surely she's drunk on peppermint and words, that fatal mixture of unforeseeable consequences—and the tears flow easily and slide down her cheeks and give her lips a salty taste, like the ocean, and wet her hands and her cigarette and her dress, and she almost doesn't distinguish, blinded by the darkness and by her crying, the man who has approached her and has sat down beside her and put his arm around her shoulders and is talking softly to her, as to a little girl, wildly in love with the moon, awkward adolescent who didn't know how to grow up, he talks to her with words Elia doesn't understand, in the first moment of stupor, because this stranger is talking to her with a voice very like Jorge's, the same slight foreign accent, the same voice Jorge has cradled and calmed her with during a thousand nights, and Elia thinks, beyond all logic that maybe it's the same boy they saw cross the street with his long-legged Pink Panther gait, and she doesn't want to dry her tears, she doesn't want to see him, because she prefers not to establish in this first moment where the likeness ends, and discover that the man who is rocking and consoling her surely doesn't have a straight, soft, multicolored moustache, like those alley cats that Elia loves so much, with black and grey and black and red and gold fur, he surely doesn't have an inconfoundable moustache over a mouth of thin lips, perhaps cruel, nor the tremendously mocking, desolate eyes of the wandering Dutchman who has furrowed again and again the seven seas, of a wolf from the steppes who has traveled them all in the snow and has forgotten all the roads now, of a warrior who returns home victorious or defeated, triumphant or defeated, after his six thousand battles, and Elia doesn't want to see his face, she doesn't want to find out who he is or what he's like, given that he can't be the only one she's waiting for, and she doesn't care if she discovers whether or not he looks like the other man they saw walking along the street, and she doesn't want either to understand his words, which aren't words said to be understood, and maybe they don't even have a meaning, only that monotonous and soothing song with which we calm children who wake up frightened in the night, similar perhaps to the senseless words Eva must invent for Clara, that big little girl she's brought to the house, to free her of her nightmares and put her back to sleep, a dreamless sleep, and Elia takes refuge in the hollow of the stranger's shoulder and sobs uncontrollably and the man whispers softly to her and cradles her and rocks her and puts his hand through her long straight hair, on her trembling shoulders, and dries her last tears with his handkerchief, and kisses her hands, her temples, her cheeks, her neck, then, for a long time, her reddened eyes, and he smells like a cologne made from herbs, lavender perhaps, of sweet pipe tobacco, of recent sweat, and he has strong hands—that aren't at all like Jorge's delicate hands—covered on the back by a thick down, but they are nonetheless soft hands, and finally Elia has stopped crying and looks him straight in the eye, at the precise moment he's kissing her on the mouth, both of them strangely with their eyes wide open, and the stranger's eyes aren't that indefinite color, aquatic, mocking, melancholic, behind glasses, they're dark eyes, without nuances, which are looking straight at her, compassionately, worriedly, solicitously, with a comforting gaze.

Before, in the beginning, a long time ago now," Eva has begun the sentence, and Clara has heard only these words, because then she doesn't listen anymore, sure that in any case, however much attention she pays, she won't understand, aware only that Eva is scolding her, of her pained and surprised look, with a hint of interrogation and perplexity, as if she were proposing something Clara could respond to, when really Clara is only conscious of the other woman's irritated voice, that impatient voice she directs at children when they persist in impossible caprices or at the girls in the office when they make mistakes in the simplest tasks, or at people in political meetings who make her argue for the hundredth time reasonings she considers self-evident. Other people's stubbornness or foolishness or wickedness always provoke that irritation, that discomfort in Eva, lucid and coherent, and when she uses this voice against her, Clara is disconcerted, and feels her cheeks burn and her ears buzz, and she wonders, at the peak of anxiety and desolation, how she could manage to be alone in these moments, thousands and thousands of miles from this house, thousands and thousands of miles from this pained and surprised voice that is scolding her for things she doesn't understand, or that she could perhaps understand, but that fall in any case higher or lower, always out of her will's reach, and Clara, immobilized in an anguish with no possible reaction or answer, would like to be far away, anywhere, however she could, but very far away, safe from the voice that is surely scolding her for her sulkiness, for her gloomy answers, for her sullen silences, for her cries in the night, for her impossible demands, far from that guy who parsimoniously smokes his pipe, with the indolent expression belonging to the supreme lord of the realm of domestic cats, of castrated felines, licking his whiskers with pleasure, sure that he understands, when actually he's never understood a thing, but why does he need to understand, if it's true that the woman never talks to him in that tone, and Clara would give anything to escape and find herself far away, even if it were in the dark subterranean world of reptiles and lizards, because there or in the deepest part of the worst hell the terrible Queen of Cats' irritation and impatience and displeasure and rejection couldn't probably reach her, but she knows she is incapable of getting up, of saying something, or of not saying anything and leaving the room and the house without further ado, incapable of such a simple gesture as standing up and walking out, paralyzed there, in front of the dining-room table, in an unbearable anxiety, with the buzz in her ears and her cheeks burning and her mind a blank, stuck on the words the other woman said at the beginning of the first sentence, and which are the only ones she has understood and listened to, "for a long time now, for a very long time now," Clara repeats to herself, and feels that for the other woman, for Eva the precise, Eva the organized, Eva the realist and the pragmatic—God, how is it possible to hate a human being so much without giving up loving her?—always stubborn in her intention to establish the facts in their exact chronology, to verify the time which has passed and what happened before and what came afterwards (Eva only capable of understanding reality by structuring and labeling it), that a long time ago must refer to a concrete past, set with pins—dead—in a coherent and logical flow, whereas if someone asked her about this time, about this "long time ago," she would surely be in suspense and disconcerted, because for Clara, the instants unbalance her, superimpose themselves one atop the other in a runaway cavalcade, and often—especially when she's talking with Eva, when she's being interrogated by Eva —any trace of coherent plot that would enable her to arrange events as in an embroidered canvas and be able to situate herself in her own past disappears, so that now, sitting at the breakfast table, as Eva scolds her, very far away now from the first words she began the first sentence with, as Pablo looks at her, powerful and mocking, with that stupid air of a know-it-all lap cat, and she has been stunned, automatically going over that "a long time ago, a very long time ago now," it's not really a matter for Clara of a temporal reference, but rather of something much more like magic, like the imprecise beginning of fairy tales—and maybe, it occurs to her, even as a little girl, Eva would interrupt her mamma or her baby-sitter or her teacher, wanting to specify an impossible "when" and while she's silent and doesn't answer or explain or defend herself, crushed and destroyed by the rough and pained voice of someone she loves so much, someone she hates so much, exasperated and annulled by the pipe-sucking and the mocking look and the disagreeable expression of that individual she hates everything about, she repeats to herself without understanding, "a long time ago," and confused images spring forth of an awkward girl captured in a viscous world of lizards, and of a woman she believed to be made of light, and who then became evanescent like smoke, and she wonders, depressed, if it can perhaps be true—as Eva claims—that she felt happy just looking at her, just observing her from afar some afternoons, just by the other woman smiling at her and looking at her, even though it was in the middle of work, even though it was in the bustling meetings and amid a lot of different people, but surely Eva isn't telling it like that, surely she's developing it as always like another story, that can appear to be the same and isn't, the story of a girl of great intelligence and sensitivity (and every time her intelligence and her sensitivity are mentioned, Clara is confused and bewildered, suspecting that someone else is being discussed, that there has, in short, been a grotesque—although very painful for her—misunderstanding), who saw her possibilities restricted by a mediocre social environment and a sick and oppressive family atmosphere, and who has now acquired—thanks to them—she always says it in plural, and Clara necessarily supposes that the unusual plural includes the know-it-all conjugal cat, and the ghost woman who doesn't even look at her—new prospects of change and development, and even Pablo and Elia must know that for Clara, that's not the question, but rather that it's a very simple story of love and unlove, and she hasn't followed Eva to this house so that the world be extended at her feet like a variegated and expensive rug on which to advance, or to develop the supposed possibilities of her talent, or to prepare for her entrance into the university, since neither the world nor her talent and much less the university matter one bit to her, and a few months ago, when Eva explained the plan she had made for her of a better life, Clara thought out loud "to live better means to live a little closer to you," and the other woman was surprised and doubtful for an instant, about to guess perhaps a reality that escapes her diagrams and which she can't or doesn't want to recognize, although immediately afterwards she shrugged her shoulders and smiled at her and cataloged it in the ample margin of her childish behavior, and Eva insists, tenaciously, that she do things, study, take walks, read, that she feel happy, and no words or recourses are left to Clara to explain that the only thing that matters to her is having her near and for her to look at Eva lovingly, and all books have lost their attraction once she found in reality what she always looked for in them, and it's the desire to please Eva, to deserve her individual approval, the only thing that moves her to leaf through books or write a poem, because what she actually would like is to cuddle up in her arms and sleep, lean against her chest and die, burn her entire life in one perfect, one impossible act of love. And even Pablo has finally understood, and looks at her cunningly, and smiles churlishly, and sometimes puts a hand consolingly on her arm, or her knee or on the back of her neck, a hand that reminds Clara, even though it's a firm, dry hand, of the awkward claws of her uncle, and then, when she rejects it, when she moves away with displeasure and with a disgust that is impossible for her to hide, the man's smile becomes grim, somber, and sometimes he looks at her as he puts a possessive and sure hand on Eva's waist, on her shoulder, in her hair, and on these occasions Clara knows she's capable of murder, shaking in her hatred with an intensity she knew only in love, with a ferocious anguish and desire to go for his throat, to sink the bread knife into his heart, to see if that would erase the condescending look and the churlish smile for good, and even Elia herself must have understood now, since she interrupts her ostracism for a moment now, her absent air abandoned, smiles at them and murmurs something about insatiable greeds, and Clara is disconcerted, because every day of this summer of sharing the same house, of sitting regularly at the same table, and of lying down on the same deck of the same boat, never until today has Elia looked openly at her or given even a sign of having noticed her substitute goddaughter alley cat presence, and however much Eva has told her and discussed with her, she hasn't been able to understand the reasons for such a long close friendship between the two women, or why Pablo disperses his sarcasms and his bad moods in front of this insignificant little woman, so grey and so opaque and so silent who, to top it off, doesn't seem to pay attention to anything or thank them for anything, when the truth is that both of them—Eva especially, but Pablo too—weave a fluffy cocoon of understanding and respect and tenderness around her, and it's strange that now, for the first time in all these days, Elia should have lifted her gaze for a moment from the tablecloth or from what's beyond the window, and for her to have looked at them and smiled at them, and Clara is not quite sure if the smile has been directed at her and that it's an affectionate expression of solidarity, because it could well be that she's smiled at Eva, who was scolding her for her bad moods and for her complaints and for her excessive demands she doesn't understand, or even that Elia has really smiled at Pablo, who strokes his pipe and licks his whiskers like a cat as he hears her being reprimanded, impossible to determine who the smile is directed at, and whether it's in support of her or an addition to Eva's scolding, or a secret, ironic complicity with Pablo, but the truth is that Elia has looked the three of them straight in the eyes and has smiled and has whispered something about insatiable greeds, like that, in the plural, although it's possible that the woman has smiled and has talked only for herself, with that very low, lusterless voice, and the three of them have interrupted their quarrel and have looked at her attentively, waiting for her to go on and explain, but Elia doesn't say anything else, her attention centered again on the toast, which she's indecisively turning around in her hand and which she then covers with jam, and she remains silent. And then Eva starts talking to them about other things, about the news in the paper—nobody but she in this house reads it—or about the children's doings and problems, so that Elia's fleeting and strange intervention has at least interrupted the scolding, and now Elia is once again as absent as ever, and Pablo has returned to his pipe, almost out, and surely Eva knows that nobody's listening to her and she is talking solely to fill the air with something, and Clara wonders if there really are reasons for her to feel guilty, convicted—because that must be what Elia was referring to—of greediness and insatiability, of the supreme crime of not succeeding in or not being able to be, or not resigning herself to being, happy, now that she has, according to Eva, such a possibility and reality has overflowed the limits of her wildest dreams, and Clara thinks that maybe the wait was too long, the accumulated unlove too deep—who once said that the past could be reversible?—the damage chronic and incurable and lethal already and there exists no rehabilitation or hope of good fortune for the hungry stray cats who've trod too long from window to window, from roof to roof, who've been excluded and rejected too many times, who've felt too many times against their sensitive nose the cold, hard slam of the windows closing, while next to the fire on velvet cushions, the powerful house cats, the detestable domestic and tamed little animals, fall asleep, and their pretty owners affectionately pet their silky fur, and look, distracted, towards the window, while all the sadness of the world rains outside on the foolish cats in love, and it doesn't help one bit that one day a more indulgent or understanding or distracted or generous woman finally lets them in through the window, that she gives them a corner near the fire, and a little bowl of milk, and even directs some friendly sentences to them, because there more than ever the cats will feel excluded and rejected and omitted and unhappy and greedy and insatiable.

Pablo is looking slyly at her, privileged front-row spectator, without parting his lips except to suck briefly on his pipe—which is going out anyway—and with that air of "we warned you, let's see how you get out of this," and Elia remains faithful to her role of the romantic heroine, overwhelmed by love's sorrows, and it would suit her to be wandering alone through a moonless forest or at least in the cypress garden on a night with a pale moon, wrapped in a black robe and with her dark hair falling on her shoulders and mixed with jasmine, and not here, absent, and looking at the tablecloth or out the window, what she has in her immediate vicinity—the bread crumbs she plays with—or what is remote and distant—the white sails on the distant sea—never at the three of them, never at the things and people that surround her, and when she returns momentarily to the reality of this shared breakfast, and one expects her to pass a pale hand across her brow and burst into a delicious "where am I?", she just smiles evasively and murmurs, "they should invent drugs against insatiable greeds," and is thinking about herself, as always—because to think about Jorge is just another more exquisite way to think about herself—not about the problems or sorrows that can affect others, and surely even if the entire world crumbled around her, Elia would find a corner to remain immersed in her own private obsessions, and she doesn't even seem to remember her son this summer, nor has she ever really been responsible for her own son, and when Eva asked her two or three times "what are you going to do with Daniel?", the other woman looked at her expressionlessly and then shrugged her shoulders, in discouragement or boredom, it's anyone's guess, Elia clinging to her pain, pampering her grief so that it doesn't die and she ends up (even in this she has to try to surpass them and go too far) shutting herself off in them like a sumptuous and terrible torture chamber, and when she asks her now "what for? even if a drug like that did exist, neither you nor Clara would want to take it," Elia is again absent and doesn't listen to her, aside from the fact that whatever another human being says or does can't distract her or dissuade her or console her, remove her for a few instants from this total suffering that this summer her unlimited self-love, her indefatigable stubbornness are clinging to, absolutely implacable this woman who thinks of herself and is imagined by others as defenseless and awkward and fragile, with those pale, helpless eyes of a little girl lost in the woods and that face which seems about to weep and it's therefore useless to expect any kind of aid, any kind of help from Elia or Pablo, Pablo anxious like the spectator who greedily awaits the exciting moment when the bull catches them in the arena, her or Clara or both of them, that doesn't matter at all, all that matters is the rapture of danger and of blood, and Clara meanwhile has blushed to her ears and clenches her fists and bites her lips and looks as though she too is about to cry, although perhaps her anxiety and her touchiness are above all an answer to the anger she feels at blushing against her will, and Eva thinks the only thing missing would be crying at this time of the morning, when she has just gathered enough courage to face the new day, and so she gives up taking her admonishings and her advice any further, which won't do any good anyway—and there Pablo's mocking smile is justified, although Eva hates him at these moments for letting it show—Clara impregnable in her extreme helplessness, just like Elia can be in her pain, implacable also the girl in her morbid decision not to accept help (or to accept only the kind of help she wants and which Eva can in no way give her). It's curious how both of them—Elia and Clara—are so alike, coming from such different worlds and having reached such diverse ages, with such similarity and that, resembling each other, they haven't felt the least bit of sympathy for each other or noticed the resemblance, that they don't even recognize themselves in the qualities she shows them, persistent in imagining themselves as opposites or different (in considering themselves, deep down, as unique) stubbornly refusing to experience the least bit of curiosity for each other, and so Eva gives up continuing her scolding and her admonishing, which are useless, and begins a monologue about other things, as she is invaded by some very concrete desires to grab them both by the shoulders—Pablo is a different story—and shake them or slap them in the face, to see if that makes them get out of themselves a little, come to the threshold of this tenacious being oneself and establish then—it seems impossible that being intelligent and in a way generous and disinterested, they don't know—that the world is full to the rim with anxieties and suffering, illness and hunger, violence and injustice and fear and death ("and you claim this will put me in a good mood or raise my spirits?" Elia asks her sarcastically), and that their minuscule annoyances—which probably aren't even about love but about self-love—their delicate anxieties of well-protected and cared-for little animals, are only an infinitesimal part of this enormous, accumulated pain, such an insignificant part that it's hardly worth noticing. Who told these three that their own suffering is the center of the world, or better yet, why has no one explained to them (with sufficient power of persuasion) that it's necessary to rectify things now, leave behind that childish image that situated them at the central axis which the universe turned upon and which sustained the stars' harmony, or how they haven't discovered for themselves a long time ago that no redemption or possible remedy exists for those who live immersed in the contemplation of their own navel, licking, gluttonously, their wounds until they poison themselves—"you can't understand anything," said Elia on the boat, with her eyes closed and her voice opaque, as if she spoke with fatigue and against her will, "you can't understand anything, you don't know how wretched I was before meeting him, you don't know what these fifteen years with Jorge have been like," as if the two of them alone had invented love, the only couple on earth to know ecstasy and rapture, others relegated to crude imitations, clumsy farces, grotesque substitutes, boorish and ignorant spectators of the prodigy, and also Clara at night (similar the two of them in this whim of believing themselves exclusive and thinking that others don't understand them), Clara touchy, Clara angry, Clara desolate and out of control, "you think you know everything and really you don't know a thing, you've never understood anything"—and maybe if Eva armed herself with courage and grabbed them by the shoulders— also Pablo, always involved (because he already said the same or very similar things the night they met and were talking on the pier, in the shadows, in front of the dark silhouettes of the anchored boats) in unfortunate loves with an impossible image of himself, which he reproaches himself for abandoning and betraying, as ungraspable and improbable and literary as the image Elia has forged of Jorge in order to love herself and in which she doesn't recognize herself at all—if she shook them or slapped the three of them in the face, maybe something deep inside them would move and the dikes, the reefs would sink and they could recuperate the magical flow between themselves and their surroundings, they could help themselves and help others and help her, because for a few months now and at intervals Eva has felt bored and very tired (incredible that neither her best friend nor her husband, who say they love her so much, has noticed), fed up with her role as the only adult in a world of children, or rather of adolescents, who, to top it off, look at her over their shoulders and say condescendingly "you never understand anything," and attribute to her, together with her nonexistent understanding, a really admirable strength and a resistance, and many years —she doesn't even remember when it began—of knowing that everything weighs on her, everything rests on her, so that if in a moment of weakness she yielded, the roof would fall in on all of them, as if her own fortitude were the only thing capable of preserving order and maintaining life, and sometimes—especially in the last few months—this tires her and frightens her and she feels tempted to give up, she feels above all so much envy of those beings who can surrender, back down, be defeated, without anything crumbling around them or anything irreparable happening, and the disagreeable sensation that she's been tricked takes hold of Eva—and it started a long time ago and far away, maybe when, as a girl, home from school, she had to take charge of the store and take care of her brothers and sisters, exhausted, scared by the absolute confidence her parents placed in her, by the unanimously shared certainty that Eva was a serious girl, capable and responsible—that they've fallaciously situated her on the middle of a drawbridge, on top of the merlons, without having consulted her beforehand (while Elia sleeps her hundred-year sleep in the palace's farthest padded bedroom, and Clara pulls the petals of daisies, she loves me, she loves me not, in the garden, and Pablo tries on green satin pants, sumptuous, embroidered jackets, in the hall of mirrors) and they've told her—without giving her time to reply, to protest—"we know you can do it, don't move, the good of everyone depends on you now," and here she is, like an idiot, facing whatever may happen, sustaining the world upon her head, so that the prince and princess aren't interrupted in the middle of their games, their exquisite nonsense, their exquisite anguish, so that they're not bothered in the middle of their dreams, Eva trapped in this rough deception of believing—they've told her so many times—that only she is able to do it, and even, to top it all off, Pablo or Elia or other people look at her cunningly and pleased—with admiration and gratitude, true, but also with a hint of mockery—as if it were a quirk of her nature to be there, unsheltered, sustaining everything, taking charge of everything herself, with others' pain and problems and anxieties, as if Eva rambled through life looking for a mess to get involved in or someone else's load to carry, "you like it, really, admit that really you like it, that you wouldn't know how to live any other way"—and Eva wonders in fact if she wouldn't know how to live now any other way, and concludes that she doesn't look for or provoke anything, that she's never believed much in her strong woman role, a role that others invented for her and in which they enclosed her as in armor, as in a shroud), only that one day a long time ago now, they situated her there, in the middle of the drawbridge, on top of the merlons, and around her there are a thousand things to do—that no one does—a thousand problems to solve—that no one solves—a thousand people to take care of —and whom no one wants to take care of—a thousand words to say—and no one feels like saying them, because even Elia, equipped sometimes with the deepest and most accurate words, has permitted herself the luxury of becoming mute and not saying a thing—and it's not that she likes to do, take charge, decide, console, solve, it's simply that things and people are there waiting—and no one does anything—and then Eva takes on, resigned, efficient, something that perhaps she never wanted to take on, but which seems to have been assigned to her in an inevitable way forever.

I t hasn't been very hot yet this summer, maybe it won't be, and at these relatively early hours of the morning—the nine church bells have just rung, which Pablo has paused to listen to, not because he didn't know the time, but for the pleasure of hearing that clean musical sound expand through the new morning—the town almost empty of summer vacationers and tourists, the streets almost free of invaders, Pablo likes it, since he woke up at dawn, with a brusque start that threw him headlong, inexorably, into total wakefulness, and chased away the most remote hope of falling back asleep because sleeping till noon is far away, the interminable awakenings that in his youth occupied all the mornings of those days when he allowed himself to do so, or allowed himself without being able to do so, and just for that, those days were a holiday, with his mother coming into the room every so often, scolding and protesting that she couldn't air the room or make the bed, consenting and deep down an accomplice to her son's laziness (like so many more of his weaknesses), since her supposed urgency, her feigned scandalous fuss, her hygienic anxieties never actually got him out of bed, and his mother was content with passing a hand through his hair, opening the window slightly, talking to him about things Pablo didn't listen to or making him drink at most a big glass of milk, without really waking him (in the intermittent stages when his mother would decide "that boy is thinner every day," uselessly worried by that son who had turned out strange, intellectual, with his head full of nonsense, and who was nonetheless her

110

favorite child, the only beneficiary of so many exceptions and so many transgressions), but all of this is part of the many things that with the passing of time have been left by the wayside, and his mother would be surprised if she could see him get up now, punctually, morning after morning, almost always before the alarm rings, entering the office a little earlier each year, precisely at a moment when he no longer has a schedule to adjust himself to or a watch to time himself by (or maybe precisely because of this), if she saw him wake up at seven during the vacations, sometimes at six, absolutely awake, with no possibility of falling back asleep, obsessively going over work problems that he believes deep down don't worry him, but which he can't manage to put aside, because even when he thinks how little they affect him and plans to leave them, he's still thinking about them (like in those curious, paradoxical stages of love, or unlove, in which days and nights are consumed by repeating to yourself that the other person doesn't matter to you, that you've probably never really liked her, that with total certainty you don't love her anymore, and you spend every hour like that thinking about her, without doing anything but inverting the meaning of the same obsession), and even he doesn't understand—probably still less than Eva or the friends who've followed the process from the outside—how a job that doesn't satisfy him has been invading him—a job he initiated a long time ago just because, which he planned from the beginning to abandon (because he never had the will to continue)—for virtually all his life, and this summer Pablo has acquired the habit, since he inevitably wakes up at this time of the morning, of getting up before anyone else and leaving the house when the others are still asleep—the kids exhausted after a day without letup or a break (and it's lucky they walk around loose through town at all hours and hardly show up at the house, just as it's lucky that Daniel is at camp), the three women exhausted, he imagines, by so much crying and gossip and nocturnal sighing, which keeps them awake until sunrise and submerges them with the first lights of dawn into a deep and possibly dreamless sleep that he envies, because Eva doesn't even move, she doesn't open her eyes at all, while Pablo shuffles around the room or makes noise in the bathroom—and Pablo has gotten used to walking down to the promenade with that illusion of his that the town, free of summer vacationers, uncontaminated by tourists, its virginity magically recovered during the night, has been given back to him and is almost the same town they loved so much a few years ago, that he still loves so much in the winter, this town where he fantasizes—to Eva's incredulity, and Elia's doubting smile, she doesn't take him very seriously either—he will install himself in a few years, not many now, to grow old and begin to die, with no other activity but to stroll along the whitewashed streets, sit and sunbathe next to the elderly with his back against the warm wall, play cards in the casino, bridge or dominoes in the café next to the ocean, maybe intervene—and he smiles—in local politics, and he thinks about this as he goes down to the promenade, greeting the shop owners who are sweeping the sidewalk in front of their doors, stopping to listen better to the church bells, going into the tobacco shop to try to get a newspaper (which hasn't arrived yet, how could it arrive if it's barely nine o'clock, but which will infallibly sell out as soon as it arrives) and then choosing any magazine, and he arrives afterwards at the promenade, and sits on the terrace—there's hardly anyone at the tables, only two boys with curly hair and long robes, nobody either on the strip of beach that separates them from the sea—with his back leaning, shielded, against the wall ("you look like a dog" Elia laughs sometimes—the Elia that laughs, not this summer's pathetic and absurd Elia—when she observes his movements in restaurants and cafés, "dogs never lie down with their backs to an open door, to any place the enemy can come from," and Pablo likes Elia when she's joking, when she kids him, he even likes Elia when she plays, Elia when she talks nonsense, Elia when she bursts into crazy laughter, Elia perennial adolescent and transgressor,

112

Elia egocentric without a doubt but very fun, that unsuspected Elia that no one knows, that flourishes only in the strictest intimacy, Elia house plant, he likes Elia when she parodies them and imitates them, "we're better in Elia's jokes and barbs than in reality," Eva has sometimes commented, and as usual she's mostly right, because it's true that the image Elia fantasizes and elaborates and even ridicules is almost always more attractive, more intimate, less sordid in any case, than the one Pablo has recently of himself, less distant from what he would have liked to become, less deep the fissure that separates him from the plans he had in his youth, without that brief point of flattering falsity ever destroying the character's verisimilitude, the exactness of the resemblance, the portrait's likeness, and so Pablo likes Elia to talk about him and turn him into a big distrustful, affectionate and slightly conceited dog, even though later the inevitable follows and Elia almost always hurls herself into interminable lyrical descriptions of how Jorge is situated in front of a closed door, or in front of an open door, or in front of nothing, or how he looks or how he drinks or how he lights a cigarette or how he cracks his knuckles or how he sleeps, because Elia's expression becomes tender and her voice transcendent in order to explain to them that Jorge sleeps like a rare specimen of a solitary plainsman, a desolate fugitive of the steppes, to such a point that it has been impossible for her to find quiet-enough kisses, slow-enough caresses, light-enough touches to manage to wake him without frightening him, without him sitting up, startled, with a brusque and defensive gesture, looking automatically for the pistols in his pajama legs. Not only does it bother Pablo that Elia invents stories and makes fables, indefatigably, about a man who, so intelligent it seems to many, has never interested him at all, and for whom he's never managed to feel a real affection, but even more irritating for him is the emphatic tone Elia adopts to talk about him, that voice of "he and I alone have invented love on earth," as if Jorge were an eagle that flies above the mountain tops, that loses himself in the

113

peaks, and everyone else were miserable basement rats, all sense of proportion and even of the ridiculous lost here, lost that paradoxical and iconoclastic sense of humor, that irreverent and delicious spark they share sometimes, because perhaps Elia was indeed at some other time, as she claims, a bashful, sad, frightened little girl, but she has also undoubtedly been years later—and before Jorge appeared, not only because of Jorge and that sublime love the two of them make a fable of—a disobedient and impudent girl, a mocking, vivacious, back-talking, sacrilegious, even frivolous girl, capable of rising to the highest peaks of joy, although all this fades and disappears as soon as Jorge appears, as soon as Jorge is talked about—and it's even much worse this summer, when he neither appears nor does anyone know where he is and, not being able to talk about him, no one is talked about—and as soon as Jorge is present, everything is grave gestures, deep looks, transcendental attitudes, ridiculous, excessive attitudes, implacable each one in the attempt to convert the least stupidity of the other into a universal cataclysm, and they all have to walk around on tiptoe, and be solicitous and grieved because Elia, as awkward as ever—in this she's completely right when she talks about herself, although in the rest, when it's about her or about Jorge, she overdoes it or is short of the truth, she misses, unpardonably too high or too low—has gone unthinkably into the kitchen and has made a minuscule cut on her thumb trying to open a can of food with the bread knife, or they must sympathize with Elia's fright or receive a scolding—Elia much more annoying than Jorge in this attempt to make them share the unsharable—when Jorge is a few minutes late, or when in a restaurant they bring him a cold plate of garbanzos or raw fish or warm champagne, and then they have to improvise an angry protest, a sympathetic mourning, a universal grief, protest, mourning or grief which Pablo alone resists taking part in, and everyone has to resign themselves to the fact that the pleasure of the conversation and of the dinner has been irremediably destroyed). So now Pablo has leaned against the wall, this early hour of a summer that's especially unpleasant and uncomfortable for him, his back protected—"the same thing dogs do," Elia would comment —facing the sun and facing the sea, and he has ordered coffee and a croissant, opening at random the magazine he bought just to buy, because no newspaper had arrived yet, as he lights the pipe with the parsimony befitting a ritual, and at these moments, sitting on the terrace of the town's café a little after nine in the morning, sadness and dissatisfaction (so hard and real sometimes at other hours) are diluted and become bearable, in a way intoxicating because of being literary, like those dense vapors that fill the cellars where good wines are stored or that tenacious aroma that lingers in closed drawers and in perfume flacons long empty, and Pablo arrives at a difficult and fragile harmony with himself, the intense displeasure that seizes him each time with more frequency subsides when he takes his pulse and his temperature, he touches and examines himself, and is even pleased for a few instants with his image as a mature man, still strong and attractive, even though he's gained quite a bit of weight since his mother lamented seeing him thinner every day (and he never was), with a certain air, it's true, of disenchantment and of fatigue, and perhaps he's appeared interesting to the two girls who have gotten up from the table and are walking towards the sea, and they haven't turned around once to look at him, although they've most likely been spying on him on the sly, and it's even possible that they are unfolding in his honor (nobody else can see them) that magical pantomime on the shore, their heads tossed back, so that the long hair reaches almost to their waists, their eyes half-closed, their arms extended, and then they've turned around and taken each other by the shoulders and linked together, have gone into the ocean absolutely conscious (now Pablo is indeed sure) of their splendid beauty erected to the morning sun, absolutely certain that interesting fellow with the pipe and the silver temples hasn't taken his eyes off them, and then they go back onto the beach, whisper, laugh, return to their table, and while one of them sits and seems to take an inexplicable interest in the process of absorbing her Coke through the straw, the other one walks slowly, and without breaking the atmosphere of a dance, of an exhibition, of a pantomime, the magical and festive atmosphere, with that particular way of walking, Pablo thinks, that only very beautiful girls who haven't yet turned twenty have (this is what he's referring to when he discourses on their power and their enormous strength), aggressive and magnificent, redeeming the world with her step and giving it meaning, the redheaded girl advances towards him to ask him to light her cigarette.

M y sadness, thinks Clara in desperation, shows her the extent of her failure. That's all I am: work that's turning out badly, a mistaken risk, an error in calculation. And Eva the efficient, Eva the sharp one, who always knows at what moment it's necessary to double the bet or raise the stakes, who never moves one chessman for another on the board, because never has Clara seen her (since they've known each other) get up a loser from the playing table, and it's almost boring the monotony with which she beats Pablo (who gets furious) and Elia (spacey), the friends who come to the house and even the old people who play dominoes in the bar—"she never loses" the fellow serving behind the bar comments with admiration and envy, "with the husband, it's a different story, he loses control, he's indecisive for too long and loses the best opportunities, but she's something else, she never loses," and Clara feels overwhelmed with pride and affection (surely she's got on her worst idiot face and is slobbering all over the floor), as if a child of hers had gotten a hundred in all her classes and even an award (and of course Eva is something else!). She feels nevertheless at the same time an atrocious fear, as she asks herself what will become of her in the hands of this woman who's perhaps never lost a game of cards, dominoes or chess, and who at the height of

116

ingenuity and brazenness communicates to those who've played with her and those she's beaten again and again "I'm a good loser, I assure you that I don't mind losing at all," when she should at least have the delicacy to say "I wouldn't mind." Eva the winner, then, Eva the sharp one, used to managing others' lives, directing others' lives, resolving what the good fortune of others consists of and making it and imposing it, drunk on the fantasy of being a god who moves bishops and pawns on the board's squares, surely this Eva hates to fail. And I'm her failure, Clara repeats to herself with an intolerable weight in her chest and her throat dry and her mouth bitter, because there's nothing she wouldn't do for her, hers since she met her, hers everything that I am, from the ends of my hair to my toenails, and if she told me to fly, I'd jump into the void and the void would hold me, and if she told me to come, I would walk on water and the sea would support my weight, and if she asked me for the volcanoes, the stars, coral beads, I would go looking for them and get them, and I'm nothing more than a whim of hers, I don't exist outside of this absurd love, and I would like to be able to turn myself into an offering, wrapped in cellophane and a pink ribbon at my neck, like a Christmas gift, and give up myself to a unique, irreversible, total act and give her that way all my love at once and forever, instead of segregating it painfully, awkwardly, from minute to minute, and it would be magnificent if Eva used it, if Eva used her, as an ashtray, as a nail buff, as a stickpin, as any of those familiar objects that she uses without paying attention to anymore, without noticing them, thinks Clara between laughter and tears, because the suffering and anxiety is terrible, but it's also irremediably ridiculous, and Eva comments sometimes "what can help you, what saves you, what I like in you" (and such few qualities remain in her that the other woman likes, because her intelligence is put more in doubt every day, and her sensitivity has transmuted into this sickly, this morbid sensitivity, and Clara rightly put herself on guard against this type of flattery from the beginning) "is your

117

magnificent sense of humor," and it must be true since Eva says so, and while the cat feels her claws slipping and letting go of the windowsill, it allows her to spread open and experience both the certainty of the asphalt against which she must break her spine in a few moments, and prodigies of humor, the grotesque and the ridiculous and the laughable of her skinny cat silhouette, an ugly stray in love, that gesticulates in the void in an absurd attempt to latch onto nothing, and in spite of everything, it's funny, Clara thinks between tears, that she's ready to give it all, to give her all, and that the other woman asks only for what she hasn't been able to give, because neither Clara nor Clara's love interest Eva in the least, and don't obtain any result but that of making her uncomfortable and irritating her, and Eva doesn't want her to turn into an ashtray or a nail buff (her morality lets her destroy her, but never would let her use her), nor does she feel capricious whims for moons or coral beads or volcanoes, and the only thing she really wants is to be left alone, for her to mature, grow up, be cured, in short, renounce loving her like this, abdicate demands and bribes, for her to love her less or love her differently or not love her at all, but for her to desist in this feverish and out-of-place passion that Eva is not aware of having provoked, nor is she capable of understanding and that she definitely does not have to tolerate, that no human being is forced to tolerate, and then Clara tries, again and again, to contain herself, to hold back, be cheerful, behave in a normal way, in some pathetic attempts that hardly last hours, because as soon as she's near Eva, all her plans fade and Clara feels a heat that burns her, and makes her pulse beat wildly in her ears, and she's a blank, like a little kid too shy in front of a teacher she's excessively afraid of, always with that discouraging sensation of taking an exam, and canceling it time after time, incapable of pronouncing now the banal speech she had prepared and outlined so well, and which should have relaxed, precisely because of its banality, the atmosphere and create a new comfort, a reciprocal trust, Eva calmed in front of the evidence that this bratty kid doesn't really love her so much, hardly needs her, isn't suffering very much, each object returned to its place in this ordered and not very big world in which Eva is god, a terribly incongruous and fickle deity without knowing it and whose almost only commandment would be in this case "you will love anyone but me," but the words fall to pieces in Clara's mouth and crumble into a pathetic sputter, and she hears her own voice as if it were the voice of a stranger and thinks "what the hell is this idiot grumbling about now?" and so much love hidden and retained in vain escapes from Clara, almost all of her desperation betrays her in her glances, never sustained, because her guilty and frightened eyes meet Eva's staring eyes that scrutinize her with an intensity so strong it could be confused with love, and that's why Clara sometimes begs "don't look at me like that," and once again everything is lost, defeated before entering into battle, and Eva defeated through her, that awkward chess piece, slippery, crazed, that slides at its own risk across the board and to top it off falls into the wrong square, and Clara can't understand what Eva is telling her, because Eva has begun to speak with a badly hidden impatience, and Clara only heeds the tone, and it's a tone of rejection, of fatigue, of disillusionment and then Clara's hands tremble, and she can't light her cigarette, and the lit ash falls on the sofa, and now she doesn't remove her gaze from the floor at all, and feels her cheeks burn more and more, her ears buzz, her throat close and it takes a serious effort to breathe and it's at these moments when she wants to be only an inanimate object, something that Eva manipulates without paying attention to, without submitting her to a test, without saying to her "don't love me," she wants to be invisible, to melt, disappear, be at the other end of the planet, to never have been born or to have died a thousand years ago, and she decides that it's imperative for her to go away, leave the house, cut, break, leave behind, flee, given that love is so useless, suffering so in vain, and there's nothing she can fight for, nothing that she has the most remote possibility of getting, and everything must on the contrary be worse every day, and she sees herself as a fragile, crazy, stubborn bird that's destroying itself against a screen without managing to pass above it, below it, on the sides or just to be still, because its stubbornness is as big as its weakness, and sometimes she has planned to escape at dawn, without telling anyone of her departure since saying good-bye to Eva would be too painful and there's no one else she wants to say good-bye to, and she has spent the night wide awake, with her things ready, and the atrocious agony of rupture, the agony of thinking that never never would she see her again, to then lose courage with the first light and understand that the long hours of suffering have been useless, because, although she'd like to, she can't leave, and other times she has announced her departure in a delirium of noise and fury, and has put her clothes in bunches into her suitcase and has pushed the suitcase with kicks to the door, hoping that someone will intervene, Elia appeasing, Pablo sarcastic, the children ignorant, waiting for the miracle to happen, and for Eva to say "don't go," but nothing happened and she had to go back to the upper part of the house and distribute, defeated, books and clothes in the shelves and inside the closet, and there were two terrible times when her fury lasted a little longer, her confidence in herself betrayed her in a crueler way, and she got to the bus stop and stayed there, annihilated, under the sun, wanting to die, die and then to enter the phone booth and ask for Eva and say "I can't stand it, tell me what I should do," and hear the contained and polite voice, perhaps as an exception a little regretful and moved (although all regret of emotion had disappeared by the time she returned to the house) "come," and so Clara has all exits closed before her, because she can't escape, she can't stop being in love, nor can she, being in love, resign herself to such a completely un-reciprocated love, and she thinks with bitterness that there's nothing left but to wait, because it seems she has contracted a very painful, embarrassing, perhaps fatal disease about which, to top it off, hardly anything is known, immune to surgery, not treatable with drugs, so that there's no recourse but to huddle, clench her fists, try to drown her wails, gather all her strength, and bear it, bear it with the hope that this terrible illness can leave one day just as it came; a surprise, with no cause, just like any fatality.

It seems that everyone is walking around half crazy this summer, or that they've seriously relapsed into the worst stages of an almost forgotten adolescence, after years and years of the four of them behaving—including herself—like more or less normal people, acceptably adult, transcendent and serious sometimes to the point of boredom, absorbed in the problems of work, politics, money, in the children's studies or in the purchase of a new car or remodeling the house, attentive to international news, to the country's realities, to the latest book, the most recent film, discussing for hours the qualities of French wines and the temperatures they should be stored at, exchanging the most hidden secrets of Chinese cooking (because some extravagant and precious interests arise in the drowsiness of respectability) and it's possible that she, Elia, has maintained, for all these years, a certain foreign and distant air, like a rather disobedient little girl who didn't want to grow up, or who doesn't confess to herself that she is finally grown up, it's possible that she and Jorge have performed with conviction the beautiful farce of an unrepeatable love that chosen couples live once every millennium—and it surprises her to have formulated it like that, to have defined to herself as a farce what from its beginning until just a little while ago (days, seconds) she's considered not simply the only truth of her existence, but the supreme truth of a superior and universal order—but they haven't been because of that less stable, less immutable and secure, in their terrible respectability, that grotesque seriousness with which they've been taking themselves, and only now, suddenly, they're living a crazy summer, in which everything seems different, doubtful, questionable, uncertain, and maybe it's because Jorge, for the first time, isn't with them and his absence breaks that granite might of diminished tetrarchs, and also certainly influential is the presence of this big, awkward, little girl who drags herself around the house with a passion too much for her strength, too heavy for her resistance and age, to which she succumbs a thousand times each day and for which a thousand times each day she gets up again, a pathetic spectacle that makes her dizzy, almost physically ill, and who follows with sorrowful but surprised eyes an Eva who doesn't seem ready to understand anything—perhaps because of this particular stubbornness in not understanding she is the only one who still maintains a minimum level of sanity in the house—and an Eva that hasn't learned, it seems, that you can't tell anyone to love if you're not willing to be loved, that you can't tell anyone to walk if you don't make way, that you can't tell anyone to drink or eat if you're not willing to transmute yourself into bread and water, and Eva moves like that sometimes through the world, awakening anxieties whose real objective she doesn't understand and doesn't even dream of satisfying, that it would seem immoral to her even to fulfill or appease, confident in the old fantasy according to which others, when they emerge thanks to you or with your help from somnolence and ignorance, can and must procure for themselves love and the way and the water and bread, and surely it's all due to Jorge's absence or the new presence of this girl, caught in a trap which she won't be able to get out of unharmed, or to herself, immobilized, obstinate in a desolation for which she admits no relief or rest or nuances (and it's now, sitting on the terrace above the sea, as she lights a cigarette and drinks, so early in the morning, peppermint, that drink befitting a flaming whore or a sad mermaid, as she goes over the others' craziness when for the first time her attitude of these weeks, which she'd considered the only one possible, appears to her as an absurd, but lucky, stubbornness), and Pablo prowling around the house with his pipe and his melancholy, in the tiring exhibitionism of so much presumed genius frustrated, so lovable nonetheless in his youthful vanity, in his desire for her to listen to him, to understand him, to pamper him, perhaps jealous of Clara as he has been for years of Jorge—Pablo, sitting now on the beach next to a splendid unknown girl, perhaps one of those very beautiful girls who possess, according to him, at eighteen, although always only for a few hours or a few weeks, the maximum level of power on earth—so close the two of them on the towel they're sharing, so sunk his face in this fragrant bunch of copper curls, as he talks into her ear and the girl laughs and they put their arms around each other's waists or on each other's shoulders, and it's as if they'd created a magic circle of secret intimacy in the little world of the yellow and blue towel, invisible both of them to others since they in turn don't see anyone; and although Pablo was waiting for her and they had agreed to meet at the beach, he didn't even notice her arrival, and Elia has renounced the idea of approaching them and has gone towards the bar's terrace, to smoke a cigarette and drink the first peppermint of the morning before getting in the water, and reflect upon the insanity of the others and upon her own foolishness and madness, and watch how the beautiful stranger stands up now, how she stretches and lazes in the sun, her figure against the blue of the sea, her hair lustrous, burnished, heavy, a dark red color, falling magnificently down her back, her arms extended towards no one, her eyes half closed, her insolent nose raised and that face of a powerful and coveted young female, of a kitten delirious with presumption and with coquetry, of a finicky gazelle who pretends to be lazy and sleepy, watch how she then starts walking, Pablo at her side, with that carelessness and firmness which may indeed be the exclusive privilege of very pretty women in a very brief instant of their sixteen or seventeen years, and Elia watches her walk towards the car, stop with Pablo next to the open door, delay a long time in saying good-bye, stand now on one foot, now on the other, her head to one side, the red hair hiding her face, her body golden, impeccable, absolutely protected by her beauty, shielded by her extreme youth, and Elia looks at her with pleasure, and for the first time in the last weeks, there are a few instants in which the pain disappears, this anxiety that hadn't left her even for a moment until it now subsides and Elia relaxes, expands, breathes deeply, half closes her eyes, savors the peppermint, so marvelous and unexpected this respite on the luminous morning, in front of the blue sea, and she feels content once again thinking that such beautiful beings exist in the world, such beautiful men and women, content also to be so extremely sensitive to this beauty, which produces an intense delight in her, curiously untied to any feeling of envy, of the least hint of sexuality, because she's never been able to envy a pretty girl however much they possess, according to Pablo, such a high quota of power on earth, nor has this visual pleasure of contemplating and admiring ever been related to the sources, surely more confused, more complicated, more hidden, of desire, tied perhaps to tactile and olfactory sensations, even provoked sometimes by the tone of a voice, the ring of someone's laughter, inextricably associated with tenderness, and tenderness, thinks Elia, arises almost always when faced with the imperfect, the vulnerable, nudity (real nudity doesn't exist in beauty, it dresses itself; those aunts, grandmothers, teachers weren't so far from the truth when they dictated "nudity in art is not a sin"), what we feel near and fraternal, and the golden body of the redhead seems, seen from here, made of porcelain or of crystal, so smooth and soft and resplendent, and Elia would touch it as she furtively touches statues upon passing, the objects she likes to have on her worktable or along whose surface she also slides sometimes a doubtful and distracted index finger, and only when the girl has gotten into the car and has driven away, and Pablo has watched her go, and walks towards Elia's table, with such a different way of walking, a little ashamed and terribly conceited, like the little boy who has committed or is about to commit a marvelous piece of mischief, a transgression for which they will probably scold him but which fills him with an irrepressible jubilation, only then does Elia know that it's not a question of a few magical instants created for her or for others on the luminous morning, the blue sea, an emblematic girl, integral part of an allegory, but rather of something very concrete and real, that Pablo has flirted on the beach with an unknown girl, and a certain laziness invades the woman, a desire to retreat and not listen, to reject this new conflicting ingredient, another crazy element in an already excessively complicated summer, but Pablo has sat down at her table, and has ordered a Coke as if he felt like the king of the world, and he's so exultant, so content, so different, so young all of a sudden, so like perhaps a Pablo who lay very far away in time and who everyone, including him, although he never ceased invoking it, had already forgotten, but who must have undoubtedly subsisted, maintained itself alive and waiting in some part, since now it has awakened and been reborn and come out into the light and is moment by moment supplanting that other Pablo, full of rancor, frustrated, wan from the last years, above all perhaps from the last months, while he explains to Elia, forcing himself to remain natural, composed, to minimize what's happened, to give a trivial touch to this beginning of an affair, a light tone, that he'd already seen this redhead other times, even one day she had come up to him in the bar and asked for a light, and they've looked at each other and smiled many times upon running into one another in town, and today she was alone (she's almost always with a friend) and he went up to say hello to her and comment that he'd forgotten his towel at home, and then she invited him to share the one she had, and she's delicious and vibrant and very intelligent, and of course devilishly pretty, although the matter won't go any further, of course, because he's much older and has too much experience the hard way to get involved in this kind of affair, and he himself doesn't believe it as he's saying it, and both of them laugh, Pablo and Elia, on the bar's terrace, facing the blue sea, drinking Coke and peppermint ("that garbage is going to hurt you," Pablo has commented and "you didn't used to drink"), more accomplices and happier than they've felt in a long time, and Elia thinks that maybe the affair will indeed bring complications and add new conflicting ingredients to this difficult summer, but he is so happy, so suddenly exultant and alive, that it's as if a breath of fresh air had entered a closed and stuffy interior, among obstinate passions, desolate narcissisms, impossible loves, unfortunate loves, yes, something fresh, new, comforting, sane, stimulating, alive, that, whatever happens, Elia can't regret in this instant that it has taken place.

It was only an illusion, the mirage of a magically luminous morning, excessively blue, with that girl rocking her splendid body—burnished, smooth, golden, with the rare qualities of porcelain or of crystal—next to the open car door, her hair falling heavily in copper curls down her back and Pablo exultant, rejuvenated, his enthusiasm recuperated—"there are some perfect things in the world, don't you think? few, but there are, like *Le Monde* as a newspaper or the lacquered Du Pont model lighter, and she's like that, an absolutely perfect specimen, a sure hit," his ingenuity recuperated—"do you really think she likes me? are you seriously saying that she looked at me with interest?"—his carefree attitude and optimism recuperated—"the things you say! why should Eva get mad? it's possible I won't even see that girl again, and if we do continue, it'll only be a fling"—that made him so tender and intimate, so charming fifteen years ago, before they got married and he stopped writing poems and began to prosper in the company or in a number of identical enterprises and their children were born and almost at the same time as Jorge and she, Eva and Pablo acquired the apartment in the city, the new car, the house by the sea, and now Elia knows it was only a mirage—summoned by such suggestive incantations—the sensation that the pain had almost stopped, that she was

126

beginning to breathe effortlessly, that it was possible to plan a "tomorrow," "next week," "next summer," in an also miraculously recuperated time, and even imagine herself alive and moderately happy in a world without Jorge—no, it wasn't exactly imagining herself without him, it was that for a few instants, she stopped thinking about him, and, with the absolute image of love fading in the forgetfulness of a moment, the reality began to become concrete and emerge as possible —and although Elia already suspected on the blue morning that such a terrible wound couldn't end like that, so suddenly, and that there would necessarily be relapses and renewed attacks, she nevertheless lived it as the initiation of a cure, and that's exactly why it's more painful now, at sunset of the same day, to suffer again in the old way perhaps as sick now as the instant Jorge said "hasn't it occurred to you that we may have stopped loving each other? we weren't going to spend our lives playing at Abelard and Heloïse!", worse perhaps than during the long hours in which she stripped the house of herself, worse than the day she arrived shipwrecked on this beach, in this sea, hers every summer, with her old ancestral and dying cat, and she has now phoned Miguel, nervous and disconcerted, "I can't take it anymore, I'm fed up with suffering like this, with having such a horrible time, do something please, give me anything that makes me sleep, numb, inert," and Miguel has spoken to her in a calm and measured voice, a special voice, and Elia thinks that he's not talking to her as to a longtime friend, whom he often runs into at dinners and meetings and with whom he has fun gossiping and arguing, but rather as he talks to any one of his patients, in a slightly professorial and protective and distant tone, very fitting, in order to explain to her (as you explain to a child or a sick person) that it doesn't seem appropriate to him to change or increase the medication, and a cure for insomnia would be out of place and there's not the remotest possibility of hospitalizing her, because she is fine, much better than a few weeks ago (this capacity to rebel against the pain and even to get angry at

127

the doctor proves it, Miguel says and laughs), and besides he's always known that Elia was a very strong woman, he's always bet on her, and now she only has to wait until Monday and come on Monday to the office, he's sure she can withstand it, and Elia wonders on what grounds, my God, can a human being dictate how much others can withstand, but she says yes, all right, see you Monday, and afterwards she hung up the phone and sat there, unsure how she's going to last until Monday if today is only Friday, and it seems impossible to ward off this anxiety, this profound uneasiness, this desolation, until dawn, and then an interminable Saturday will follow and another night and an odious Sunday—Sundays were always odious—and another night, and Elia gets up and goes to the café of sad songs and dim light, ready to mix barbituates, antidepressants and alcohol until she bursts, perhaps because she has really gotten angry at her doctor—although thinking about it makes her laugh—she's gotten angry at her doctor because he's abandoning her until Monday and because he treats her as if she's sick, she's gotten angry at everyone and everything, in a bratty little girl's tantrum, a little girl who takes refuge in a corner and hurts herself and says, "when they see what's happened to me, they'll be sorry," although it can be a good sign, she recognizes, that so much desolation, so much grey sadness, so much emptiness, has changed now into anger, and she is above all furious with herself for having decided to clear the world of herself, exile herself from time, resist living, without the courage however to commit suicide, too passive to kill herself (but going out into the streets every morning with the firm hope that a balcony of a cornice will collapse on her head, crossing the street without looking, hoping that a car will run her over), for having wanted to go down a dead-end street, because there's only one way out, and that is to accept once and for all that Jorge doesn't love her, that Jorge has stopped loving her, and it's better for her to swallow this truth now, this very night, along with the pills and the peppermint, since it seems inevitable to first drink all the bile to be able to get out of the sea of bitterness, and Elia repeats in different tones, in different voices, "Jorge doesn't love me," she says it aloud, whispers it, shouts it, sings it, asks it, as in one of her old theater classes, without worrying, she so timid sometimes, if anyone is looking at her or thinking she's crazy, what the hell, maybe she has indeed become ill, and besides, everyone is shouting to be able to make themselves heard above the music, drinking, smoking hash or marijuana, dancing feverishly, rubbing against each other as if, from this body-to-body contact, light were to spring forth, and maybe there's no other way to remain lucid, and lucidity for Elia is reduced tonight to this: accepting that Jorge doesn't love her anymore, that Jorge has stopped loving her, that he never actually loved her with the unique and imperishable love that he promised or that perhaps the two of them, accomplices, made a fable of, and Elia repeats it with different intonations in the café, determined to swallow all the bitterness at once, to gulp it down in its entirety or burst, while she lifts her glass towards the fellow with the microphone and the guitar, the fellow recognizes her and smiles at her and also lifts his glass towards her and begins, in order to please her—the poor guy hasn't understood a thing—the song of these last few nights, and Elia shakes her head, rejects with a gesture of her hands, laughs, protests, because no, it's not true that living on dreams is the true way, it's necessary to annihilate dreams first, it's necessary to accept "Jorge doesn't love me" and she tells it to herself in a murmur, in a lament, her head to one side and her eyes suddenly full of tears, to the fellow with the soft hairy hands, with the voice that has a slight foreign accent, who in short doesn't resemble Jorge at all and who has sat once again at her side without saying a word, and begins now to kiss her, to caress her, and Elia closes her eyes, and is also quiet, unpardonably drunk on words, on drugs, on alcohol, maybe only on so much pain transmuted into anger, taking refuge in this corner of a dive where there's undoubtedly too much noise, too many people, too much smoke, where they're all too young, and where, who knows why, she feels comfortable and safe, and when her friend, mute up to now, begins talking and says "stop drinking, don't take any more concoctions, let's go outside so you can get some fresh air, I'm sure Jorge was a jerk," Elia stands up docilely and lets him support her, and follows him and lets him do everything, and the man holds her close to him, both of them standing on the sidewalk, motionless for a long time, like two kids, Elia thinks, like two abandoned children, because the man suddenly seems—and it's the first time she's stopped to consider him, the first time she's observed him from an angle other than that of a hypothetical ghost chaser—as sad and as abandoned (maybe as drunk too) as she, holding her like this in the dark alley, with an intensity that must necessarily spring from fear or desolation, since it can't be from love, his head stubbornly hidden on her shoulder, as if he didn't want her to see his face, or look in his eyes, and squeezing her hard, hard, so hard that he's hurting her and cuts off her breath, and Elia is surprised by this robust, solid body, this coarse musculature, very different from the thin, fine, smooth bodies of fellows who work among books and who play a game of tennis on Sundays, bodies on which a soft down grows, and in which the ribs are drawn like on the characters of frescoes and medieval altarpieces, and Elia starts laughing amid her tears, because she has remembered the end of a nineteenth-century novel and it would be so ridiculous, so ineffable, to die like this, in the street, crushed by the strength of an embrace, and the man lets go of her, separates her a little from himself, looks at her, hurt, "what are you laughing at?" and Elia, "nothing, nothing," and he gives up immediately asking any more questions, sighs, puts his arms around her waist, leads her slowly to the beach, both of them wobbling, a pair of staggering old drunks, Elia thinks, although she immediately rectifies it because it occurs to her that the man is much younger than she, and again he has rested his head on her shoulder, and now he lays

130

her carefully down on the sand between two boats, under the stars, under a sliver of a moon ("I'm a woman who in another time possessed the moon," Elia meditates, melancholically, a little ashamed of how ridiculous and bombastic the sentence sounds), the sound of the ocean very very near, his jacket serving as a pillow, and Elia feels sad, dizzy, tired, empty inside, and everything seems so absurd to her, although perhaps this sensation too is due to her drunkenness, and again she laughs and again the man asks "why are you laughing?" and Elia refuses to answer and is quiet, aware that she's offending him, but incapable of explaining to him that she's loved for a long long time, almost a whole life, the thin body of an awkward and ungainly intellectual, a smooth soft body, covered with a fine down like a bird's plumage, along which she so used to like to slowly run the tips of her fingers, and feel under the other person's so fine skin the unexpected hardness of his bones, and she feels a certain surprise and a hint of displeasure for this strong, coarse, hairy, sweaty body, who hasn't even acquired its firmness on golf courses or tennis courts, not even swimming or sailing, and she can't explain to him either that for many summers, as they strolled along the beach with their arms around each other, either Jorge or she had proposed, "one night we'll sleep on the beach, on the sand or inside a boat, under the stars, wrapped up in a blanket," until that never-fulfilled plan began to form a part of their private mythology, like the meeting and the oath with the tetrarchs in the piazzetta, or the log cabin, the shelter made of tree trunks that he'd promised to build some day for the two of them (his primitive man side, genuine man returned to nature), and which was never built, they'll never return to Venice either, nor will they sleep, embraced, on the beach, wrapped in a blanket, between the fishermen's boats, because those are things that they said just to say, that they fabricated for the pleasure of inventing, and now Jorge is definitely far away, overwhelmingly absent, and this strange boy who has sat next to her some nights in the café (while the Argentinean with the beard and the microphone repeated with conviction that to live on dreams is the true way), and who has kissed her, caressed her, has dried her tears, has almost cradled her with words, as if he were consoling a little girl (and maybe that's why Elia hasn't realized until tonight that he's a young fellow, much younger than she is), has brought her now to the beach (surely because he has no other place to take her), and kisses her untiringly on the eyes, on the throat, on the mouth, on the breasts, caresses her waist, her thighs, the warm hollow between her legs, asks her "are you cold? are you comfortable? do you like being here with me?" and Elia nods in silence and lets herself go, maybe because she's so sad and so tired, or because she's finally drunk too much peppermint, or because the ocean shines so beautifully under the pale waxing moon, or because the boy's error moves her, he has in his naïveté taken her, it seems, for a real live woman, not a zombie exiled from time, or only because for a few instants, when he approached her the first day and talked to her in his slight foreign accent (the same day they'd seen the fellow walking along the promenade with the unmistakable Pink Panther gait), he seemed so incredibly familiar to her and she was about to confuse him with Jorge himself.

C lara wraps herself up in the sheets and raises to her chin the light cotton blanket that Eva always leaves at the foot of the bed, as the cold, together with discouragement, gradually overcomes her and she feels rigid and trembling on the warm night at the beginning of August, because first there was a prolonged phone call—strange for Eva to talk for such a long time on the phone—and then the children shouted for her from the kitchen because they had all been at the beach, it seems, bathing nude in the brackish and lunar night—a sliver of pale moon that's a little thicker, a little more reddish, every night—and they and their friends came home (always Eva's house is the best supplied, the most ready to receive them) with the hunger of genuine werewolves bewitched by the moon, although the full moon is still remote and none of them is the eldest of seven brothers, and they shouted for Eva, and Eva went to them as soon as she hung up the phone, and surely placed in front of them, on the kitchen table, very tall pyramids of sandwiches and leftovers from the adults' dinner, big glasses full to the rim with milk or Coke, and then she returned to the living room, without remembering at all that Clara is waiting in bed as every night for her good-night kiss, and the three of them are conversing, although she's not able from her room to understand the meaning of what they say, and hears only the voices, which seem, in the distance, isolated and parallel, Elia's voice, tenuous and prim, like the whisper of a shy girl who monologues untiringly with herself, the voice of an agonizing mermaid on the edge of the pond of the deepest unlove, because when Elia speaks, whatever meaning what she says may have, she seems to be repeating a monochord complaint for which there exists neither consolation nor answer, and Clara hears from her bed the voice of Eva the forgetful, Eva the fickle, Eva the treacherous, who has left her today without her good-night kiss, and it's a calm and clear voice, which is busy surely with routine things, like the nocturnal bathing of the children who then eat like wolves, or the political commentary on TV, or the last book she's read or is reading or plans to read, or the need for the carpenter to make something or to buy another anchor which doesn't invariably coil every time they manage to anchor, the only sensible and sane voice in a world of crazy people, Clara thinks, tenacious in making reason prevail amid so much foolishness, Eva the clairvoyant, Eva the blind, she thinks, and is invaded by this violent and sudden wave of tenderness that is inevitably loosened when she stops to consider any characteristic, any weakness of Eva's, and it's true that she still thinks many times of Eva as a strong, lucid, protecting figure, warmly maternal (even though she hasn't come to give her the good-night kiss), who marauds without arrogance along the borders of omnipotence, but she has also begun to imagine her other times as a

133

myopic and fearful little girl who, humming or jumping rope, goes into a mine field, and whom someone should warn and stop, and even, other times—or maybe it's in fact one time, since the contradictory images are simultaneously super-imposed in time—she sees her as a little child who is playing innocently with the pistol her daddy has forgotten, a revolver whose mechanism and whose reach she doesn't understand but with which she can inflict on others, inflict on her, ir-reparable damage, and Clara wonders how not to be afraid of a child who's aiming a loaded gun at us without knowing it, and how is it possible above all to so love someone who inspires so much fear in us, because Clara has always been timid and afraid and humble, but she doesn't ever remember being as deeply ashamed of herself, so terrified as now, with such an intense desire to hide and disappear in the furthest corners of the house, or to get into bed, like tonight, in the dark room, wrapped up in the sheets, divided between the very violent eagerness for Eva to come and the fervent desire to be forgotten, her attention centered on the three voices that, muffled, reach her from the living room, Elia's voice, which goes along shedding melancholies and languishings, Eva's voice, which claims alone to impose the norms of the most innocuous everyday living, and making its way between them, the man's voice, and Clara wonders if they are indeed conversing, because heard like this, from far away, they seem three isolated voices developing three parallel monologues and without any possible point of contact, the three of them talking alone in the living room only to themselves, and in Pablo's voice, which interferes and imposes itself on the voices of the two women, there's something that frightens her, something she can't define, and which perhaps appeared a few days ago, although only at this moment, when she hears the voice without being able to understand the meaning of his words, has she been capable of detecting it, and although always, from the first day she met him, and hated him, he's seemed to her a pedantic and affected guy, a bad actor who stubbornly overacts a grandiloquent and literary character, hardly convincing, it's true that now he's more theatrical than ever, and in his affected voice melancholy, boredom and disillusion have been replaced with a mysterious self-sufficiency, a joy that to Clara, without knowing why, seems threatening, as if he considered the three of them, condescendingly, from the top of the stage where he's interpreting the role for himself, with a smile that Clara doesn't understand either, and perhaps that's why it frightens her (now indeed Pablo licks himself like a big, gluttonous, shiny cat), as if he'd discovered all by himself the tree of life, or the fountain of eternal youth, and he were forgiving the three of them, or maybe only Eva, her ignorance, magnanimously, and he were containing with difficulty the desire to leave them dumbfounded with the revelation of some prodigious, knightly—scoundrelly—feat, and so Eva was first talking on the phone for an eternity and then detoured towards the kitchen and prepared mountains of food for the starving wolves and then returned to the living room, and has forgotten that Clara is waiting for her in bed as always for her to give her the good-night kiss, and Clara thinks that she's not going to be able to sleep without that kiss, that she's not going to be able to contain her anxiety, but she knows she's not capable either of getting up and going to the living room to get her, that she's not capable of calling her, because she doesn't want to risk a new very painful rejection, and she starts crying quietly and rocking herself between the blanket and the sheets, and feels so bad, so unpardonably bad, and begins to tell herself the sad story of a timid girl, bashful and afraid, who, upon waking one morning, found love in her arms, and it was a strong love, a healthy love, a beautiful love, she'd never seen anything so beautiful until that instant, it was a love that seemed capable of filling the world and redeeming it, a love that illuminated her inside, and she almost couldn't believe it had been born to her, so timid, so awkward, so afraid, a love like that, and then, in a not too remote past, she took it to the woman made of light, because that miraculous love had been born magically from her and for her, and the silly girl felt proud, she felt happy for the first time in her life, and she took the love, dressed it in ostentatious finery, a pink ribbon at its neck, and she took it to the woman as an offering, as a homage, as a gift, and nevertheless Eva didn't want to receive the offering, accept the homage, take the gift, Eva had that expression of surprise, a suspicious look, and said "this is love," as if she were accusing her of something, or as if she had tried to cheat her, or as if it weren't evident to everyone that this was love, that this was called love, that it couldn't resemble anything but love, and she stood there like an idiot, with the enormous love weighing very heavy in her arms, and the love that had been marvelous and had been able to fill the world had now a frustrated and grotesque quality, and Eva added with displeasure, Eva proceeded with annoyance, "I don't like you to love me this way, you don't have to love me this way," and she, aghast, not understanding what she was hearing, because how the hell could anyone manage not to love this way if that were precisely how she was loving, how could she love less or love better, love better and love less, and how could as bright a woman as Eva propose such stupid and unattainable things (and she felt for the first time the fright of having put her life in the hands of a very dedicated schoolgirl who had read all the books, who had learned everything in books, and who had never understood a thing, because maybe in her textbooks there was no chapter about skinny, foolish stray cats who maraud across rooftops in search of a pretty owner who they can call mamma) and Clara has told herself a sad story that has made her sadder and sadder, so that now she's crying in torrents, drowning among her sobs, divided again between the fear they'll hear her from the living room, that especially Pablo will hear her, Pablo the malicious, Pablo the sarcastic, and the hope that Eva does indeed hear her and come to her and the night isn't yet lost, and she tells herself the story or tells nobody, that she backed away with her bashful love, with her rejected love, her battered love, and that she put it back together as well as she could, and time after time sent it to the woman, she tried to make it pass through unnoticed, like smuggled goods, so they'd let it in, permit it to live in the shadows, make a nest in any corner of the palace but time after time Eva recognized it, Eva identified it and raised the drawbridge, "this is love," suspicious, "this is love," rancorous, "this is love," accusing, "this is love," gradually more irritated, wanting to kill it and without daring to, but annihilating it little by little, with the hope of perhaps being able to finish it off with innumerable small deaths—so painful—castrating it, beating it, so that the love has been returned to her, is returned to Clara, in a more sorrowful state each time, and it's more difficult for her each time to recognize it—this is love, of course it's love, what else could it be but love—to put it back together, and what was so beautiful, healthy, strong, capable of filling the world and of warming her and illuminating her inside like a flame, is now a deformed creature, mutilated, miserable, that hides, ashamed, under the bed or behind the curtains and wardrobes, like a dog who's been treacherously shorn to nothing and can't bear the humiliation of this nudity, the vexation of this despoilment, and each time—Clara moans as she grabs the soft, dry, warm hand of the grey figure who has entered the room and has come near her and has sat on the edge of the bed, and who isn't Eva the desired, Eva the badly loved, Eva the feared, nor is it Pablo the hated, Pablo the fatuous, threatening Pablo, but rather the grey figure of a foggy woman in the ultimate remoteness of her own inexhaustible sadness—and each time is worse, because at each new mutilation, at each new blow, at each new rejection, the love becomes more unbearable, she's more unhappy and more bored and more fed up with us, with my love and me, and a love that isn't accepted and can't die either is so terrible, so terrible, Clara sobs, and she embraces the foggy and melancholic woman's waist, buries her face in her soft perfumed lap, and the woman runs a light hand through her hair, gives her little pats on the shoulders, separates her from herself, makes her lean back again on the pillow, takes her hair out of her eyes, and begins to talk, holding her hands, in her opaque, quiet voice, a little hoarse, which isn't the voice of a mother, but rather the voice of another child, perhaps as frightened and pained as she herself, who tries in any case to calm her in the middle of the night: once upon a time, Clara (and although she has hardly ever spoken to her until now, and it's the first time that she's said her name, she says it in a warm, familiar way and begins her story as if telling stories to this little girl were an every-night habit, and she were renewing, like Scheherazade, one same story only accidentally interrupted by the previous day), there was an emperor in China, and he was powerful and handsome and rich and strong, and I don't remember exactly how it happened, I think the emperor had fallen in love, and perhaps because it was a very happy love, or because it was an unbearably unfortunate and sad love, or because it was, I don't remember, an impossible love (a love as unfortunate as yours, thinks Clara, a love as impossible as mine), the truth is that the emperor gathered together all the wise men of the court, summoned all the wise men of his scattered realms, and asked them to find a phrase for him, and for any man, a unique phrase which would fit and be adequate for any of the multiple circumstances and vicissitudes of life, and the wise men shut themselves in and deliberated for a long, long time, and finally one day they came out of their confinement and went to communicate the phrase to the emperor, and the phrase was "this too shall pass"—do you understand me, Clara? I know it doesn't help you much now, that you hardly believe it, but think about it, Clara, this too, I assure you, Clara, this too shall pass.

She's waiting for him on the outskirts of town, in jeans and a blue T-shirt, and she strikes Pablo now, standing there, her body a little to one side, and her head bent, near the gas station, as a skinny redheaded little rogue, a worried little ragamuffin who's run away from home and who's waiting for the first stranger to pick her up on the highway, a fugitive princess disguised as a boy (Elia the lover of tales would imagine) because she feels the desire for adventure, or because they want to marry her to a fat, rich, stupid prince, or maybe because daddy king chases her all over the palace grounds with perverse, libidinous intentions, but the truth is that Elia didn't want to accompany him—not even to the edge of town —she doesn't want to know the girl and it's possible that she doesn't really approve of what's happening, because Elia the romantic, Elia the protesting, Elia the nonconformist, the one believing all is fair in love, everything is possible through love, the one who has sung in beautiful verses of the triumph of orgiastic passions over established institutions (although there has been, it seems, in her life, one sole passion, which isn't even, seen from the outside, very orgiastic), has become now strangely conservative and cautious when it's a question of her best friend's husband, and shows herself to be inclined to prophesy hidden risks, to predict vague misfortunes, when he forces her to declare herself, as if the three—four, because Jorge too—of them hadn't always had so many reservations about relationships, so many doubts about monogamy, as if there hadn't been other women in his life ("occasional, stupid flings, so brief that Eva didn't even have time to discover them or to see herself as forced to let anyone know she knew, now it's not the same," Elia insists stubbornly every time he urges her to talk about the subject, and he urges her often, because he needs, in a certain way, her complicity to be able to abandon himself to this affair with absolute joy, her approval to be able to live it without guilt and with entire freedom), as if there hadn't been other men too in Eva's life, or haven't there? (and here Elia is always quiet and shrugs her shoulders and obstinately repeats "it's not the same," without Pablo knowing exactly if the affair is or seems different to her because the girl has an importance the other ones didn't, or because he's living the relationship with her with an intensity he had forgotten about and thought lost forever, or because Eva isn't the same as in other times, or maybe, and this he doesn't dare suggest, because Elia herself is struggling with the knowledge or the suspicion that Jorge too can be traveling the highways of this dislocated and estival Europe with an unknown girl at his side, a girl who laughs and listens to him and rests her head on his shoulder and kisses him on the cheek, as close as she can to his mouth, so that he has to turn his head a little to receive the kiss and the car begins a slight zigzag along the highway, and then she drops a careless hand on his leg, on the inside of his thigh, and Jorge's heart does a somersault, as if he suddenly returned to his seventeenth year, and catches his breath, as if it were again the first time he was taking a girl home from a summer party, and in short he lets the car slip out of control towards the opposite lane or the ditch, and perhaps it's these fantasies about her own abandonment that make Elia so cautious and fearful and reflective), and it's true that when the girl—his, not Jorge's, if one does exist for Jorge—gets into the car and kisses him, as close as she can to his mouth, and rests her head on his shoulder and drops a languid and innocent hand on his thigh, as if she were unaware, as if she really had actually dropped a glove, it seems to Pablo as if the air were impregnated with a wild, meaty, animal aroma, scandalously young, which would surely make Eva's nostrils and even Elia's wrinkle with a certain distaste and makes him feel like growling, like the ogre in fairy tales, "it smells like human flesh here," like warm, female flesh, like the fragrant flesh of a pup still fed only on milk, and the air is filled with this penetrating perfume, slightly acrid, in a certain way excessive and vulgar, and with the girl's salty laugh, also very like the reckless purring of a young feline, and she laughs without really knowing why she's laughing, what she's laughing at, in the same way that disturbing and involuntary smell bursts with no reason from between her breasts, or from her curly, thick, shiny hair, and Pablo lets the car slide towards the ditch and advance a stretch further, amid the pine trees, and

140

grabs the girl by the shoulders and separates her from himself, immobilizes her against the car door, stares at her, without blinking once, and she's left in suspense, incapable of continuing her laughter or of meeting his gaze, agitated and confused, like a little trapped animal, who knows nonetheless that it's a game, and that the entire game revolves around her, and she breathes unevenly and out of rhythm, and her breasts tremble under her navy blue T-shirt, which doesn't look at all now like boy's clothing, and it seems inconceivable to Pablo to be experiencing something like this, a marvel that it's happened to him, that once again and at this point and after so much dead time, it's happened to him, and that the girl is so beautiful and so young, and that she's there for him ("what are you doing here with me, if all the boys in town are surely wanting to take you out?" and she shrugs her shoulders, "I love you," without emphasis, laughing, blinking very fast but looking him in the eyes now, "I love you," and Pablo, "you're crazy, a crazy girl, why do you love me? tell me, why do you love me?" dying for her to explain and to listen, but the girl shrugs her shoulders again, laughs, blinks anxiously and doesn't risk saying anything), as he still holds her strongly, stuck to the other side of the car, curbing her and restraining her for the pleasure of feeling that everything in her is searching for him and calling for him and is impatient, the lips that open and close, voracious, frantic, dampened by the touch of her tongue, her breasts with their hard and erect nipples trembling under the navy blue fisherman's T-shirt, like two blind young beasts, frolicsome twins, eager to jump on their prey ("my skin hurts from wanting to touch your skin so much" she moans in a hoarse voice) but Pablo still keeps her at a distance, as he inhales the acrid perfume that bursts from the furrow between her breasts, the dense laughter that is born in her throat, a silly, adolescent laughter, without any reason, as spontaneous and wild as the aroma, and he imagines under the jeans, amid silky chestnut curls, the humid warm sex that is opening and calling him, and now Pablo keeps her at a distance with only one hand, the girl has become quiet, and puts his other hand on the warm nest, on that eager mouth "if you don't explain why you love me, I'm not going to touch you, we won't do anything if you don't tell me the reasons you love me," but she moans and weakens and gives up and closes her eyes, and when he finally lets go of her, she crumbles on top of the man like a mountain wanting to fill up the valley, like a river flowing inevitably to the sea, and Pablo feels the mountain overtaking him, the river overflowing and he loses his footing, and as he still tries to tell her in a slow, deliberate voice "you're crazy, to screw in a parked car like this near the highway, at our age, at my age," in a last effort to control himself and control her, he knows the dikes have broken, the murals have exploded, and that he's on the edge of one of those very few and rare moments for which it's worth having been born and having remained alive.

The porter is in his lodge behind the desk, reading a newspaper, and Elia tries once again to open the door with ease and cross the lobby—so ample, so illuminated—with naturalness, as she makes fervent invocations to the pagan gods, to her private demons, for the fellow to be really involved in his reading and not to see her, but she has to say good morning to him as she passes, and her voice comes out quivering and broken, the voice of an idiot, and the porter—brown hair, eyebrows grown together, grim—raises his eyes from the newspaper (maybe he discovered her from the moment she opened the door and has pretended not to see her in order to trap her later like this, at the last minute, treacherously?) and she directs a brief but categorical glance at him, a glance that allows no discussion, that spreads across the land her airs of "I'm a personal friend of the doctor and his family, you know, and I've come a thousand times before to dine in this house, so do me the favor of not considering me one more nut visiting her shrink," and Elia trips over the edge of the rug and rushes headfirst into the elevator's protective shadow and suddenly feels an intense desire to burst out laughing (and all she needs is for this guy to follow the elevator's ascent from below), because it's incredible that at this extreme level of desolation and of anxiety, about to touch bottom or to transpose the limits, beyond—it would seem—good and evil, she's still worried about what the porter of a building which isn't even hers can say about her, and who perhaps on the other hand, and this must be the bad part, is right, since she is in fact only one more, just one more woman who's been beaten by life and who couldn't take it, who toppled and ran on all fours to the psychiatrist's office, in search of multi-colored little pills or of someone in whom to deposit a now impossible faith, in search, in short, of a miracle, one of so many forty-year-old women who have been abandoned by a man ("we're not going to keep playing at Abelard and Héloïse the rest of our lives . . .") and who couldn't bear it, who still hasn't been able to stop swallowing so much bitterness, rebuild another world atop the ruins, because the castle made of cards toppled, the fortress of sand that between the two of them they had laboriously erected, and she doesn't know which card to choose or where to begin again, although maybe her worry about the porter's insolent air, or the fact that she made it until Monday—what else could she do?—in fact signal the beginning of a slight improvement, point towards the road of a remote but perhaps possible cure, because it's true that she didn't see the porter or the nurse who must have had to open the door for her—as she opens it today—or anyone (since she doesn't even remember who brought her or how she arrived here alone) the first time she dragged herself to the office six weeks ago now, and not even on all fours, dragging herself, in search of something, anything (just as she could have run to a sorceress, the neighborhood witch—she's spending the summer after all in a town of witches—a card reader, a heroin pusher, a Buddhist monk consecrated to Zen meditation: Miguel's phone was simply closer at hand, and Miguel had seen her once already, in bed, a few days earlier, at Jorge's insistence surely), anything that would permit her to survive until the following morning, because a miserable and extreme level of suffering exists—she's discovered—in which anxieties referring to a more or less remote future (in any case unlikely), the worry of not knowing what to do with what's left to us of life, lose meaning, and one interrogates oneself desperately about how the hell to manage to last until the next dawn, to clear the very high wall, bristling with the night's barbs, what rare ability or what dark and powerful magic will make the blood keep flowing sensibly through the veins, make the heart keep beating industriously, make the lungs fold with the monotonous fatigue of breathing, and Miguel gave her an ample repertoire of pills and capsules of different colors and shapes, which Elia can line up like little toy soldiers, place on the tablecloth like the ingredients of a sacrilegious communion, and Miguel said, and Miguel repeats to her "there are people who make love the center of their world, and this strikes me as mad enough, but there are others, very few, like you, who reduce the entire world to being the center of your love, and when love ends—notice you're the one who says it's ended, not me, because what you're telling me means that Jorge is going through a difficult time, that he probably has doubts, that he can even be a little or very tired of this romantic, obsessive, exhausting love that you invent, or both of you invent, but it doesn't mean that your relationship is over, or that the marriage is broken, or even that he's stopped loving you, because there are other ways of loving, Elia, however much you don't believe it, that have little to do with Abelard and Heloïse, and all that nonsense of my solitude begins two steps away from you—so when love ends, or when you think it's ended, you've lost the world together with love," Miguel concludes, and Elia thinks yes, Elia accepts it, that it might be true, that surely she awarded love and awarded the world—a long, long time ago—the wrong roles, places that didn't correspond to them, but this comes from too far away to be changed—why does Miguel insist the past isn't irreversible?—

from so far away she can't remember herself feeling any differently, living it in a different way, and maybe it's due in fact, as he suggests, to an always busy and often absent father, to her fatherless childhood, or to a very powerful, magnificent, invading mother, not in the least maternal, to that basic lack of affection, or because she was born like that, retracing the roots of her illness even farther back in time, timid, fearful, unsure of herself, not at all pleasing and thinking herself incapable of being liked, without accepting herself at all or therefore being accepted by others, an entire childhood then, an entire adolescence and a first youth sunk in the wells of her fear, her sadness, her solitude—"until you met Jorge?" Miguel asks without curiosity, with the fatigue of someone who already knows the answer—yes, until Jorge arrived, and Jorge chose her among all the rest, because the Jorge of fifteen years ago could have chosen any girl and gotten her, and as she was not going to begin accepting herself after this prodigious choice, Jorge took her out of the well and carried her with him and everything bad was left behind, Jorge said look at yourself in my eyes, and she discovered in his eyes a different Elia, of whom she'd not even been aware, an Elia who could please, who could be useful, who could do beautiful things and provoke love, and suddenly—for the first time— the evil, the stupidity, the sordid madness, the cowardly cruelty, the basic injustice that govern the world became bearable—they never had been before—because there were two of them to face it, two of them to brace themselves against it and combat it, you see, even death became in a way acceptable, and surely because of that I came to know the world, I was able to have a world and to take it on, when I made it the center of my love, and it's not, as you say, that I'm only intent on, obsessed with, whatever creates problems for myself, or that I don't have a world or that it works badly for me, because actually I don't have separate accounts, nor do I have different drawers at my disposal, one for my profession, another for the enjoyment of sensitive things, another for my social life or for friendship, another for money's problems or satisfactions, another finally for love, each thing supposedly in its drawer, and me refusing to appraise and use the full drawers and stubbornly crying over the only messy or empty drawer, it's not like that, Jorge is not one more drawer, one more category, Jorge is the key that let me open all the drawers every morning, do you understand, everything came to me and everything was useful to me and everything was made possible for me because of his love, and his unlove submerges me into the most absolute nothingness, and it wouldn't make sense—is that what you're proposing to me?—for me to sit every morning for a long time in front of the mirror, sometimes as a little girl I did, you know, when I felt the worst, because things like that are only attempted when one is absolutely wretched, and still today I feel sorry for myself when I remember myself there, in front of the bathroom mirror or the big wardrobe, one finger raised as if I were getting ready to impart a masterful lesson, the tears running down my face and getting my dress wet, ready to repeat again the supposedly magic formula—and it never worked, of course—that perhaps someone had transmitted to me or was perhaps of my own invention: "I'm happy, who doubts it? to deny it would be idiocy," is that what you want, for me, almost forty, to renew the same litany and enumerate every morning in front of the mirror in a calm and convincing voice the multiple reasons I have to be happy and which nonetheless are useless to me?—"you've forgotten some," Miguel interrupts her, phlegmatic, resigned, without ever losing his calm faced with her speeches, "for example, that you have a magnificent son, an exceptional boy"—yes, it's true, surely Daniel is an exceptional boy, and he should probably be enough for me to feel fulfilled, but it doesn't matter what things should be like, it only matters what they are like or in what way they're lived, and I'm like that, and I'm not going to change anything by repeating the lesson a hundred times every morning in front of the mirror, because it turns out Jorge isn't one more element in my life,

146

not even conceding that he's the most important, I don't know how to explain it to you, it's as if I possessed an immense piece of machinery, new shining, recently oiled, and I only needed to move a minuscule lever to put it in motion, and there wasn't a lever, or as if I had an enormous palace, and don't make that sneering face like here-come-my-fairy-tales, an enormous palace with a thousand rooms full of treasures, one for silver, another for gold, another for diamonds, another for rubies, but there existed one sole, irreplaceable key and I'd lost this key, it's like (to give an example that doesn't come in the least from fairy tales) possessing millions and millions of a currency that has no legal value, or a huge book covered with very valuable formulas in a code the key to which has been forgotten, all of it dead, all of it unusable, "and that very thing," suggests Miguel now, "is what's happening with your sexuality, another probably overflowing drawer to which we've lost the key, and that poor fellow from the café will busy himself and be desperate on top of your body in vain, useless for him to shave his beard and let his moustache grow and dye it three colors, for him to wear glasses and crack his knuckles and smoke a sweet tobacco, and even learn to walk like the Pink Panther, because however much he tries he won't ever be able to become Jorge, he'll never be Jorge," and now Elia laughs, looks Miguel straight in the eye, "yes, I'm afraid it's useless," and they both laugh, and for an instant, only a few seconds, like on the beach the other morning, the pain yields and Elia experiences a certain relief, a very brief breathing spell, a glimpse of well-being, and afterwards, still smiling, she explains to her psychiatrist that not only is he very right, but that the reality is even worse, since it's not a question, as he claims, of her sexuality being enclosed in a drawer, and the only possible key is love, and the only love imaginable is always called Jorge, which would make the situation complicated and difficult but probably not desperate: what happens is that for her sex and love and Jorge constitute one sole, indivisible reality, and not even at a

147

theoretical level is she capable of separating them, and she wouldn't know or couldn't imagine a sexuality without love, or a love that wasn't Jorge's, or a love that wasn't at the same time sexuality, because everything came to her together, she discovered it all together, it was given to her together, she has lived it together and together she has lost it forever.

"No, you're not interrupting anything; it looks like I won't accomplish much this summer," Elia has answered him with a dry and slightly sarcastic laugh, sitting, like so many other times, at her worktable, only that you can't hear the typewriter's hum—she hasn't even bothered to turn it on today—and there's no paper in the carriage either. Elia is simply sitting there, absorbed, staring vacantly out the window at ghosts (or at the same sea as every summer, which today has, on the unpleasant morning that has made the boat or the beach impossible, a dark blue shade under leaden clouds), and when he justifies himself beforehand, "I know you don't really like me to talk to you about this, to get you involved in this . . .," the woman in the chair turns around and faces Pablo, who has sat down, as always when he comes to chat with her and interrupt her, on the edge of the sofa bed, and looks at him, a hint of a smile playing on her lips, and Pablo doesn't know if it's a residue of the initial laughter referring to the little she'll accomplish this summer, or anticipated laughter for what she presumes he's going to explain to her, and now Elia shrugs her shoulders, "you can't help telling me; you wouldn't talk about anything else! And it's better for you to tell me than to have it shouted by the town crier or to send raffle tickets for it to friends, or for you to stop strangers in the street one by one to tell them about it," and suddenly serious, suddenly grave and serious, "what is it you feel? are you in love?" and he's perplexed for a few seconds, less because of the question's content than because of the intensity with which Elia awaits the answer, as if she were consulting the oracle about her own destiny, or about something that concerns the common destiny of them all, and then Pablo answers hurriedly, without stopping to reflect, "I don't know: I'm very happy," and he realizes, as soon as he's said it, that it's the precise answer (Elia also sighs and nods, as if she saw her suspicions confirmed and all the questions had been resolved), that it's exactly that, he's very very happy, completely delighted, a delight he hadn't experienced the likes of for many years ("since you met Eva?" Elia has asked, and he assents with a gesture of his head, with an evasive movement of his hand, yes, in part yes, although that was different, it seemed so much work and so difficult to conquer her, she in a way so above all the others, so coveted, so distant, it made him afraid to know she was so sure of herself and demanding, so that when, unexpectedly, she accepted him, the victory didn't even seem believable, since deep down he'd never thought he'd get her, and the fear persisted, hidden away, that it was only a mirage, a joke, or that he'd gotten her only to lose her immediately afterwards, and Eva had said yes, but she hadn't had the slightest expression of faintness or of abandonment, Eva never said at the crucial point of the contest—that she didn't live either for that matter as a contest—"I've discovered your name, stranger, your name is love!" and the anxiety had been so great, the victory seemed so unsure and gratuitous that perhaps part of what could have been experienced as delight had evaporated by the wayside, "since when then?" Elia insists, very curious and relentless, avid listener always of tales and stories, insatiable as a little girl, although there is now in her curiosity a special nuance and Pablo thinks that more than questioning the witch about her personal destiny or the destiny of others, it's as if she were carrying out a sociological poll in order to clarify an unknown that obsesses her; "what's going on with you today about love?" and Elia laughs—these last days she's recovered laughter, even though it's a drier and more muffled laughter, as in a minor key— shrugs her shoulders, "nothing, I've discovered that I don't understand it, that I don't know the slightest bit about love,

how long has it been since you felt as happy as with this girl?",
"a long long time, since a few months before meeting Eva,
before meeting you, too," "and what happened?", "she left:
she was a foreigner and had to leave, when I met Eva, the girl
was no longer here"), a delight he didn't believe was ever
possible to recover, and which had nonetheless been waiting
crouched in some hidden corner of his being, since it had been
reborn unharmed as young as his delight of twenty years ago,
and which wasn't only, as perhaps it was in the first days,
delight because of the girl's beauty, because of her youth,
because she was so astoundingly near perfection ("like a
newspaper or like a lighter" Elia laughs), beautiful from any
angle, under any light, at any time of the day or night, whatever her expressions and her clothes, a beauty without fissures
or parentheses, a beauty that doesn't require effort or artifice
at any moment, not only is it because the girl has placed her
prodigious beauty in love at his service (surely she was never
so pretty before and won't be ever again) and she is stirred and
suffocates every time they meet, every time he comes through
the door and approaches her, and she trembles and catches her
breath every time he touches her, and she holds him tight
tight as if she were always afraid of losing him, avid and
devoted, with tender, damp eyes, which move him, and she
never tires of touching him, kissing him, saying tender and
ridiculous and pampering words to him, and she never tires of
playing the game of love with him, that she seems to have
learned now for the first time even though she may have
played it a thousand times, always ready to continue and
begin again, absolutely indefatigable and insatiable—never
has she shown fatigue, sleepiness, hunger, thirst, while they've
been together—looking at him again with those damp, astonished, incredulous, dilated eyes, red to the roots of her hair
and breathing with difficulty, "I didn't know it could be like
this, I didn't know . . .," the same as if her body had been
awakened or born at the touch of the man's body (previous
touches and caresses disappeared, erased, annulled), and she

150

had been acquiring in Pablo's arms awareness of her own skin, "I've never felt anything like this, I've never felt anything, there was never anything before you," bewildered by the discovery, crying with pleasure and gratitude, docile and enraptured, and his, God, so intimately his, because she indeed had lowered her defenses, or not even that, all defenses had simply stopped existing, they had vanished in smoke, in nothing, like her past, and she indeed had said at the crucial moment, "I've discovered your name, stranger, your name is love," as natural and limitless in this surrendering as in her miraculous beauty, and all this had been and was marvelous, an unexpected gift at a time when one had stopped believing in Santa Claus and doesn't hang up the stocking, but there was more, he had renewed for this girl an ancient speech, interrupted for years and years, perhaps for lack of a listener and because one tires with time of talking to oneself, and how he talked and she listened, and surely she didn't understand at times what he was saying, or half understood it, or understood it badly ("did I tell you she didn't even know why we went to Colliure? and when we left, I told her: now you know, Colliure is the town where Machado is buried, she rebutted: Colliure is the town where we bathed under the rain together, one of the places we've been together and where we've loved each other") but that didn't matter at all, it was enough for her to listen to him like that, so attentively, hanging on his words like a dedicated little schoolgirl, her head to one side, her thick red hair falling over her shoulders, and those humid, absorbed, marveled eyes of a gazelle in heat, it was enough that she listened to him and looked at him like that for things Pablo had given up on to seem possible, plans he'd renounced a long time ago, causes he'd abdicated from—"oh so many lost things that were never lost, you kept them all," Elia hums without irony, and Pablo "you know that I've even begun, after so many years, a new book of poems?"—and Pablo talks to the girl about himself, and the girl imagines him, idealizes him, invents him, gives him back, in short, an image that isn't true, that is at most vaguely similar to the image he dreamed of himself at twenty, but it's nevertheless flattering and comforting for one to be seen that way, "it makes me feel like working, surpassing myself," and Elia, very serious, Elia a drag and a puritan, "but what about Eva?" as if Eva had anything to do with it, as if it weren't a question of two different and perfectly separated things, "why do you insist on asking me about Eva? you know how important she has been and is to me, the most important part of my life, along with the children," "just that she doesn't delight you," and Pablo recognizes that, no, she doesn't delight him, at least not that way, and he doesn't risk telling Elia, as the witch probably would, that human love—and we know no other—functions almost always like that, in the best cases like that, that the in-love love, the passion love, doesn't last forever (the love Elia proclaims and which she supposes, between her and Jorge, imperishable), that love, like everything else, is suspended and wears away, that there is an inevitable deterioration, and it's replaced—always in the best of cases, like his and Eva's— by a subtle net of experiences and goals in common, by respect, by solidarity, by affection (this is what makes his relationship with Eva permanent), but delight, genuine, rapturous delight, however lamentable it seems to Elia, you have to look for it as the years go by in other places, or resign yourself to living without it.

He ("that poor guy who gets desperate and busies himself uselessly on top of your body" Miguel had said) has only been, thinks Elia, awake beside this sleeping man, one more element of the decor, and I was only looking for a comfortable decor in which to accommodate my grief, an interior landscape in which to shelter a pain that neither has nor admits any consolation, and which nevertheless is even worse when I'm alone at night in this bed, and everyone in the house is asleep, and I look at the ceiling and at the grey rectangle of the window, waiting for dawn (and then the night is a very high wall, unsalvageable, bristling with barbs and broken glass, on whose other side there is nothing anymore), and this sadness is also worse when I go out in the boat with Eva and Pablo, and that intimate atmosphere is established (like the one produced in cars on long trips or on trains sometimes, fit for complicity and confidences), and everything is so similar to other summers except that Jorge isn't there, and the two of them know me well and have for a long time, and they still keep waiting for me to start talking and tell them or cry, and I can't (with them least of all, and I don't know why) tell them anything about this pain that's drowning me, cry on their shoulder or in their lap, and I'd feel so bad, and the sadness gets worse when I ramble through the town's streets or along this house's porch, like a ghost who has, from pure absent-mindedness and misfortune, forgotten her chains in the tomb, a crazy somnambulant who's been let loose through careless-ness (perhaps Miguel interceded) of the guards, and that's why I go off so many evenings to the café, because I feel better in a way in a closed, small environment, dark and damp like a lair, where I don't know anyone—they're all so young—and where Jorge never took me (and it seems sometimes that I was with him everywhere and he left the world contaminated with his footprints, making it uninhabitable for me without him) in the farthest corner, my back well protected against the wall (I don't like to have my back to an open space either, although I don't confess it and I laugh at Pablo), my head hidden on this fellow's shoulder, this fellow who also goes there almost every night, and sits beside me, and kisses me and caresses me and is quiet, and has a rough, thick, dark beard instead of a tricolored moustache, and he even smells dif-ferent, but something about him keeps reminding me none-theless of the Pink Panther's loose gait and clumsy gestures and I hold a tall glass in my hand—I like to feel the smooth cold surface against my palm, hear and see the ice cubes crash into each other in the green liquid that gets cloudy—and the guy with the guitar sings into the microphone again and again, because I ask him to and because he knows I'm going to ask him to, "living on dreams is the true way," and the sadness doesn't diminish, but becomes perhaps (because of being more literary, in the worst sense of the word, because not only do I live my life sometimes as if it were literature, but I choose besides the most awkward, cheapest style for my life) less unbearable, and I even feel accompanied up to a point, with the company that can be offered to us by a cat that's fallen asleep in our lap, a dog that licks our legs and looks at us, and maybe it is poor company, but it's also the only one we have available or the only one we can accept, and even though we don't give much importance to the sleeping cat, to the dog who's licking us, we know that we would miss them terribly if they disappeared, and their devotion moves us and we're grateful to them, and maybe that's why I've let my Pink Panther take me out of the café, like the other night, and hold me for an eternity against him in the dark alley, so tight that he hurt me and left me breathless, as if we were the only desolate inhabitants of a depopulated earth, the last specimens of a noxious species about to be extinct, and I've let him take me to the beach and lay me down on the sand—his jacket as a pillow—between the fishermen's boats, which almost all have women's names, with the full moon above—now it is indeed full moon—and in my ears the sound of the sea, and the night had the improbable beauty of a melodramatic decor, of a romantic landscape, of a postcard, and I was drunk on literature, on sadness, on peppermint (above all on sadness) and it would have been pure artifice perhaps, pure stage machinery, pure farce, except that the poor guy moved anxiously on top of my dead body, that he looked at me, begging and desperate, that he said meaningless things to me, crazy words that were born perhaps from a lunar spell, "you don't know what you are to me, you don't know what it is for me to be with you: you're what I've always looked for, all my life," amplifying that always, that my life, to eternities, as if he had exhausted time's possibilities with the scarce thirty years that can fill his life, and he believes he's looked forever, that I was what he was waiting for, a woman who's beginning to get old, who has lived dreaming a silly game and who refuses now to wake up, who drags herself through town like the dead body of a zombie or like a ghost, who cries and requests cheap songs and drinks peppermint, who runs on all fours to the psychiatrist's office (hiding, to top it off, from the porter) and communes daily with her doses of antidepressants, who has believed herself authorized to erase the world, to ignore others, because her personal and miserable love story has ended badly, a woman who in short knows nothing about anything, because she doesn't even talk, and he doesn't even ask, and maybe it's this almost total void of knowledge and facts that has fueled all the fantasies, it has occurred to Elia, perhaps falling in love is basically founded on that, to assemble on top of some minimum realities the delirious scaffolding of one's own fantasies, impelled by the pressing and imperious need to love, because in the precise instant in which she tried to contradict him and interrupt him, "but what are you saying, how can you love me if you don't even know who I am, or what I'm like, how can you have fallen in love if you know nothing about me, who the hell are you really loving?", she became confused and suspended, and the words that had begun as a scolding died in a not very convincing murmur, that neither asked for nor expected an answer, because Elia suddenly remembered herself on a summer's night fifteen years ago, embracing a man under the full moon, the two of them standing next to the car as they said good-bye, and he hugged her so tightly that he almost hurt her and cut off her breath, but not with the desperation of a little boy lost in the middle of the night, but with the firmness of someone who has found something very much his own and has taken it forever, and then she had asked him (with some fear that it had all been a dream and that she would never see him again) "when will I see you again?" and he had separated from her a little, looked at her, moved, but smiling, and told her very slowly "tomorrow and the next day and the next and the next, every day we have left of life," and ever since then Elia hadn't felt any more fears or doubted again, and indeed one day had followed another, and another, not for an entire life, but for years and years, and, however it ended, whatever happened, that had without a doubt been love, great love, the kind of love that people search and hope for ever since adolescence and, when they find it, makes them ready to abandon everything, begin everything anew, take everything on, and it had been a real relationship and they had so many things together and had even had a son, and nevertheless that summer's night, saying good-bye to each other in the parking lot of the nightclub where they'd met a few hours earlier, where Eva, who was there with him, who went out with him sometimes and had told a distracted Elia about him, had introduced him to her, and where they had exchanged a few very strange words, unconnected, whose resemblance to what they were thinking or feeling would have been pure coincidence, and Jorge had taken her onto the dance floor, and after three steps they had stood, motionless, petrified, in the middle of the dance floor, among the other couples who kept spinning around them and then vanished, the two of them merged in such a tight embrace that it seemed they would never be able to let go, to make a single movement more, to return to the very remote table where Eva together with other friends were perhaps waiting for them, and Elia had felt faint, completely dizzy, literally sick, and after being anchored for eternities, still on the middle of the dance floor, she had had to tell him, "I'm sorry" (still unable to move) "but I feel sick," and he, "what's the matter? what's wrong?" and she, "nothing, it's nothing, it happens to me sometimes," and it had never happened to her, she had no knowledge ever that something like this could happen to anyone, but she couldn't confess it (years and years went by before she told him in detail how she had experienced that night), "I feel sick, dizzy, almost dead from the intensity of your skin meeting my skin, because it's too disturbing to be in your arms, even like this, both of us dressed and on a dance floor" and Jorge had taken her then into the garden and had made her drink a glass of water (useless to protest "I'm not thirsty") and they had strolled among the flower beds and had sat on a bench and kissed each other, and she insisted nonetheless upon going home alone, in her own car, because she simply needed a pause to take a breathing spell and try to understand the unimaginable, to try to get used to such an unexpected and excessive happiness, but that night, in the parking lot under the moon, when she suddenly had the apprehension that it all could have been nothing and could vanish like a dream, and she asked him "when will we see each other?" and Jorge answered, "always, every day of our lives," and everything was, in that precise instant, decided and sentenced, and the two of them had jumped together into the void without any fear, without the least vacillation, although they were aware that there was then no turning back, in that instant, what did they know about each other? Elia has asked herself, astounded, on the beach, as she tried to convince this foolish guy, who looked at her, desolate and busying himself uselessly and repeating that he loved her, that his love was in vain, and inconsistent, and she asks herself the same thing now, and awake still in bed, next to the man who has finally fallen asleep (because tonight, perhaps because the full moon was so beautiful, the decor so artificial and literary, or because she'd drunk a lot of peppermint and felt too sad, more sad than ever, or because she was ashamed of having used and kept using—because of his resemblance, more remote every time, to the Pink Panther, because of the fact that she confused him with Jorge the first day she saw him—a poor guy who was now telling her he loved her, or because she had the sudden, certain, total awareness that she could never even begin to love him, and this made her feel guilty and bad and stingy, or perhaps because he seemed to suffer so, desire her so, and it seemed incongruous to her, out of place, that someone could love her like this, that someone could

could depend on her with an intensity comparable to the one that bound her to Jorge, that she could be for someone else what Jorge was for her, and she succumbed then to the old temptation of playing God or at least Santa Claus, of giving the man a happiness she couldn't get for herself, who knows which of these reasons, or if it maybe happened because at a certain moment of the night, under the full moon, all the sadness and frustration and abandonment condensed and merged and transmuted into sensuality, a very strange sensuality, but sensuality anyway, and Elia felt excited and desirous for a few seconds, and believed that she should probably try her luck, that maybe Miguel was right after all, that the miracle might be possible, and she took the man home and put him in her bedroom, and let him undress her and lay her down in bed and on his knees beside her, kiss and lick and caress her, while he drowned in a torrent of tender words of incredulity faced with his own good fortune, and very deep, very far away, Elia felt something that could be related to pleasure, but then the man stood up and put a hand on each breast and came close and lay on top of her, and everything happened then in a second, like a flash of lightning, the vision of Jorge, standing above her, one of his hands on each breast, approaching her mouth, and then the stupor that it was someone else there, the incredulity that it could be someone else, and all her body dead, cold, except that intolerable biting between her legs, at every thrust from the man, who stopped a moment and looked at her anxiously and didn't understand, how could he have understood, "what's the matter? what's wrong?", and she shaking her head, nothing, it's nothing, go on, thinking, let him finish once and for all, biting her lips not to cry out in pain, but also not to burst out laughing, and it would be an uncontrolled laughter, on the edge of hysteria, and hysteria has little to do with the peculiar form of her madness, as she wonders how the hell she'll tell Miguel next Monday that she was raped here in her own bed, by a respectable fellow who repeated that he loved her, at her almost forty years, and that it seemed atrocious to her) and now, next to the man who's finally fallen asleep, after all the tenderness and all the delirium and all the flattery, after talking to Elia for the first time all about himself (and she was too distant, too pained, too tired to really listen to him), the woman has calmed down, and the pain has disappeared, and it's even pleasant for her to have a living and sleeping body next to hers in bed, much better than sleeping alone, and Elia, soothed and insomniac, renews the discourse she had begun a few hours earlier, on the beach, and she asks herself again, perplexed with regard to love (the in-love love, passion love, since there's no evidence that permits her to suppose the existence of any other kind of love, it's not just to call love that heap of little reasons, often sordid and miserable, that keeps couples united beyond love), that delirious scaffolding of crazy fantasies sustained on nothing, or on almost nothing, or maybe on the very yearned-for need to love, a scaffolding that doesn't seem very solid, rather gratuitous, not at all important, almost foreign to the seriousness of adults, something, in short, that is impossible to take very seriously, and which nevertheless causes us—against all logic—atrocious and prolonged suffering, incurable wounds whose scar hurts us throughout our entire life, blows that we'll never recover from, common sense and dignity and even the most elementary appreciation of oneself lost, but which can also exalt us to ecstasy, put in motion parts of our being we didn't even suspect we had, make us built marvelous, lasting realities, descend to hell and ascend to paradise, and can, above all, make us so happy, all of this bound by tight and secret knots, by mysterious roads (that Elia doesn't know yet, but she does know that everything is definitely tied together, and there isn't, as Miguel claims, a drawer for each thing, that enables us to arrange them and isolate each one in its place) to that confused, unknown, uncontrolled world, that's called nature, sexuality or pure instinct.

S he glides furtively along the dark hall, again a muffled, hard beating in her ears, and her heart in her throat, and the same fear, or similar, as her childhood fear (because as far as her memory reaches, Clara remembers herself as always fearful and frightened—always sad too, so that her life until now seems one long, tiring and useless battle against fear, against sadness—only that the fear is different today, a specific fear whose causes, however, she can't locate or discover, and which has little to do with her childhood and adolescent fears, which had been prolonged almost without variation until yesterday, until the first days of her arrival in the town, fear of staying alone in the house, of going out alone, of advancing along the interminable hallway to her aunt and uncle's dark bedroom, where they've sent her to look for something they didn't need in order to help her, supposedly, to control her terror this way, her fear of the dark, fear of the dead who are alone and cold in the cemetery and who sometimes talk to her or look at her strangely (from below the earth) with their eye-less sockets, afraid of being sick and of dying, that they'll bury her alive and that black cockroaches, hairy spiders will walk across her body, and of screaming then and no one comes, afraid of being asked the lesson in class and being incapable of separating her lips to answer and being mute there in front of everyone, like an idiot, afraid of the icy voice, the discouraged eyes, of a teacher who confesses she's never liked children, afraid of the other children, those who—they don't need to confess it—don't like her at all, afraid of mockery, of their deliberate and perverse incomprehension, of their incomprehensible cruelty, of the harm they do her, that they do each other, that they inflict on animals, terrified of the children's parties where everyone seems to have such a good time and where she suffers the successive agony of a thousand tiny deaths, the parties her aunt—and she's afraid of her aunt too —forces her to attend, in a horrible organdy dress full of bows, carrying a little box of chocolates, afraid of the violence that seems to surround her—her and everyone—everywhere,

160

afraid of (mortal) sin and of hell (an eternity of eternities), afraid of having to confess, of not being able to, of confessing badly (repenting is never enough, the intention to make amends never seems convincing and sincere), of impure actions—that she doesn't even know exactly what they are but which she intuits to be terrible—afraid of everything, so that when Eva asked her impatiently a few days ago "but what the devil are you afraid of, tell me, why do you always walk around scared?", she didn't know what to answer, partly because her fears had been multiple and contradictory, and partly because she realized then, in that precise instant, that they had been left behind, annulled and replaced by one omnipresent fear, and she didn't dare answer "I'm afraid of you," afraid of displeasing Eva, of boring her, of disappointing her, afraid also of being rejected, said good-bye to, beaten, forgotten, and it was in a way a relief to be able to centralize her strength and unify her fright in this total fear that didn't leave room for any other, but now, and she can't specify exactly since when, maybe since the night Eva forgot to give her a good-night kiss and the three of them were talking for a long time in the living room, and then the foggy old rheumatic undine came, surely because Eva had heard her cry and asked her to—with her damp words of comfort—"this too, I assure you, Clara, this too shall pass," without knowing if she were telling herself a story or talking for Clara or discoursing for no one—since then maybe this fear has changed, and however much it keeps referring monotonously to Eva— is there anything in her life that doesn't refer now in one way or another to Eva?—it's probably not of the harm that Eva can still do her, and which she will undoubtedly, inexorably do her, but rather of the harm that someone or something—a diffuse and threatening presence seems to hang around the two of them in town and in the house, a presence she can't identify and which she associates vaguely with Pablo's unusual voice that night in the living room, so euphoric and confident without cause, a voice that Clara didn't know in him, and

which terrified her—could do to Eva, and now she slides
furtively along the dark hallway, and she feels the same fear
or similar to her fear as a little girl in the interminable hallway where all dangers were spying on her, from the sewing
and ironing room, with its dim lights, the brazier lit, the sound
of the sewing machine, the smell of starch, the persistent
voices of the women who only interrupt their gossiping or
their stories to listen to the advice for the lovelorn spot on the
radio (some afternoons they tell, and Clara listens to them
fascinated, frightful horror stories), to the aunt and uncle's
bedroom, that seems nonexistent and unreal from pure unat-
tainability, so infinitely remote, separated from the warm and
safe den where the women sew and iron and chatter, along
this atrocious hallway, which Clara walks along as a little girl
with a never-vanquished fright, perennially renewed, very
close to the wall, holding her breath, slowly, slowly, trying
not to make the slightest sound, so that they don't hear her or
become aware of her presence or her passage, and those
shapeless, demonic beings don't attack her, the kind the
women talk about and which undoubtedly remain hidden and
watching from the shadows, with her back against the wall
then and very slowly, more frightened as she moves further
away from the safe den, advances palm by palm along the
hallway, and light, warmth, the sound of the chatter, the
affected voice of the female announcer are left behind, with
her back against the wall, hardly daring to breathe, except
that the wall is interrupted at each respite by the holes—even
darker—of the always-open doors that lead to the different
rooms of the house, and there's no defense or protection possible here (she won't even have time to scream and for the
faraway women to hear her), and there's no recourse but to
wait and gather strength and really hold her breath, and then
cross quickly and terrified, in front of that frightful hole from
where the werewolf, feverish from the full moon's spell, can
catch her (he's the youngest of seven brothers, the women
explain, and the victims are left so disfigured it's impossible

162

to recognize them), the old man who puts children in a sack and draws out their blood or their fat (a very rich and powerful man, whose sick son survives only if he's fed human flesh and blood, and has turned the country into a dreadful market of cadavers), the dead people she's seen sometimes in church and who look at her through their closed eyelids, from their empty sockets, and cry because black cockroaches, hairy spiders cover them and they're very cold and nobody comes to console them (some of them, the old women in the sewing room say, the women mumble as they sew and iron, have been buried alive, and when years later the coffin is opened they're found with their hands half eaten and only an indescribable grimace is left of their face) and that very brief time it took to cross in front of the hole of a door in the dark hallway lasted eternities, and now too Clara feels a muffled and wild pulse beat in her ears, and her throat is closed and dry, and she advances very slowly, stuck to the wall, more and more apprehensive and afraid as she gets further away from the security of her own bedroom—with fear, although it's a different fear—and she advances towards the room where Eva and Pablo sleep, because Eva has spent the whole day in the city, and she didn't dare ask her "when are you coming back?" and when night came, she went to bed early, her hope that Eva would come back today lost, trusting that asleep the time would pass more quickly and probably tomorrow when she wakes up Eva will be here, but she heard the two of them later move along the hallway, and now she knows Eva has returned, and it's no longer possible for her, knowing this, to wait until tomorrow to see her, she can't resign herself to sleeping without her good-night kiss, without asking her how she is and finding out if the trip went well, and she jumped out of bed, barefoot and in her nightgown, and hurled herself into the dark hallway, and walked with her back stuck to the wall, as when she was a little girl and they sent her to look for something they didn't need, into the aunt and uncle's room, with the fear—worse than all fears—that the woman will get angry

163

at her, that she'll look at her, surprised and displeased, that she'll scold her—what are you doing here, Clara, at this time of night?—and the bedroom door is, how strange, open, a light escapes from it, and Clara approaches with reserve, and there, on the bed, are Eva's two legs, bent, the knees up, and separated, as immobile as two columns, and between them, Pablo's greying head, she sees only his head, not his face, like she sees only Eva's marble and inanimate legs, and there's a muffled sound of sucking and licking and drowned exclamations coming from the grey head, and Clara crouches down, and remains there, her back against the opposite wall of the hallway, watching, astounded for a few instants, without understanding, without thinking or feeling anything, trapped there like a wild beast—however much that she's the one who's watching, who's followed the tracks and has discovered them, she is the trapped one—incapable of not looking, of risking the slightest sound, of leaving ("Clara, why don't you leave and go home, before everything gets too complicated now that there's still time?" the gloomy old undine proposed to her this very morning, the moldy, rheumatic undine, the grim eldest sister of the little mermaid who abandoned the seven seas for her prince, and her voice sounded far away, indifferent, as if she were talking to her from the deepest part of the pond, and she spoke just to speak, because how can what Clara does or doesn't do matter in the least to her, and Clara, rancorous, "what are you up to, what are you and Pablo up to against Eva?" and the pale figure insists in her shadeless voice, muffled by the thick layers of water, "what are you saying, really, Clara, leave now, before you're too trapped," and it was grotesque and almost funny for her to be told that, as if she hadn't spent days and weeks already hopelessly trapped, as if she could still decide between staying or leaving) and now she's petrified there, huddled in the hallway, progressively more afraid they'll discover her, that Pablo will lift his head for a moment and discover her, without wanting to look, without being able not to, like as a little girl she couldn't stop listening to the terrible stories the old women in the ironing room told, fascinated and horrified, like she's not able either in a movie theater to stop following the movie from between her fingers however much she's covered her face with her hands, afraid now they'll discover her and scold her—God, what if it's Eva who gets up and discovers her!—but also progressively more indignant, because how could these two forget the open door? her temples beating furiously, her heart out of control, suffocating her and drowning her in the dark hallway, and her gaze fixed, immobilized on that very strange image—it actually looks like the fabulous creature of an imaginary bestiary, an enormous spider with only two golden claws and between them the hairy grey head—and then the legs shake, twitch, contract, reject him, and from the place where the pillow lies comes an agitated voice, disfigured by emotion—"come inside, oh come, please, come now, come inside"—which is nevertheless impossible to confuse with Eva's voice, and it's not, as she suspects for an instant, the moldy voice of the de-angeled undine, it's the voice of an unknown woman, who has sat up and clung to Pablo's shoulders, has grabbed him by the back and made him get up, turn around, cover her, penetrate her, and the two bodies shake, twist, awkwardly, ugly—again Clara thinks that it's a fantastic animal, a repulsive but imaginary being, which gesticulates hysterically with its eight paws and lets out some more and more inarticulate, less human sounds—except that Clara has stopped caring what they look like or what they caw, or what they do, they are only an unknown girl, a man she detests, copulating disgustingly and violently in the bed—they haven't even remembered to close the door, to make sure the children wouldn't see them—and the only thing that at this moment troubles her and upsets her is the evidence that Eva isn't here, that she can't have come home, that she's still far away in the city, that she'll have to wait until tomorrow to see her, the only thing that makes her indignant and stirs her up is that they're doing it in Eva's bed, that they're making love precisely in her own bed.

S he will be waiting for him already (even though it's not yet the hour of their date, but always, when Pablo arrives, he finds her waiting breathlessly for him, consumed with impatience, ready to explain to him—as soon as she's recovered her breath and has been released from his arms—the new tricks she's invented to make the last hours go by more quickly: "does the number 6,666 mean anything to you?", "no, I don't think so, what is it?" and she laughing, embarrassed but laughing, "the minutes we've spent without seeing each other, the minutes I've spent without you," and he, "you're crazy, crazy, God, what a crazy girl!") in the apartment they've finally managed to get so they can be alone, and which she has converted in a few days into a kind of dollhouse —or into an image of a home, Pablo thinks, only that he prefers not to think this—where they play at making meals or at being mommy and daddy, a house full of plants and flowers and posters and junk—some of it so so ugly, and this, instead of displeasing him, moves him, just as he's enchanted and touched deep down by the fact that the girl had no idea why he'd taken her to Colliure, or of who was buried there, or why his daughter is named Guiomar—and on the bed, leaning against the pillow, a moth-eaten and dusty felt teddy bear ("my father gave it to me the day I turned five," "just a little while ago, I don't understand why you've dirtied it and ruined it so," and she, "what? eternities ago, the eternities that fill this dead time I spent before knowing you," "your prehistory?" Pablo asks, because she called it that one day, and he felt slightly afraid but so flattered—and it amused him that she would use the same expression as Elia when she refers to the time before Jorge—and it's remained as a joke between the two of them, "yes, my prehistory") so she will be waiting for him, impatient, her pulse accelerated, her pupils dilated in the astounded eyes, her lips moist, moist also the warm lair between her legs, naked under the light robe he bought her in one of the towns they passed through, when they didn't yet have a place where they could meet or any intimacy other

166

than what the car offered them (it seems to both of them now that that was many many days ago, although it can't have been more than six or seven), she waits for him and time is passing and Pablo doesn't see any way of escaping from here, from the living room to which he's been summoned by one of the children—"Mom wants to see you, she's in the living room" —and where the three women are waiting for him, stiff, uncomfortable, lugubrious, they've made him think for an instant of the witches who presaged dark misfortunes for Macbeth, of the Parcae who spin and weave and cut the thread of life, three figures of death, three lethal figures— Elia, whose eyes he has searched for without managing to meet her glance, more remote than ever, more foreign, establishing abysmal distances between herself and the other three inhabitants of the house, as if nothing that can happen here concerned her at all, and only an arbitrary fate has made her abandon her spectator seat in the front row and planted her in the middle of the stage, between actors who must necessarily ignore her presence, look at her askance, given that she doesn't figure in the plot or in the writing of the play, and she's not willing to participate in a show she doesn't even approve of, and she is only that: a spectator who has taken the wrong seat or has been made to go on stage against her will; Clara bristling, blushing, and out of breath, about to cry, biting her lips and making fists in a supreme effort not to cry, more incongruous than ever this solid and dense body of an adult woman and this expression of a retarded and frightened little girl, definitely grotesque, and Eva between the two of them (sitting like this in front of him and in the back of the living room, the three women evoke—more than an illicit gathering of malign witches, or a somber meeting of the Parcae, ready to cut perhaps at any instant the thread of life—a lugubrious council, an absurd court, which can turn out to be perhaps threatening, which is undoubtedly dangerous for him, and which is also, however, unavoidably ridiculous, the three of them there, so rigid and stiff, so grave and solemn, as if they should authorize or veto his passage from the Estigia lake and grant him or not the diploma of a good man or simply of a mature one, when the truth is that Pablo cares little at this moment about their verdict—it's been many years now since he's taken an exam —and the only thing he wants is for them to let him leave— the girl is waiting for him and she must have lost count now of the minutes, her tricks to make the wait bearable used up— for them to put off until later the great scene, the colossal quarrel that he begins to see as inevitable), Eva pale as death, with trembling lilac-colored lips, so different from the Eva he knows, from the multiple, diverse but coherent Evas that he has been unveiling throughout the years, so unusual and strange, asking for testimony in a broken voice and with a solemn attitude, with such an affected dignity that she should be expressing herself in French or in rhymed alexandrines, as if she were invoking the immortal gods and a bolt of lightning should descend as soon as possible from the sky to strike the guilty one dead, and now Clara, sweating blood, blundering over her words, confusing her sentences, trembling from head to foot, tears running down her cheeks, is arriving never-theless at the end, formulating a complete accusation, without any holes—how can this little brat have guessed or discovered so many things?—and showing herself ready to maintain it and prove it right there, in front of the jury, because Eva has threatened her into testifying, and it's possible that the girl has wavered, afraid, for a few seconds, but then she began talking and said everything she had to say, more than any tribunal could have dreamed she'd say, and then Eva, paler and more melodramatic and unknown than ever, has turned to Pablo and asked him if it was true, and Pablo has recognized that yes, that in general—discounting what is attributable to the notorious malevolence of the district attorney—yes it was true, knowing that nothing can free him now from the storm and that the situation of the three of them is going to be hard and agonizing from today on, but still trusting that they'll let him leave, that they'll put off the inevitable, the rest of the tragedy or the one-act farce, until a little bit later, because all of this is so grandiloquent and so banal and so false, and there is on the other hand a girl who loves him and who is waiting for him, counting the seconds in a furnished apartment that she's tried to turn into a home, a living girl, he would like to explain to them, but he understands that it may not be the most appropriate moment, a young and beautiful girl who listens to me and tells me she loves me, who will probably have hugged the pillow, desolate from my lateness, and must be telling her misfortunes to a dirty and moth-eaten teddy bear her daddy gave her not long ago.

This impossibility of sharing, thinks Elia, empty, hollow, flying above reality, exiled from time (perhaps she's finally turned into, like the little mermaid, a bubble, and floats here and there propelled by the wind, and it's even possible that one day she'll recuperate, if children are good, her woman's soul, which Jorge unearthed for her and then took with him along with everything else, maybe that's why Miguel scolds her about the recklessness of reducing the world to the mere center of love, although after all Jorge couldn't take away from her more than he had previously given, and before him there existed only the prolonged underwater childhood of an asexual and melancholic little girl who would read and dream, and anyway, why would she want a woman's soul at this point, when it hurts so much, it would be better to float and turn in the wind like a pensive bubble), this impossibility of becoming interested in others once has even lost all interest for herself, this growing repugnance for what they tell, this reluctance for them to involve her, to mix her up in their affairs—other people's affairs always seem more stupid and banal, if not sordid and miserable, and Elia wonders how her own affair would have seemed to her if she'd seen it lived by someone else—now that her own has ended, this resistance to their disturbing her somnolence, taking her out of her stupor, drowsiness, making her get out of herself to offer them support,

169

help, understanding, when she is so tired and everything is—
maybe because of her daily communion with the pills—so
remote and indifferent, Eva and Pablo tugging on her from
opposite sides to win her over as an accomplice, to convert
her into an ally, Eva and Pablo raising her untiringly as a
witness and as a jury, since that first day in the living room,
Eva insisting "you knew about it, Elia? you knew about it and
didn't tell me anything? you've let him make a fool of me in
front of everyone?" and she, so uncomfortable, progressively
more uncomfortable and angry as the other woman persisted
in accusing her and in stubbornly refusing to understand, yes,
she knew, but how was she going to tell her, and who were all
these people in front of whom she would feel a fool, who
were they and why did they matter so much to her, and Eva,
without listening, accusing them both of betrayal, repeating
obsessively that her husband and her best friend, her only
friend, the two people in whom she had placed an unlimited
trust, had ganged up together against her, and had perfidiously
betrayed her, and now never again could she believe in anyone, and meanwhile Pablo trying to talk to Elia aside for a
moment, to ask her to phone the girl, for her in some way or
another to notify her and calm her down, tell her he couldn't
go today but he would get in touch with her as soon as he
could, that nothing was wrong, Pablo so worried about his
date and because the girl was waiting for him and what she
could be going through or afraid of, that he wasn't even paying
attention to what Eva was screaming, because at this point of
the quarrel Eva the intrepid has lost her head and all control
and was insulting them both, screaming at them both, without
caring if the children could hear her, without letting Clara get
near her to try to console her or appease her, pale as death and
spitting out, in an agitated voice, hard words, dirty words,
words they didn't even know she'd picked up since they'd
never heard her use them, and some were vulgar and others
archaic and picturesque, as if she lacked words in her habitual
vocabulary and had to borrow them from the worst ghetto

170

slang or from our Golden Age tragedies, but Eva's reaction, so violent and unexpected, to what was going on (because not even she, although she refused from the beginning to participate in Pablo's optimism, so tailored to his desires, and much less to foment it—"they're two different things, why should my wife get angry?"—had ever expected anything like this), wasn't as serious as what followed, because Elia could understand an initial reaction of rage and jealousy, some first moments of madness that one regrets immediately afterwards and tries to rectify, and the first day's scene in the living room wouldn't have been so terrible if after a few hours or the next morning Eva had reflected and changed her attitude, but instead of subsiding, Eva's desperation, her excessive fury, that unexpected jealousy that no one among her friends could have diagnosed—so opposite was it to what Eva had always said, to her way of understanding and living love, the relationship of a couple—before it all exploded with this terrifying violence, it did nothing but grow and fester, as if an evil, lethal, unknown plant had germinated in the basement and were invading the house, filling it, undoing it, each day Eva more different from the woman they'd known for years, because some frightening days, each one the same, followed that first scene in the living room, the three of them in the boat every hour, going out almost at dawn, as soon as Eva awoke and woke them, and returning in the dark, to fall exhausted into bed, going out in good weather and in bad weather, with the sea calm and with stormy waves, with the south or with the north wind, in front of the disapproving looks of the fishermen who remained on the wharf and shook their heads: these city folk who let themselves joke with the sea, and never, never, as far back as Elia can remember, had they spent so many hours sailing, as if they were escaping from something or pursuing something, and that was—the decision to take off towards the wharf and cast off—the only thing they agreed on, and Eva was probably acting impelled by the desire for Pablo not to have a chance to see the girl, by the eagerness to have him permanently, without parentheses, within reach of her reproaches, and Pablo probably preferred the boat because that way the action took place outside town, outside the house, where the children could listen, friends could find out, but there was above all in the three of them (by chance of a tacit agreement, they had eliminated Clara from the boat, or maybe she had eliminated herself, because she hardly left the house, and walked around at all hours silently, her eyes red, like a lost soul, moping around the garden and the empty rooms), an eagerness to get lost at sea, to merge with the sea, to be absorbed, devoured by the sea, and they didn't cast off like city folk who know nothing and let themselves, sheltered by this ignorance, make reckless jokes with the sea, it was something else, in a way, a ritual gesture, an invocation to old pagan marine divinities, and one sunset when the sea had become especially rough, and when Pablo tried to return to the port shielded by the coast, Eva grabbed the helm from him and directed the boat into the middle of the sea, advancing headfirst into the waves, and the boat was thrown and hurled and beaten, and the three of them were covered with foam, and the water penetrated into the boat and rose and they should have bailed it out, they should have taken the helm from Eva's hands, interrupted her gesture of provocation and challenge, they should have headed towards the shore, but they didn't do any of those things, they sat there, motionless, clinging to the boat's railings so a wave wouldn't drag them along with it, drenched to their bones, their hair stuck to their faces, and the three of them knowing that if the motor stopped, if the boat overturned, there was no salvation possible, and it was precisely the reality of the risk, the imminence of the danger, the beauty of the grey sea, of the enormous waves, of the dark sky, the roughness of the sea and its beauty, the fact of challenging it, and grazing the limits like that, passing them, breaking them, that plunged the three of them into an intense exaltation, the drunkenness of danger, Elia thought, more powerful than any other drunkenness but

172

that of love, and isn't love the supreme risk, but the motor didn't stop and the boat hadn't overturned and other days and more days followed, the three of them alone in the boat, Eva and Pablo struggling in those grotesque, those sordid and absurd matrimonial fights—never had Eva and Pablo been so conjugal—that there was nothing but one same argument repeated ad nauseam, and which, from the looks of things, lost meaning or interest if she weren't present and didn't listen to them, because they needed an audience in order to upbraid each other and assault each other and insult each other, and then go crazy and throw everything overboard and then—when it seemed to Eva that they had gone too far, that they could reach the point of no return—once again at full speed, backtrack, both of them persistently annulling and denying the words already said and irreparable in themselves, trying to repair the situation however possible, and conclude that nothing had happened, or at least nothing too serious, and then a few minutes of artificial harmony, false affection, cloying tenderness, and then, because of some banality Pablo had said or because of some foolishness he hadn't said, Eva started all over again at the same point she left off this interminable and exhausting game, and Pablo and Eva, from the looks of things, needed an audience, even though it was made up of only one spectator, and to top it off, they needed this audience to manifest itself, and it was useless to claim not to be listening, to lie face down on the other end of the deck, to try to remain uninvolved in the reduced intimacy of the boat, unless she felt like swimming back to the shore—and the shore was too far to reach swimming—or ask for help and shelter in one of the boats that crossed near, and so Elia listened reluctantly, and kept herself whenever possible in the field of ambiguities or compromises and then, when both of them pestered her with questions and there was no way out, she assented or censured, and then invariably one of them—or both of them at the same time—got angry and scolded her, and as it was, this stage of the three of them together at sea, drowning in storm after storm, surviving tempest after tempest, still wasn't the worst, because one night Pablo announced he was going out, and Eva, tiresome, insistent, pressured him until he ended up confessing that he was going to see the girl (where else could he go? and why did Eva insist if she didn't want to hear it?) and then Eva locked herself in the bathroom and they had to beat on the door, threatening to break in, and when she finally came out she was as pale as death, she staggered, and although too superficial to put her life in danger, the cuts on her wrist were showy enough to stain her clothes with blood and cover the floor with drops as she walked, and they had to scream and get frightened and make a tourniquet and bandage the wounds and give her a little cognac to drink and put her in bed, and Pablo naturally didn't leave the house that night either, and it seemed to Elia that she was attending the mediocre presentation of a long-running tragicomedy that the three of them knew by heart, and therefore no surprise was possible at the incidents of the plot or the unfolding of events, and now the three of them had ended up interpreting poorly (too bad that Clara, the only one who could have played her part with conviction, was at those moments out of the house) one of the crucial scenes, the one where the deceived wife crowns the long series of reproaches and aggression and bribes with the apotheosis—end of the second act—with a coarse suicide attempt (a never-sufficient dose of barbituates, an attempt to hurl herself down the elevator shaft when there are people present and near, horizontal and shallow slashes on the wrist) and the husband believes it or pretends to believe it, he doesn't want his incredulity to provoke a second attempt which may by chance be true and efficient, and in any case he is frightened and yields, even if it's only a temporary abandonment, and the woman marks down some more points in her favor in this struggle with no rules and with no time-outs in which it seems all arms are allowed and all blows are authorized, only that in the skirmish, she has risked her wild card and she's lost one of her aces, and it's going to be difficult for her to continue this escalation of madness and violence much further, all of it so well known, so hackneyed, so vulgar, a never-changing story, an immortal triangle, made up of characters who are, as in the commedia dell-arte, prototypes: the husband who upon entering middle age feels bored with the daily routine, dissatisfied with the life he's lived, with the work he's done and hasn't done, with the opportunities he's missed, and is enraptured by a young girl who kept his youth and his dreams intact in order to give them back now, the wife who feels herself aging too, and becomes, if she hasn't always been, jealous, and upon discovering her husband's infidelity, rants and raves and falls apart, and the other one, the young girl, who is almost always only that, a young girl, and in this case Pablo fits the role pretty well, he has hardly introduced any personal variations, nor has the girl, who is a girl like any other, only more beautiful than average, and nothing would surpass the norms or have too much importance—it wouldn't at least for Elia, who could easily remain truly uninvolved and wait for the storm to subside—if it weren't that Eva is acting the part of the humiliated and offended wife, and it's out-rageous to see her act this part that has nothing to do with what she has manifested and propagated publicly and in private, spoken and written—all her life, a part that at bottom is in-compatible with what Eva is, with what she has symbolized for many people, for years and years, and Elia has been present, frightened, at the metamorphosis, trying to close her eyes so as not to look, plug her ears so as not to listen, wanting really to stay uninvolved, transformed into a mermaid or foam, wanting to be very far from the town and the house, and without being able to leave, trapped by her own inertia, by her passivity and her tiredness, trapped also by the show, which assumes for her a special gravity that she refuses to recognize, an unavoidable threat, because Eva is her friend, her best friend, the only person with whom she has for years shared certain experiences, a particular sector of her intimacy which she has never revealed to Jorge, and the only person with whom she could keep sharing them in the future—the only person to whom one of these days she would end up telling what she's felt and suffered this summer—as close as sisters, Eva almost an ennobled duplicate of herself, and in the monstrous image the deforming mirror reflects now (she never wanted to look in them, not even as a little girl, they always frightened her) something very much her own is getting lost and is crumbling, something intransferably her own, as if it were her own image, and not only Eva's, that was unavoidably altering and deteriorating.

So that was it, Eva repeats, somberly, sarcastically, disconsolately, as she again and again sees the light appear in the cracks of the Persian blinds become golden with the dawn, intensify in the morning, suspend at noon, diminish later until it disappears at dusk, on the other side of the window, so that was it—overwhelmed, ruined, inflamed—as she turns over in the bed and faces the wall, so as to not know that outside the days keep passing as always and life is prolonged for everyone in more or less the same way (the children stick their heads through the doorway sometimes when they're going to leave or when they've just come home, and ask her if she feels better, if she needs anything, they come into the room, hesitantly, grope to give her a kiss on the cheek and they go, and it's possible they feel surprised, even perplexed, because never, as far back as their memories reach, do they remember their mother sick, nor has Eva ever, in all these years, stayed more than two days in a row in bed, and even then programming everything, directing everything, from there—with that stupid idea of hers—God, how grotesque it seems now—that if she's not there or has a moment of carelessness or abandonment, the world will collapse, or at least these private family surroundings will, and they constitute the world for her, and it's possible therefore that the children are disconcerted, but not even for them has the floor really moved and their life goes on and it's useless for Elia to repeat to her—deep down perhaps without conviction—"you have to come out of this, you can't collapse like this, we need you, the children, Pablo, me, so many people, we all need you," because Eva knows now that nobody needs her, not even the children, and much less Pablo, who enters and leaves the room with a grave air, with a heroic gesture, with a solicitous expression, as if he were doing his good deed of the week or of his life, as if he were competing for the prize of best husband of the year, when it's evident that he's thinking only about the other one, that he's dying to leave everything and run to that redhead's side who's waiting for him, and he doesn't even try to hide it, and he pretends to appease Eva, to calm her suspicions and fears, "don't be silly, it's something else, you know, it has nothing to do with you," and Eva falling in the trap, "what's she like?" hating herself for asking but unable to contain herself, "is she pretty? is she young?" knowing she's committing suicide, "but do you love her? does she love you?" despising herself, at the final level of disgust towards herself, of total unhappiness with herself, "how is she in bed? how do you make love?" and Pablo, with the voice of a responsible husband who knows his place and doesn't abandon it, with the voice of a complete and good man, resists a little, "why do you ask me these things? afterwards it will be worse," and Eva, with that obstinacy we only have sometimes in regards to what can destroy us, "no, I'd rather know," and then Pablo explains that there's nothing special, it's a summer fling of the most banal type, except that the girl is indeed very very beautiful, and so incredibly young, not only because of her age—and Eva interrupts him: "how old is she?"—maybe eighteen or nineteen, he doesn't know, but he wasn't referring in any case to her chronological age, he means that everything about the girl is fresh and fragrant, with a fruity skin, and the long fine legs of a filly, of a frightened and crazy gazelle, and that smell of puppy and of warm milk, like cologne or talcum powder, all mixed, and that red hair, thick, heavy, that falls in ample, lustrous curls to her waist or inundates the pillow with a waterfall of liquid fire—and here Eva feels sick, and she repents and blames herself for having asked again, for having pressed him and insisted, but she knows deep down that if for any reason he were quiet, she would persist again until he continued—and she's so spontaneous, innocent in a way, with those big, astonished, moist eyes, as if everything were new for her, and being new for her it is for him too, you know, as if there were nothing in her past, as if she didn't really have a past, and had just been born upon meeting him and were discovering through him her own body upon discovering love, and Eva, wanting to strangle him, twist his neck, but still maintaining her composure, "she loves you then? do you love her? are you telling me that you love each other?" and Pablo makes an expression of doubt, and then a gesture of stupefaction and incredulity, as if not even he himself could understand or believe it, "yes, it looks like she loves me, that she loves me a lot," and when Eva insists—"and you, tell me, do you?"—he concludes that no, that he doesn't love her, if by love one means what there is between the two of them, between Eva and Pablo—what's left for me, Eva, desolate, asks herself, what can this serious and respectable feeling be or what value can it have next to the fruity skin and the moist eyes of an eighteen-year-old girl in love, what ground is left to me, and why the hell do I want it?—he's already told her from the beginning that it's something else, the girl is a perfect object, and Eva, drowning in bitterness and despair, "perfect for love, right?" after years and years, almost an entire life blaming her half-jokingly for her simplicity, for her lack of imagination, for her inhibitions and her puritanism, "do you mean to tell me you've finally found your ideal erotic partner?" and Pablo is quiet and sighs, grieved, and denies nothing and Eva wonders, frightened of what secret offenses he can be avenging, how her husband has been able to accumulate so much rancor and so much hate against her, without anyone, probably not even him, realizing it, while they seemed to love each other and constitute a happy couple without big problems, because a lot of accumulated resentment is needed in order to talk like that, in order to make her feel so miserable, in order to cause this useless and terrible damage to someone who like her is not able to defend herself, and it occurs to Eva for the first time that this girl is a source of pleasure and illusion, a magic reunion with his own dying youth, a recuperation of lost time, something that flatters Pablo and restores his confidence in himself, a desire to live and undertake new projects, but it's also in a way a balancing of the books—only that she doesn't know which bill is pending and needs to be settled—and it's useless therefore for Elia to insist that Pablo loves her, that Pablo needs her, because he surely loves her, but with a love that at these moments isn't worth a thing to Eva, why is she or anyone going to want this secure, monotonous, boring, respectable love when she knows there exists somewhere else a different, wild, excessive, flashing love and it's possible that Pablo does need her for some things, but it's even more certain that she constitutes for him a weight, a hindrance, an annoying duty, a snare in the wheel, lead in the wings, and she would so much like to throw him out of the room and the house and her life, be able to tell him truthfully "go to that girl and don't ever come back," but she can't), she turns over in bed and faces the wall, and repeats to herself "so that was it," and she finally asks Elia, who is clumsily shuffling around the room, trying to arrange the sheets, put order in the dresser, open the window slightly, "so was that it?" and Elia, surprised, without beginning to understand, "was what it?" and Eva turns towards her and looks at her, "what you both were feeling when you felt bad, when you feel bad, what made you crawl on all fours, as you say, and made you run with your tail between your legs and your tongue hanging out, to the psychiatrist's office or to the warlock on duty, and stuff yourselves with pills or drugs or alcohol, and talk about death, and lean over the elevator shaft and assure everyone that you couldn't take any more and go to bed with your face to the wall, was that it?" and Elia, now immobile next to the bed, holding between two fingers the bottle of sleeping pills that she just found on the night table, dubious and a little uncomfortable, "yes, I suppose so, what did you imagine? a friendly sadness, an elegant melancholy, an exquisite and literary anguish, perhaps something like the vague nostalgias of adolescence?", yes, she had imagined something like that, never this in any case, never could she imagine this, being tied here, to this bed she hates, with an unbearable pressure in her chest, and her mouth overflowing with bitterness, and a total malaise, as if her organism were completely refusing to continue—she was frightened a little while ago by her image in the bathroom mirror: hair lank and without any luster, lips cracked, eyes red, features contorted, like that terrifying transformation we see at the movies when someone finally drives a stake into Dracula's heart and in a few seconds his face passes through all the stages of life and of the decomposition that follows death to finally become a skull—unable to eat, to sleep, even hardly to breathe, unable to think about anything but this fixed obsession that's killing her, the two people she loved most, the only ones perhaps whom she fully trusted, the two pillars her world rested on, have ganged up to betray her, both of them are now going to abandon her, and she can't face it, she doesn't even remotely have the strength to bear it, to get up from this bed, to go far far away, so far that when she comes back, everything will be over, and Elia, as if she still guessed her thoughts as she has guessed them for years, and answered no, not to the last thing she said but to what Eva is thinking, "nothing's going on, I assure you, we both love you as always, nobody is going to abandon you," and Eva is quiet, but she knows it isn't true: if Pablo loved her, he would have taken her in his arms days ago, he would have lifted her chin to make her sustain his gaze, and like that, she in his arms and her eyes on his eyes, he would have said that this redheaded girl is nothing, that he doesn't care at all about her, that he'll never see her again, that this will never happen again, that it's only been a stupidity without consequences, and if Elia loved her, she wouldn't now leave the bottle of sleeping pills on the night table, with a sigh, she wouldn't limit herself to giving her a kiss on the cheek, to looking at her, worried, before leaving the room, if Elia were truly her friend, she would throw the bottle of pills into the trash, she would get her out of bed, even if it meant beating her, she would put her in the bathroom to blow her nose and make sure she brushed her teeth, and arrange her hair in tight shiny braids, she would dress her in her best Sunday clothes, her party clothes, and she would take her out of here—God, someone should realize she can't bear it, that she can't get out of this alone, someone should take pity on her and take her out of here—she would get involved up to her neck, and would take her far, very very far away, to a place they've never been before, where Pablo couldn't, even if he wanted to, find them, instead of being so stupidly cautious and respectful, keeping herself at a distance, and claiming to be objective, and asking questions of principle, and analyzing carefully when which of them is guilty, which one is right, as if they were studying a theoretical case in a textbook, and feeling disappointed because Eva is not on this occasion up to the circumstances ("I'm sorry, Eva, maybe it's because I don't know how to see you in this role, I'm so used to the two of us fighting on opposite sides," as if Eva could enjoy assuming the role of the hysterical and jealous wife, defender of the most traditional morality, as if she wouldn't have preferred a thousand times over to be in the other one's role!) and feeling uncomfortable because Eva is committing unpardonable errors of style, when it's not a matter now of being right or being wrong, not that there is any objectivity that's worth anything, it's a matter only of subsisting, of her best friend collapsing, and if Elia loves her, if she doesn't want to abandon her, she must support her then unconditionally, beyond all justice, and let's not say all aesthetics, she must take sides, assume complete responsibility—since Eva has lost her capacity to resolve or to act for herself—sink in shit up to her

181

neck if necessary, and take her out of this bed, of this house, of this town, of this hell.

The camp is halfway between the top of the hill and the sea, surrounded by shrubs and pine trees, much friendlier this French coast, much greener, much more rounded, than the craggy, abrupt, desolate, inhospitable and lunar coast that Elia has loved so much since she was a little girl, that she has sailed along summer after summer, until she knew its most secret twists and turns, its most hidden bays, the most unsuspected, the most beautiful marine depths, and the color of the rocks at different times of day, the color of the sea under different skies, the direction and danger or mildness of the winds, and now, on this French coast, where Daniel will have spent the summer, the two of them have sat on a fallen trunk, somewhat separated from the other boys, on the peaceful, sunny, really splendid afternoon at the end of August, almost now an autumn afternoon, without looking at the boy at all, her stare fixed on the distant sea, with her atonal voice, deliberately atonal and slow, Elia has been developing point by point the long speech she's been rehearsing for him throughout the last two weeks, from the moment she understood that the summer was ending and that she should face, one way or another, the problem the boy posed and which until then she hadn't wanted to think about, a speech she had had to change again and again as the conviction that Jorge would never come back gained ground in her, the certainty that, however much it hurt them both, the end had come, and there's no possibility of fixing it or compromising, however much Jorge insists in the letter she received from him three days ago (and which she carries around with her permanently, like an amulet, stuck to her skin, as if she wanted to concede to them, to him and to the letter, one last chance, the chance of a magic absorption and assimilation by touch) in which his trip is about to end and he is going to return to the city and everything can resume between them, in the same way, or almost the same, and they have to think about the boy above all, and about what they've achieved and built and lived together through more than fifteen years, about the affection and the respect—"I've never loved anyone as I've loved you, Elia, and I never will love anyone as much"—and the interests in common that subsist, unalterable, indelible (this is what remains, it seems, when love has died, when you no longer play at being Abelard and Héloïse, when you can never return to Venice, this is what, indefatigable, hour after hour, Eva and Pablo talk about in the house, this is what they both persist equally in saving at any price, at all cost, this is what, whatever happens, whatever has happened, can't ever be tossed overboard, and Elia wonders what it is, what it's called, why the hell it's worth so much and matters so much to them), but however much Jorge insists, she knows now better than ever, she's probably discovered for the first time, that there's no going back, nothing to save or recuperate from this shipwreck, and this is what she's trying to explain to Daniel, her voice calm and her eyes on the sea, trying not to show how nervous and frightened she is, explain to him that she will leave the house, maybe the city, but that doesn't mean she loves him any less, or that they're going to stop seeing each other, since they can be together some weekends, maybe spend vacations together, and now unexpectedly Daniel's voice rises up in the quiet and luminous afternoon, a firm voice that admits no discussion (so unusual for a boy, so like Jorge's!), "I want to live with you," and Elia has to interrupt the line of speech she had prepared and looks at him, disconcerted, astounded, with such a look of astonishment that the boy can hardly keep from laughing, although he's looking at her straight in the eye with his hard eyes, "it seems that strange to you that I want to live with my mother? it hadn't even occurred to you?" and Elia, "but, Daniel, darling, I don't even know where I'm going to live . . ." surprised now at herself, seeing how strange indeed it seems that not even as a remote possibility, not even for an instant, as she's been going over and over the problem of the boy and what she was going to tell him, has the solution of taking him with her occurred to her, so evident is it, or was, or it seemed, that the boy, like the house, like the furniture, like the friends, like the life they've lived these years, rightly belongs to Jorge, exists for Jorge, and that she had to leave as he had found her fifteen summers ago, naked and divested, with her only baggage her absurd girlish sadness—which she has recuperated now, whole, identical, unalterable, as if it had been waiting for her all this time—and the poor cat Musli, who was then a kitten and who's now about to die, the cycle of the cat's life coinciding with the cycle of her love and her happiness, "you'll have to live somewhere, and wherever you live, I can live, or do you think I'll be in the way?" the boy insists with this adult voice that admits no retort, with his eyes staring insistently, a touch of a smile still playing, however, on his lips, "no, of course not, Daniel, but your father . . ." and she interrupts herself suddenly, because she was going to say "loves you so much" and that could mean for the boy that she doesn't love him just as much, and Daniel, accentuating the smile, "we don't have to stop seeing each other, we can be together some weekends, maybe spend vacations together," and in the depth of his light, brilliant, not very big eyes behind the glasses, a mocking and impish spark ignites, and Elia observes that Daniel, just like Jorge, laughs with his eyes, laughter escapes from them both through their eyes before it reaches their mouth (and there's nothing in the world, she thinks with a pang, that she's loved as much as this laughter) and Daniel maybe has, also like his father, the same horror of melodramatic expressions, grand phrases, that literary and excessive way of hers of understanding life, and now Elia laughs, relieved, the tension broken, they both laugh, looking each other straight in the eye, very close to each other, on the luminous and quiet August afternoon, and the woman feels so relaxed and comfortable—she doesn't even dare believe it— so content, because after days and more days of preparing her solemn speech, imagining scenes more and more painful and

184

anguished, everything has turned out so easily, so simply, with this skinny and ungainly boy—God, he's so skinny! skinnier every day, all arms and legs, surely his ribs stick out from under his skin—sitting next to her on the fallen trunk, a freckled, big-nosed boy with small shining eyes, not at all handsome, and so absolutely intimate and charming, deciding for her in a tone that admits no retort, as if he were trying—and it's a strange idea, because in spite of his adult voice and his serious air, he's still an adolescent—to protect her, as if he wanted to make things easier and help her, help this awkward and fearful mom, so distracted and so disoriented, whose eyes are stupidly filling with tears, when she realizes that Daniel, like Jorge, detests scenes "did you know, Daniel? did you know what I came to tell you?" and a little embarrassed, now, not looking at him, "is it very painful for you?" and the boy, shrugging his shoulders, tossing his fine brown hair back with a movement of his head, "it's your decision, you know, it's got nothing to do with me" and here Elia can't repress some words that as soon as they float in the air seem so false, so much like a soap opera, "I'm afraid I haven't been the best of mothers . . ." and Daniel bursts out laughing and again the malicious spark ignites in his eyes and he gives Elia a quick kiss on the cheek down which finally a tear runs, "Mom, I've suspected it for a long, long time," and again they both laugh, sitting face to face, looking each other straight in the eye, and then he, "will you come get me the day camp ends?" and Elia, "if you want . . ." without understanding very well what's going on, without knowing with certainty what this boy is like who is at some moments so intimate and her own, and at others seems almost a stranger (maybe because a summer away from them has suddenly matured him, made him grow up, made him leave behind the child he still was in the spring, or maybe it's Elia who's looking at him in a different way, who's learning to see him in another way without intermediaries, exactly how he really is) but without a doubt so relieved and almost, for the first time in several months, happy.

He has told her in a fit of desperation, of anger, of fatigue, because he can't stand seeing her like this anymore, for days and days, not wanting to get out of bed, not letting anyone open the window or turn on a light, refusing to eat, complaining of insomnia, or immersed in that strange sleep (so deep that it's hard to wake her, and nevertheless a restless sleep in which she moans and cries) that the sleeping pills and tranquilizers provide at intervals (and he anxiously counting each time the pills left in the bottles, verifying that the doses she takes are excessive, gradually higher, but not dangerous yet, and leaving the bottles in their place because he doesn't dare hide them or throw them out), he can't take any more of her sullen, festering, miserable silences that aren't even parentheses of calm, but rather a threatening stillness between storms, or in one same storm momentarily interrupted, the air populated with electricity and shadows, the closed and un-healthy atmosphere of the bedroom dense with rancor, until Eva has once again recharged the batteries of her inexhaustible fury and hurls herself into a new savage outburst and then the absurd accusations, the unimaginable insults, the ferocious sarcasms, sinister, terrible threats that don't forgive anything arise because Eva seems capable in some moments of destroy-ing the world in her eagerness to wound him however she can and hurt him, capable of—she says—leaving him without the children, without friends, without prestige, and even without money and without work, Eva the scrupulous capable of the most sordid baseness, and then something breaks inside her, something gives, and the crying, the repentance, the lamenta-tions follow, reviling herself with a fury similar to what she's been using against him, and there are no words that can calm her, make her reflect, because she doesn't even listen, and Pablo has woken sometimes in the middle of the night, and has found her wide awake, vigilant, sitting up in bed, looking at him with an intensity of hatred that frightens him, and then sometimes he has gotten closer to her, kissed her, caressed her, hugged her, in a final attempt to calm her, and Eva has clung to him some nights with a desolate fury, has put him in her bed and forced him to make love to her as they never had before, as if Eva's ire, her desperation, her wounded pride had swept away inhibitions, had cornered fears, had annulled shame, after so many years (here also hatred stronger than love) and perhaps Eva is fantasizing what the redhead is like in bed, and tries to imitate her, surpass her ("what does she do that I can't do? what does she give you that I can't give you?") and this drags her along in an anguished, tense, false frenzy and they love each other as if they were on the edge of annihilation, mutually trying to devour each other, break each other's spine once and for all, crazed, ferocious, engaged in a combat that admits no time-outs, in a struggle that could be said to be to the death, and afterwards Eva asks "did you like it? did you? is that how you wanted it?" and Pablo has answered each time that yes, and it's true that up to a point the pleasure was intense and prolonged, and it's also true that for all these years he has been fantasizing, greedily, about what being in bed with Eva could be like if she abandoned herself to a certain audaciousness, to certain forms of fervor and craziness but now, at the moment this has happened, he feels perplexed, and in a way uncomfortable and frightened, pressured and ordered, and when Eva asks "are you thinking about her? are you thinking about that girl while you're with me?" Pablo swears he isn't, but the truth is that yes, he is thinking about the redhead, who knows nothing—if Eva suspected it . . .— of this almost homicidal fury, of this savage frenzy, of these complicated caresses, of these sumptuous and lethal fantasies, the redheaded girl who surely doesn't have much experience or much imagination, who lets herself go gently, her body trembling, her lips half open, her eyes moist and astonished, the girl who tells him she loves him, and who these days is quiet and cries on the telephone when Pablo explains they can't see each other today either, that the situation is very difficult and painful and complicated, and she accepts and swallows her sobs and continues to wait for him, and Pablo thinks these days about her with an unknown intensity and desolation, because at no other moment of the affair had he loved her so much, had he taken her so seriously as he is loving her and considering her now, as the risk of losing her increases, because he can't take any more brawls, screams and crying, he can't take seeing Eva suffer like this anymore, and that's why, in a fit of desperation, of anger, of fatigue, he has promised "all right, I'm going to go say good-bye to this girl and I'll never see her again," hoping that Eva would react and protest and restrain him, that she would say that she couldn't accept a resolution like that, that at that price she doesn't want it, that she will never be able to forgive herself if Pablo breaks it off like that, pressured and against his will, with the girl, and this rupture will always remain between them like a ghost, and what began only as a pleasant summer fling between a forty-year-old man and an unknown young girl will turn into something extremely valuable and important, almost a true love, Pablo hoping then that Eva will speak, that she will give in, that she will restrain him, hoping until the last minute that she won't let him leave the house like that, but knowing now already deep down that Eva will not say a word, her lips puckered and pinched, her eyes staring vacantly and obstinately at the ceiling, as if she didn't want to find out about what, because of her, is going to happen, as if she were trying at the last instant to remain uninvolved, symbolically wash her hands—do what you will, Pablo, I haven't asked you to do a thing—and only at the last minute, when he's leaving the room, she abandons her muteness and asks him, "you really have to see her? can't you send her a note, explain to her on the phone?" and Pablo feels wildly like laughing or murdering her on the spot, "not this time, Eva, this time I'm going to tell her in person," and Eva is stupefied, really surprised, because not once have they talked about that affair throughout more than fifteen years and she couldn't imagine that he still thought about it, and it's true, Pablo thinks, that it's a long, forgotten story and besides, it never had any real importance, and if he's evoked it now in a spark of intuition it's only to wound her, to punish her for her unimaginable suggestion, and Eva, "what did you say? what are you talking about? I had nothing to do with it, it wasn't my fault in the least," and Pablo, sarcastic, bitter, "of course not, Eva, of course not, those things are always one's own fault," and he leaves the house without waiting any longer and goes to the apartment where the girl has waited days and days—more than a week —for him and he's overwhelmed by the sensation of repeated situations, of already-lived acts, that he's betraying someone, that he's betraying himself for the thousandth time, and it's no longer a matter of that skinny, freckled, crazy girl, who didn't want to get involved, commit herself to anyone, and who ended up saying "I've discovered your name, stranger, your name is love," even saying, "your country will be my country, your god will be my god," and whom he swore to go look for in her northern country and never did, because it was hardly more than a vaporous and romantic youthful idyll, and she must have already forgotten him a long time ago (as he had forgotten her, because he only brought up the old story to wound Eva better and punish her) surrounded by a husband, some children, some friends who never will have heard of a Spanish student she knew in Barcelona and who wanted to be a poet and whose name was Pablo, more than a thousand years ago, that's not the question, and nevertheless, that English girl with the freckles and this girl now, of this summer (so exuberant and so docile and so in love and so beautiful, who's been waiting for him here, on the threshold of maturity, on the edge of the definitive loss of hope—or at least of a certain kind of hope—at the beginning of disillusion, and who has made him in a way find his own youth, the last fluttering of some dying dreams which now have their heart full of lead and will never take flight again, appear strangely united and related, as if the two girls—so different in everything, and so identical nevertheless in their way of loving him—were in fact one person, or were at least equivalent figures, or two milestones in time that mark the beginning and the end, it's not known of what, maybe of his years of plenitude, of his life as an adult, and now, while in the living room full of posters and flowers that she tried awkwardly and wrongly to turn into a home, Pablo explains to her without daring to look at her that they can't go on, that it's been very beautiful, unforgettable (and the girl will never know to what point he's been exact and sincere in saying unforgettable), what they've experienced together, but it's over, since Eva has taken it very badly and is suffering so much—"you know, I warned you, I confessed to you from the first day that my wife along with the children was the most important to me"—while she cries and cries, hardly opening her mouth, and assents with a movement of her head to everything Pablo gentlemanly, scoundrelly, cowardly betrays, he knows that it's positively the end, not only of a love affair—as it may be for the woman, who's suffering undoubtedly in these moments in an unbearable way, who will suffer for days and days, who will be scarred perhaps forever with this wound, but who still has the future in front of her, open like a fan with multiple possibilities—but of his attempts to live life as he used to believe long ago it should be lived, the end of illusion—or a certain type of illusion—of the possibility of surrender, of getting out of himself, of the possibility of loving like an adolescent, like a seventeen-year-old boy—who ever said that other ways of loving exist?—of the possibility even of writing, of working at what he likes and at the same time doing some useful job valid for others, and now the girl cries disconsolately and wordlessly, her hair dull and messy, her nose red, her eyes small and irritated, her features altered (for the first time, Pablo notices, she's not beautiful, as if he had found the ways to destroy a beauty that seemed unalterable, that seemed invulnerable), and the man talks to her apparently sure of himself, in a moderate and composed tone, worried only about consoling her without committing himself, without committing himself at all, and he knows nevertheless with complete certainty that in this affair, he is the loser, that he's irremediably lost himself or a very loved part of himself, that life has given him, by way of being generous or perverse, one last chance, and he hasn't been capable this time either of taking advantage of it, and now there won't be any more, and it is, now indeed, the definitive end where, along with youth, the possibility of dreaming and taking flight is buried forever.

S he hears her voice filling the air, "do you really have to see her? couldn't you send her a note, explain to her on the phone?" and for a few instants she wonders, astounded, who has spoken, what fucking bitch has been capable of usurping her voice and using her now to risk such stupid and miserable suggestions, because it's not likely that she could have provided Pablo with something like this, it's not conceivable that she has even to herself been able to think it, except perhaps as one of the many fleeting ideas that cross our minds rapidly, like meteors, shapeless, without time to materialize into anything, to crystalize into anything, so that we aren't able to recognize them in their progress nor afterwards remember them as ours, and nevertheless, there's the voice now—icy, secure, firm, odious—so like her own (although how could that powerful voice be hers when she's trembling so, and is so confused and frightened?), filling the air, and Eva would like to try to draw it back in like the net at sea still empty of fish is drawn in, lower it like a flag that appears at dawn, unexpectedly and foreign, on the top of the mast and for which we are not willing to fight is lowered, only that here there's no withdrawal possible, no opportunity to rectify, because (more attentive to the sound, the timbre, the tone than the meaning of the words) Pablo has immediately accepted this voice as hers, and when, going out the door, he looks at her with a ferocious cunning she didn't know he had in him, with a density of contempt never accumulated before against anyone, "no, Eva, no," she understands that the words have been irremediably identified and marked, filed in a secure place but very close at hand, ready to arise again on any occasion, and float there, unalterable, between the two of them, because Pablo will not forgive her now having said them (written on that long list of wrongs and offenses, of secrets and hushed motives for rancor, that Eva, stupefied, has discovered this summer, and which Pablo seems to enjoy prolonging, and it's even possible that deep down he likes to see her act this way in order to add new negative entries in the books, and she wonders how she could have been so blind, how she could have lived years and more years next to a man without even suspecting to what point he sometimes detested her), and never—how strange—will Eva forgive, not only that Pablo has motivated them with his conduct, not only that he has immediately accepted them—without protests, without doubts, without an astonishment that would have opened the way to apologies and rectifications—as if he had been waiting for them, as if they had been foreseeable in some way, foreseeable in Eva, but above all that he's been capable in these few weeks of bringing out the worst in her, making her most sordid and sad and mean qualities stand out, of bringing to the surface traits that surely Eva in her worst moments feared or suspected, that the others always denied roundly and untiringly, but of which in any case there had never existed any evidence, all of them—but most of all her friend Elia and her husband Pablo—obstinate in singing and multiplying her praises, in holding up in front of her a magnificent full-length mirror, magical, cheating and flattering, where she looked marvelous, more than fifteen years of exalting her qualities, admiring her, envying her at times, leaning on her always, affirming her in the lavish belief that she had become unique and irreplaceable, essential for the regular course of the stars, lucid enough to undo spells, powerful enough to scare away ghosts, to maintain she didn't know what on her shoulders, the happiness or the sanity or the health of the world, and she suspecting that no, a little frightened always, with the slight apprehension that at some point perhaps they were deceiving her (probably without even their suspecting it) but so flattered too, so comfortable almost always in this strong woman role, mother superior, protector of the wounded, director of a kindergarten, so happy above all that they love her and so desirous of never losing this love because of disillusioning them in their suppositions—as she has finally and irremediably lost it upon deceiving them now—and it's even possible that the grotesque pantomime, the ridiculous farce, began quite a while earlier, she as a young girl coming home from school with the key hanging around her neck, next to the pendants and medals, judicious enough to unlock the house and stay there alone, waiting for dinner, with no mom or dad, she taking care of her younger brothers and sisters, so responsible—"there's no chance of anything happening to them while they play, I'm sure that with Eva there, nothing bad can happen to the children," and Eva not so sure, not at all sure, Eva trembling, although not daring to protest—replacing the mother, occupying the mother's place in the house and in the store, when the mother got sick, and everyone looking at her, pleased, admiring, valuing, smiling, that admirable young girl who could play the part of an adult—only she wasn't—going over and over how trustworthy she was—"I have absolute confidence in Eva; she's never lied to us," "I trust this girl totally; not even in her thoughts is Eva capable of the least baseness," "I don't know how we would get along without her; she's wise and responsible enough to take care of the others and of herself of course"—and Eva aghast, Eva suspicious, Eva disconcerted, fearing herself capable of the most vile lies, of the worst baseness, knowing herself in need, or simply desirous, of any type of shelter, protection and care, and even of repression and vigilance sometimes, envying in secret so many other young girls, whose mothers judge them, it seems, "capable of any fiendish prank" (and they said this while they were perhaps happy deep down, drooling) since they couldn't "trust them at all" (how marvelous, God! sometimes, not to be trusted at all!)

and the uncomfortable, the growing suspicion that love for her (not for everyone, not for other children, not for other women) was a matter of collecting merits, as prizes and gifts in the store were attained by accumulating coupons, the certainty that she could, without resting, compete and stand out and surpass herself, figure always among the best, if anyone were to pay attention to her, love her, because there are fragile, touching, awkward, lucky beings, those who are loved just because, who are loved for nothing in particular, maybe even with some defects, some deficiencies, that make them more loved than ever, beings who abandon themselves, docilely and passively, and unarmed, to love as to a shower of gold, whereas for others, for her, love has been something to achieve laboriously, something that's conquered in battle, that is imposed perhaps on others, and throughout her entire life, the terrible suspicion has assailed her in flashes that nobody was loving her for herself, that nobody has ever truly loved her—in her fear, in her anxieties, in her sadness, in her basic insecurity, in her miseries and discouragements—they've simply considered her too admirable to risk loving, extraordinary in everything, too valuable to not be able to desire her, to renounce possessing her, to let the chance to get her pass by, how could Pablo let a woman like that escape, so superior in everything, when he knew he would never find another woman like her—and that seems like real love, but isn't love: she has suspected it forever and now finally she knows it with certainty—how could Elia renounce the friendship, the identification with someone who seemed so admirable to her (although in fact Elia should have understood, closer to her in everything, and she would have understood without a doubt if she weren't always lost in some metaphysical examinations and exquisite existential anguish centered without exception on her own navel) and for fifteen years they have sung her praises in chorus, they have kept her sitting by force on the throne they'd invented for her, they have forced her to look at herself in the lying mirror, they have impelled her to match up

194

to both of their fantasies, they have exhibited her proudly before friends and strangers as if she were a trained monkey, a valuable and exotic bird (they've in fact left her so frightfully alone), and Eva has let them, has cooperated in the mistake, has shared the game, has played her part in the farce and even has believed in it sometimes, many times, because they offered it to her in exchange for love, so much love (I needed them— she thinks now—with a desperate urgency, with a total anxiety, they were the only two pillars upon which my life was sustained, and I've depended on them as they have never really depended on me, at no moment, not on me or on anyone, because they don't even know that this type of dependency can exist, this kind of love, in spite of Pablo's dark looks and his grand phrases and his complaints of a lover, according to him, never his match, in spite of affirmations reiterated for years that it was he who loved me and I was the one who limited myself to being loved, in spite of everything that he assures he's sacrificed for me, including this girl, not the other girl before, this girl now, beautiful and a novice and helpless, so ignorant and so silly and so irresponsible, allied from the cradle with the groups of those who are loved just because, those who abandon themselves with open legs, their sex moist, their hair of fire inundating the pillow, and wait for love to cover them, to penetrate them like a shower of gold, and the poor things don't know how to struggle or defend themselves or console themselves when a jealous, impossible, possessive wife, like me, bursts onto the scene, well, in spite of all this, Pablo has never depended on me like I've depended on him, nor has Elia, in spite of those literary and artificial theories with which she covers reality like a page, and those extravagant essays about the center of love and the center of the world, or the other previous ones she's been indoctrinating us with for years and which situated her and Jorge in the exceptional role of the only possessors of love in the second millennium after Christ—it was a miracle she didn't begin counting the days and years from the summer night they met, imposing on all of us the new age of Jorge—high priest and priestess of an esoteric cult, officiating magnificently at the altar, while we others crouched in the last row of parishioners), and now both of them have betrayed her, they've broken the deceiving and flattering, deforming mirror that offers her only a degraded image, distorting her, the pillars have given way and the world is going to cave in, and maybe it is in fact due to their letting her down when for the first time in years her specialness has been put to the test (as that voice also probably failed, with that other girl), it's probably all due to her not having passed the test and having defrauded them, very difficult to establish who let whom down, who has betrayed whom, in this matter of multiple betrayals bound together, and "this time no, Eva, this time I'm going to tell her in person," Pablo has spit ferociously and rancorously from the doorway, and she, stupefied, shipwrecked, but what are you saying, losing her balance, what are you talking about, so different, so different these circumstances from the ones Pablo has now referred to, that Eva shouldn't have even understood, and the allusion would have remained inoperative then, innocuous, dead, not at all dangerous, in the air, but the bad thing is she has understood, she did know right away what he was talking about, and however much one part of her has remained aghast, really dislocated by surprise, it's as if another deeper part had been waiting for years and more years for this delayed reproach, and she struggles now desperately, in water up to her neck, justifying herself, I had nothing to do with it, defending herself, drowning, choking on anxiety and salty walter, it wasn't at all my fault, but Pablo has left the room and the house without listening to her anymore, without giving her a chance to try to restrain him, of probably rectifying (it would have been useless—she confesses, disconsolately, to herself, feeling sorry for herself and hating herself—I would have given what's left of my life to be able to say to him "don't break up with this girl because of me, go on with her, live your love affair to wherever it takes you," but I couldn't,

I haven't been able to for all these days, and I couldn't now either if he had stayed, if he had come sat on the edge of my bed and were listening to me), and it's as if everything had been said and sealed and filed, because when Pablo linked her words of a few minutes ago, her miserable attitude of these days, which seems to Eva herself the words and attitude of an imposter, of a stranger, with that act of hers years ago now in which she doesn't recognize herself either, that she's never begun to understand, to forget (nor had Pablo forgotten it, even though not one single time—and this seems a betrayal also to Eva—did he even mention it), an act to which she has returned sporadically but insistently, repeatedly, for years and more years, with an equal sting of perplexity and displeasure, a guilty apprehension, a glimpse of a bad conscience, that has forced her to go over and over in her mind what happened then, arrange and line up the incidents, weigh reasons and motives in order to convince herself very soon that her attitude was correct, the best attitude possible, that her behavior was completely justified, since what happened was what would have happened anyway, Eva free of all guilt then, Eva absolved, rehabilitated and absolved, and nevertheless the trial has never closed with her absolution, because always again, after a few days or a few years, when she remembers fortuitously what happened then, she has watched the same doubts reappear, she has again experienced an identical discomfort, similar perplexities, and it's been necessary to begin anew, revise the case again, always again absolved, always with the passing of time obliged once again to prove it, and now Pablo has linked in a second, with four or five words, what's happening now with that banal little affair, it didn't even seem very important then, which ended such a long time ago (one summer morning, a little while after she and Pablo met, fell in love, decided they would live together happily ever after, as in fairy tales, while Elia had already begun to make a fable of her novelesque and passionate romance with Jorge, and for weeks they hardly saw each other, each one immersed in her own love affair, and

197

Eva hardly had time to discuss anything with Elia, to consult her about anything, although surely this wouldn't have changed the situation and everything would have happened more or less in the same way, and Eva would have been there, in the park, one summer morning, sitting on the bare and parched grass, next to Pablo, a vacillating, contrite, sorrowful Pablo— only on that occasion was the overflowing happiness of their first days together interrupted—who was writing reluctantly, like a lazy and idle little boy, the good-bye letter, a letter that had to be written, that he would have written anyway without her, because he couldn't leave the girl in ignorance and deceit, he couldn't let her wait for him there in her northern lands, thinking it was only a question of time, a problem of work or money, before they got together again, he couldn't leave her like that, waiting, and the girl had to know that another woman had appeared, that they were going to get married, that for one reason or another Pablo had abandoned her, she had to know, Eva still repeats now, obstinately, Eva convincing for others but who isn't able to give herself credit, somebody had to tell her, Pablo would have written her sooner or later anyway, but why that urgency, why above all was it she who was dictating that letter almost word for word, a letter that Pablo was writing reluctantly, guiltily, sadly, why didn't she give him time, when they had so much, why didn't she let him resolve things in his own way, although it would in all proba- bility be a worse way, wordy, cowardly, even dishonest, why didn't she wait and remain uninvolved when it was so evident to everyone that she had already definitively won the match? She loved him so much, did she really do it because she loved him so much?), Pablo has chosen these two points to identify her—this is the frightening, deforming mirror, cruel amuse- ment-park mirror, that he holds in front of her, and how is Eva going to recognize herself?—and an entire life gone by meanwhile, almost half of her life is suddenly annulled, in a way it doesn't count at all, and it's as if these long years in which she's stupidly believed herself loved, respected, indispensable, secure—because there were Elia and Pablo ready to prove it and show it, stubborn in having her believe it, ready, with one word, with a kiss, with a smile, to scare away any hint of terror, any inopportune doubt, any possible suspicion—had never really existed, annulled even the possibility of seeing them exist in memory, since they've only been a parenthesis empty now of meaning, a stupid farce, erased irremediably by her miserable words of just a few instants ago, by her attitude in the park one morning so many years ago, which are it seems the only points of real reference, the only thing Pablo recognizes about her without wavering and identifies her, and he has left the room and the house, at the curtain of the second act in a romantic tragicomedy, without giving her a chance to explain, a moment to retract or rectify, and now he must be next to that girl, she crumbling and defenseless, her legs open, her sex moist, her eyes also suddenly flooded, her cheeks wet, the pillow seeping, her fiery hair inundated with tears, he explaining to her that the shower of gold is over for them, or maybe only convincing her that they have to be more careful in the future, and the girl needn't cry so much or worry about anything, since she was born predestined to figure among the awkward ones, the unarmed, the ones who always win, the ones who are loved just because, for nothing in particular, and in her life, with Pablo or without Pablo, the warm, flashing, splendid torrential showers of gold must follow one right after the other, and later at some moment of this same night or of the next few days, Pablo will come home, but he won't be the Pablo now of a few days ago or of a few minutes ago (as he wasn't the same Pablo either after writing the letter that she dictated to him in the park, even though Eva has taken such a long time to realize it), he will be a different Pablo, who will have abandoned, for her or for the children, who knows really why, the girl he loves, or maybe doesn't love, only of whom, in his own words, he's enraptured, who has restored to him the happiness and illusion that Eva hasn't been capable of understanding or sharing or above all preserving, the girl in whom he's finally found—or that's what Eva has understood—a kind of erotic partner to match his fantasies—only that: no reason then to feel jealous—that girl who loves him so much, and who has known how to convince him that she loves him so much, who lets herself go, unarmed, trembling, with her eyes closed, who swears to him that she was born to experience love in his arms, and the Pablo who returns will be a resentful and rancorous man, a very powerful being who will have renounced, for her, illusion and love, perhaps his last love, the only possibility for rapture that destiny reserved for him on the threshold of maturity, and he will never be able entirely to forgive her, never leave off in some way reproaching her, never give up trying to make her pay for it, a man whom Eva won't know how to look straight in the eye or call by his name, with whom she can't imagine on what basis daily life will be able to begin again and proceed, a man—however strange, however unjust it seems to Pablo and even to Elia, after this heroic sacrifice of his, his spectacular renunciation—that Eva will never again entirely forgive either, because how can she forgive his reducing her to this miserable state, his raising in front of her this terrible mirror where she sees herself as a monster, grotesque, unrecognizable, how is she going to forgive him for those days and more days, imprisoned on the cot, hating herself and despising herself and wanting to die, just as she will never forgive Elia the touchy, Elia the hair-splitting who hasn't been capable of interposing herself between the two of them, of breaking the mirrors, of getting her out of this bed and taking her to the other end of the world, to avoid however possible Eva's reaching these ultimate levels of depression and grief because right now Elia will have heard the discussion, the words that have crossed between the two of them, before Pablo's exit, and she will no doubt have discreetly closed her bedroom door, and she will be wondering perhaps how her friend could have sunk so low, how she could have lost to such a degree her sense of decorum and respect for herself, planning a study or a poem about the misery and profound grief of the human condition, or of woman's condition, or of the wife's condition to be even more precise, assigning points to them, to Pablo and to Eva, and also to herself, as if they were undergoing an exam, and perhaps it's people like Elia who are guilty for her having spent her life taking exams, up to her ass and with her tongue hanging out in a grotesque effort to live up to the circumstances or to herself or to the absurd image that others had fantasized for her, and now she has flunked, zero for effort, zero for conduct, and it turns out she hasn't lived up to anything, and there's not going to be a third or a fourth or a fifth chance, and even if there were, it wouldn't matter, since Eva wouldn't take the exam again, this is over now, and it's very possible that Elia the exquisite, Elia the dubious, Elia the extravagant, the narcissistic adorer of her own navel, the supreme priestess of love and truth, or what she has decided to establish for everyone as love and truth, is right after all (Elia who has no doubt shut herself in her room, sorrowful and ashamed, embarrassed that Pablo and, above all, she have been capable of behaving like this, terrified when faced with this lack of dignity and style, too prudent to intervene, to cast everything aside, starting with her principles and her shame and her eternal and so useless preoccupation of fixing the limits of the channels of reason and of justice—as if someone could claim to be right in that type of ambling—too discreet to burst into the room and take sides and scream at Pablo that he's a miserable jerk, get hoarse from screaming that he's been behaving like an asshole, throw him out into the street just from yelling at him, and get her however she can, out of this bed, with blows or with caresses, it doesn't matter, just so that she makes her understand that, outside all justice and against all reason or lack of reason, above or below all the defects of style and the failures in conduct or in urbanity, she loves her and is her friend), surely Elia's right, like so many other times, and she has lost the most remote sense of dignity, the slightest spark of respect for herself, she's lost forever the right to the sash of honor because of failing every class one after the other, surely she's never been so marvelous or so strong or so responsible or so anything, and she's like many other women, like almost all of them, a woman who very soon will be forty and can't bear the image of her husband in bed with another girl, and goes crazy with miserable jealousy, with uncontrolled fury, and commits against others, but above all against herself, the worst idiocies, and maybe it's not even for love, she's not at all sure that she loves him that much, but above all because she has an uncontrollable dread of solitude, a terrible fear they'll abandon her, her friend and her husband, and leave her alone, on the edge, forever alone and abandoned and without love.

N ow the trapdoor has finally closed over her head, and everything is darkness and uproar as if everything had been turning at once and their voices merged into an unbearable howl, and Clara sinks into a sticky and damp molasses with no hope of ever touching bottom, and her suffering has overflowed (it overflowed a few days ago, when she arrived at the house and found Eva in bed, secluded in her room, and she couldn't go in and see her because Eva didn't want to see her—"she doesn't want to see anyone," Elia said to console her, but it wasn't true, because Elia herself and Pablo and the children do go into the room—and she knew that something terrible had happened during her absence that they didn't want to tell her about, Pablo doesn't even talk to her, he doesn't even say good morning, while he wanders somberly through the house, like a big, awkward husband-cat who ruminates on the offenses of destiny, with a manifest desire to kill someone (it could well be her), the children because they don't know or maybe they do know and act as if they don't, and carry on their normal life, always outside, and Elia— she's not sure—maybe she didn't want to tell her so as not to hurt her more—as if it were still possible to hurt her more— and instead of answering her questions she just said: "why did you tell her? why didn't you leave when I told you to?" and Clara doesn't feel like explaining to her that she didn't leave because she couldn't and when she told Eva what was happening, what everyone but she knew, she never suspected that it could upset her like this, unleash such a degree of madness, such unjustified desperation, "why has she gotten like this? how can she care so much that a guy like Pablo, whom she surely doesn't even love, has a sordid affair with an idiotic girl?" and Elia "it's not that simple, Clara, it seems it's not that simple," and Clara thought that actually things were very simple for her, if you love someone you put your life in their hands, and anything that affects the other person or that the other person does has infinite repercussions and importance for you, if you don't love the other person, what he or she does, says, or suffers hardly affects you, it's that simple, because love is a terrible illness—if I get out of this love alive, she promised herself, I'll never fall in love again—that leaves us unarmed, helpless, paralyzed, in an upside-down world, that makes us clumsy at the exact moment we need to be graceful, when we need our intelligence, because if I hadn't loved her so much and perhaps so badly, if I had been able to control my feelings, things would have worked better between us from the beginning), and now the suffering has overflowed its limits, Clara's limits of resistance, and beyond the pain there is no longer really pain, only this strange sensation of sinking into darkness, into viscosity, into a clamor, or of having remained trapped inside a crystal ball, and everyone else—if they exist, if they are more than mere shadows—is outside and far away, irremediably lost, unreachable, like the passersby who walk along the cemetery's paths and even let some flowers fall, but whom it's useless to call to explain to them that everything is so damp and so cold, that everything is so full of black cockroaches and hairy spiders, and the hallway that leads to all horrors is very long and she advances, slippery, heart in her mouth, fleeing the doorways, each time further away from the room where the low lamps are still on, the

203

smell of starch, the women's voices, the warmth of the
brazier, so far away that—she discovers now—it's not possible
to recuperate it ever again, because there's no longer any road
on which to recede, and that house and this house, and the
pretty cat owners who leave the windows open at night, the
women of smoke and light who lower the drawbridges of
enchanted castles, the snake women who harass her without
respite, and without love, have turned out in the end to be the
same, so alike, like emerging from a well and glimpsing the
light only to fall once again into the well, and to have learned
that the light is an unattainable mirage, a brief parenthesis in
the darkness, so real, of the well, and now the last telegraph
cable has broken, the last telephone line, the last and very
fragile bridge between herself and others, and there's no possibility of calling or asking for help, and she sinks alone into a
tumultuous and dark and endless viscosity, and this is no
longer really pain, and an irremediable fatigue invades her
like a dream, like laziness—everything becomes irremediable
when one reaches this state—and the effort has been so intense
and so hard and so painful, she has put so much of herself
("what for?" Eva, skeptical, would perhaps ask, if she deigned
to consider her still as a problem, trying to verify for what
reasons Clara has botched so many and such excellent possibilities, "what have you struggled for and what according to
you have you suffered so much for?" and she would have to
accept that for nothing, nothing that the other woman could
understand, to reach a very very high and luminous window
and cross through it and approach the fireplace, to escape
from herself for the first time and establish—through Eva—
contact with others, to open up like a flower, to ripen like a
fruit, and fruits only ripen in love, and the corollas only open
for love, "only for you to let me love you, be near you," and
Eva would have said crossly and demythifyingly, liquidating the
question as always with one stroke of her temper, "it's not true,
you wanted everything, nothing would have seemed enough
to you," and maybe talking like that, Clara recognizes, Eva

would have been very right), and everything has been useless from the beginning, everything was condemned to the most absolute failure even before the beginning, it's only been a lamentable misunderstanding, "I'm very sorry, Clara, really, and I think it's been mostly my fault," the voice of an invisible Eva has said from the back of the bedroom and from the shadows, and Clara, squinting in an attempt to discover her in the darkness, to see her one last time, since there's no longer any doubt that this is a good-bye, and Eva's is an uncomfortable and bristling voice, as if she were doing violence to herself in order to speak, as if she had to conquer an initial rejection and were proceeding only impelled by her damn sense of duty, of equity and of justice, while in Clara the certainty deepens that Eva has never understood anything, that she's never had the slightest idea how she was inside or of what was happening, that not once has she really looked at her and listened to her, but rather that she first brought her to this house and now is throwing her out of it for reasons equally gratuitous and arbitrary, "I'm very sorry, Clara, but the way things are"—and how would she know how things are or what things are at stake?—"maybe it would be better for you to go back to your house," Eva has said in this craggy and difficult voice, divided between her bad conscience and the repulsion Clara incites in her, and at this moment the trapdoor has shut over her head, and even though she'd been expecting it for days, and she knew that it would inevitably happen, so evident is it that Eva can't stand her, incapable of forgiving that it was she who formulated in words what everyone knew, who risked saying out loud that Pablo was cheating on her, and not because she blames her—as she could blame her—but because Clara's image has remained bound to those moments, to that revelation, monstrous for Eva, and in all that summer storm, when it ends, her marriage with Pablo will come out hurt but still standing, her friendship with Elia will come out weakened but undamaged, and in sum, Clara will have been the only one expelled, sacrificed,

chosen as scapegoat or as victim—she and that other girl
whom she has already stopped hating—even though she was
expecting it then, and knew it was going to happen and has
been trying to prepare herself for days to face the blow, now
that it has really happened, it has caught her by surprise in a
way, and she feels that the trapdoor has closed inexorably
above her, and she notices that the pain, that well-known
feeling, immediately recognizable and labeled, that admits
gradations and ups and downs and attenuations, with which
it's possible in a way to agree upon and temporize, against
which there exist tricks and recourses, has vanished and been
replaced by a dreadful feeling, with no possible gradations or
nuances, total, and Eva has said something about didn't she
want to give her a good-bye kiss, and that later on, when she's
back in the city, they can see each other sometimes—that
stupid executioner's pity—but Clara is already out of the
room, although she doesn't really know how she's left, she
doesn't remember or imagine herself at the moment she
turned around and crossed through the doorway—crossing to
the outside through the window that closes behind her—only
that she's there with Elia, in the entryway and the summer sun
beats fiercely down on the curtains and the birds sing wildly,
and Elia shakes her, gently at first, then roughly, she seizes her
by the shoulders and hurts her—strange that a shadow woman
would have such strength and those strong hands—Elia
makes her sit down in one of those ridiculous chairs with
straight and rigid backs, chairs to receive visitors in country
houses, and they almost never enter this cold, impersonal and
strange room, Elia looks her in the eye, for the first time she
looks her straight in the eye, she's talking to her—why is it
that even in these moments when she has no one to run to, no
one to confide in, not a single person in the entire world willing to become interested in her, whom she can ask for help or
tell what's happening (although what use is it at this point to
tell anything?), Elia's figure, that shakes her and looks at her
and talks to her, keeps seeming so blurred and distant and even

unlikeable?—Elia shakes her by the shoulders and scrutinizes her with her gaze and talks a lot even though she does nothing more than go over and over the same thing: "you have loved another person and this other person hasn't loved you, you see, and this is not the end of the world, there are thousands of people that this happens to, it's a simple story, as Sagan would say, who I think you liked so much, remember, you have loved her and she has never loved you, 'c'est tout,' remember, do you understand, Clara, 'c'est une histoire simple, il n'y a pas de quoi faire la grimace,' it's happened to many people before you, it's happening to many people, it's happening to many of us," and here Elia laughs, and Clara thinks that it's not possible, that nothing like what's happening to her can ever be happening to this strange woman, and nevertheless she is right about something, she repeats to herself, as she leaves the parlor and the house, and Elia looks at her, worried, vacillates, lets her leave, as she walks alone through the streets and doesn't even remotely know where she's going, she only knows she can't go back, that she'll never return to that house, and that she'll never return to her relatives' house either, to that house Eva now suddenly calls "your house" as if she'd forgotten that it never resembled a home, that it was never "hers" at all, as if she had ever had a house, as if stray cats who wander along rooftops, skinny and sad, ever had a house, although this was just one more foolishness, all those stories about cats and dead people and women of smoke and snake women and frog men, a heap of foolishness, of childish fantasies even she's never believed in, and didn't get her anywhere, because everything is very simple, that's where Elia is right, everything is surprisingly simple, Clara has loved someone very much, and this someone has never loved her at all, "c'est tout," as Sagan would say, only that if it's like that—and she knows it is—Clara can't go on, Clara doesn't want to keep living, and she doesn't care if it's happened to thousands or millions of other people before, she's indifferent that it's happening to them now or that it will happen to them in centuries to come, it's no use, she doesn't care one bit, because it's not a matter of statistics or of founding a league of unloved lovers, and there's no solidarity or identification possible, and the only thing Clara knows with certainty is that she has loved Eva with all her soul, with all her heart, with all her mind, with all her skin, above all perhaps with all her skin, and that Eva definitely doesn't love her, irrevocably she'll never love her now, very simple, c'est tout, as it is also very simple that she can't bear it and doesn't want to survive in a world without Eva, and she walks now through the streets very quickly, her tearless eyes fixed on a distant and undefined point, like those stray dogs, also condemned to death, that have always obsessed and moved her, those abandoned street dogs infinitely more lost than the stray cats, much more defenseless and dependent and desperate, those poor dogs, more straight-lined and speedy (more lame too) as they feel more frightened, as they know they're more disoriented and lost, as if they wanted to hide that they have nowhere to go, that there's no house to return to, or that they've been thrown out forever and they can't go back now, and so there's no hope for them, for her, no way out, only walking and walking, walk while you can, as long as your feet hold you up, your breath lasts, with a grave face and a resolved attitude—as if someone really were waiting for you somewhere, as if someone were missing you, when all that's waiting for you are the wheels of the car that will crush you against the asphalt—in some way the race will finally have ended, a way out will have arisen—or the rope, worse, of the dogcatchers who will take you to a harder and dirtier and more bitter death.

I'm going to get you Daniel I promised you I would and now I'm going to get you it's a magnificent evening the beginning of dusk of a day crazed with light that whitish dazzling blinding excessive light that I can't take that makes me find shelter in closed interiors protect my eyes with dark sunglasses that acquires as it dims with the end of the afternoon an unusual splendor a suspension of gold and the air is quiet like a sigh and in the background always in the background of all my landscapes the blue sea and I would like the hillsides to be covered with Spanish broom as they were once years ago I don't know if you've ever noticed how beautiful the yellow of the Spanish broom is on luminous days of quiet air and blue sea but that other time a long time ago now and you weren't with us nor had you even been born yet and it wasn't summer of course because neither the Spanish broom nor the mimosas another yellow splendor dimmed as the excessive sun dims on August evenings flower at this time of year but even without the yellow flowers of Spanish broom on the hillsides the evening is magnificent and I like it what silliness to go get you on an evening like this so immobile so beautiful having the sea all along the road to my right the same sea your father is right when he laughs sometimes and says that I'm rotten with litera-ture since really it's not very important whether the evening is one way or another and that we meet each other you and I in one or another place and nevertheless for me it has a perhaps ritual meaning perhaps symbolic or maybe merely aesthetic pure whim to be careful about the decor pure fancy for the events to develop in appropriate places and it's possible that throughout the years traveling has been for me nothing but carefully choosing backdrops for love scenes in which to situate like in a painting or on a stage the figure of your father loving me or my figure loving him and those trips that made you so mad because the two of us would go and we'd leave you alone were only another pretext to try out my senses of taste touch hearing smell in different places finding again on the way like on a sacred pilgrimage the reference points of other moments of our lives together and it was during years and more years from before you were born until now until I don't know exactly when maybe a few months ago or a few days maybe it began a long time before I even realized or maybe it's not finished happening yet I don't know how it was as if nothing but Jorge could interest me as if nothing that wasn't tied to him could interest me in visiting or knowing or experiencing or discovering as if everything came to me through him about him I don't know if you can understand as if your father were the mirror that reflected me and I existed only in the reflection my real corporeal solid three-dimensional me reduced to a simple pretext for the image Miguel says that instead of making love the center of my world I made a mistake and reduced the entire world to being the center of my love and this or something very similar must have happened and so when your father left me when the image in the mirror broke when I lost love I was left with nothing or that's what I thought at least with nothing including you and writing because even my writing even though Eva and Pablo are right and it did exist in me before knowing him as a way of conjuring away death making fears flee exorcising ghosts mitigating solitude it existed as my only possible defense against horror because other people when something happens to them something wounds them something hurts them pray or drink or take drugs or beat someone up or go to the country or feel sorry for themselves in someone's arms or are bewildered in a thousand ways but for me the only possible reaction to the horror and the horror is so many things the horror is that people die and aren't happy and that you yourself have to die and aren't happy because I never was really happy before I knew Jorge and happiness seemed to me for years another one of those cruel lies they deceive and confuse us with to make us quiet to force us to say yes and besides one's own and others' and always inevitable death besides the fact that almost never does anyone achieve happiness and no one understanding anything and no one explaining anything there was the injustice and the violence and the strong trampling the weak maybe also in an attempt to confront death like that trampling relentlessly monotonously without ceasing throughout history filling the fissures of time all the spaces of the planet the strong trampling the weak without respite or pity and the weak dreaming of becoming strong to be able to then trample injustice violence brutality hunger death the suffering of children who don't understand anything who suffer without understanding you know Daniel that the worst for me what I can't stand without interposing screens of drunkenness or madness between myself and lucidity is that people or children or animals because first I believed it was only animals or children but then I learned that adults also suffer like this absolutely defenseless and without understanding with that astonished incredulous fascinated look that I can't bear without wanting to die and many years ago I saw a picture in a magazine I don't know in what country of Latin America it was but the rumor had gone around that there was rabies or another similar epidemic I don't remember and then to top it off it turned out not to be true but even if it had been that wouldn't have changed anything in the picture for me because in the picture there was a little boy maybe seven years old a badly dressed little boy sitting on the sidewalk and hugging a dog very still both of them very calm without even one gesture defenseless in a total way totally incapable of defending themselves of escaping incapable of understanding that was the terrible part of the picture it captured the precise moment when in his look still veiled by incomprehension and incredulity the horror insinuated itself as two men approached one from each end of the street with clubs ready to beat the dog to death it's only a picture I know and everything ended a long time ago but the grave thing is that things like that occur to thousands every day in an endless chain that will end only when the history of man on earth ends and silence is made and in a way the only possible peace begins and sometimes a dog dies and sometimes men die and sometimes children die and nothing is justified or redeemed or explained once faith in a provident God is definitely lost hope in an improbable communion of saints so much death and so much suffering invading everything and oneself paralyzed in the horror of excessive lucidity impossible to do anything or almost anything and before I knew

Jorge I could only write faced with what hurt me which was almost everything with what I didn't understand which was everything faced with so so many things that made me feel like killing because writing is my spontaneous visceral un-learned reaction faced with evil not better or worse than others I suppose and that's why I wrote before I knew your father and Eva and Pablo are right when they assure that I didn't begin to write for him that it wasn't he who gave me my voice and words and that I would have kept writing anyway with Jorge or without Jorge maybe actually because I don't know how to do anything else nor do I know how to defend myself any other way but it's also true that I have only written for him basically for him since the day I met him because from that moment on and until a short while ago writing was for me above all one more way of getting close and explaining myself to Jorge why would I want to explain myself to anyone else writing was one of the elements of our game played by two never I'm sorry Daniel by three because in order to get to Jorge the roads seemed few to me and I had to invent them and because poetry gave me the possibility of telling him some things that I didn't ever dare tell him directly face to face since I have in me a certain modesty that I've never com-pletely conquered even with your father and the fact that what I wrote for him turned into a book was published in the form of a book and got favorable reviews sometimes adverse others and even that it sold always seemed to me an absurd blunder that my books should sell that a few people who weren't Jorge who weren't even our friends who didn't even know me would go into a store and ask for them or choose them from the shelves and leave their good money at the cash register or on the counter and take away a wrapped copy under their arm I've never seen it you know I never saw any-one buying a book of mine and maybe that's why I can't believe it pure fallacy like so many others mere fiction among fictions just like I've almost never recognized myself either in what the critics say against me or in my favor and I feel like interrupting them don't bother please gentlemen there's been a mistake this isn't for you this wasn't meant for you nor for those unknown people who, deceived, buy copies in bookstores actually they should have stamped on the cover written only so that Jorge will read it but your father was happy with my books and with the sales and with the reviews or at least it seemed so to me and perhaps I invented it to find new stimuli and incentives to work who knows but it seemed to me he became proud and content and smiled at me and patted my back like his favorite greyhound who won all the races and if I had insisted on convincing him that it was a misunderstanding and my poems were in no way literature but rather naked gestures of love it's possible he wouldn't have liked that although certainly your father has loved me very much and I believe him when he tells me in his letter that he'd never loved anyone as much before nor will he love anyone like that in the future very firm very strong very complete your father's love for me very superior probably to my crazy absurd love in which I wanted to redeem all my fears all my failures so so many frustrations so much fear for years of never being really loved really understood so much fear of never living as a couple and of not being capable of living alone maybe to this is due the disproportionate the excessive the absurd qualities of my surrender of my centering everything on him and this made him uncomfortable and sick sometimes and now I think that your father would have preferred that I love him not less but indeed in a different way or that he began to prefer it once the first two or three years had passed and I'm almost sure that the certainty that I was writing for him would have been more bothersome than flattering to him the conviction that this wasn't one of my exalted and novelesque fantasies but a literal truth and really the truth was that I wrote before I knew him as a conjuration as an exorcism as a defense always in self-defense so that the dread of having to die and that others had to die didn't annihilate me the dread of the total uncertainty about what can happen to us in the

next instant the dread of so much pain accumulated throughout time around the world and which seemed to weigh heavily
sometimes all together in my breast because I was more fragile
more sensitive more foolish because I was born perhaps worse
equipped to live more inclined therefore to accept living on
dreams as the true way since reality seemed too terrible to
bear too terrible for any human being to lucidly assume and I
believe that until I met your father until the moment of the
night when I met your father I always thought it would have
been a thousand times better not to have been born not to
exist as a human being on the planet earth I believe I had never
seriously said yes to life but then your father appeared Jorge
appeared and he took me as he passed by just as you snatch a
white flower off a hedge covered with flowers and he took
me with him and everything was so fast so unexpected for me
since I had never dared you know hope for so much that I
didn't even have time to react or to think he decided everything for me and in a few seconds in very few words we'll see
each other every day for our entire lives he said that first night
when we hadn't even slept together yet when we hadn't even
made love and we knew nothing about each other and in a few
seconds with hardly any words everything was said everything agreed upon everything sealed and then I learned and I
still believe it in spite of everything and against everything I
still believe it I learned that certainly man's existence on earth
is atrocious in many ways in many many moments but that
with all certainty love only love is as strong as death can raise
up against death like a banner in flames like a sacred ensign
only love is strong and terrible like death and however much
it's true that in the end death has necessarily to win the match
before this end there can exist some spaces of time in which
life transfigured into love triumphs over death and in the
beginning during the first weeks I slept with your father I
would wake up sometimes in the night more afraid even than
before knowing him since for the first time I now had something very valuable to lose something extraordinary which

they couldn't divest me of and I would wake him I don't want to die and your father would hold me tighter and cradle me don't be afraid silly we'll never die and that was enough for me because around your father there was a halo of security a space and I'm referring to an almost physical space in which nothing bad could happen to us and I was safe from everything even dying but then later much later further on I understood and I didn't wake up frightened in the middle of the night anymore I didn't tell him I don't want to die anymore because in your father's arms in the love with your father there was such an intensity such a plenitude of life that death lacked importance and after making love with your father I've never known anything like it I believe there's nothing in the world that can be compared to it nothing like the love between a man and a woman who love each other afterwards I was at peace with everything reconciled with the entire universe ready to accept even the inevitability of death and for the first time in my life I said I don't know to whom I don't know to what exactly if to God or to life or to reality or to dreams I said yes and still now Daniel even in this moment in which divested of everything I'm going to meet you as though to a meeting with a stranger if there were anything I could desire for you something I could deserve for you from the fairies or destiny I would desire this because I've never known anything that can be compared to it and I don't believe it exists and from then on I no longer wrote against death against horror I no longer wrote in self-defense nor in defense of anyone since death had lost quality and entity and even likelihood and there was no need then to protect myself once the marvel of living as a couple was discovered my fears annulled my ghosts scared away by the marvel of two people confronting them that someone would fight at my side elbow to elbow and cover my flanks or the retreat and there was no point I couldn't reach no goal I couldn't attain if your father was with me and covered me and then also for the first time I could say yes to myself I could accept myself as I was because really what I was or wasn't had no importance from the moment your father had chosen me as he passed by like someone who snatches a rose and he had chosen me as his and the writing metamorphosed then into another form of loving another road by which I could get closer to Jorge because he has been for years the only road by which everything came to me and it seemed to me for years that the roads that led to him and to be able to love him more were few and there was no other road nor any other way superior to writing until you came until I invented you to love him better to be able to love him in zones I'd never been able to reach that always escaped me all those years before our meeting in which he existed and wasn't with me years to which I hadn't found a road that I missed as something very much my own and very lost because the present wasn't enough for me not even the future to love him and I wanted to love and accompany him in his past too when he was an adolescent when he was a young man and even further back when he was a little boy and maybe this has been the most dangerous of my dreams the craziest of my multiple crazy fantasies in which so so many things besides were mixed because to have a child to conceive lucidly and fearfully and voluntarily a child was to assume the most immeasurable of risks it was to undoubtedly surrender hostages to destiny but it was also the most rotund evident and unrenounceable way of saying yes to life yes to death yes to the adventure of the human race on the planet earth it was to participate fully in the grand game of which before I had always wanted to be outside and you were for me above all a magical route to recuperate your father in the past to have him as a little boy and you were then the best means that I had at my disposal that any man has at his disposal to say yes to life and before I as a poet had always claimed that mirrors and copulation are abominable since they reproduce us and multiply us always until I met your father and in him a man who didn't seem abominable to multiply and whose image it no longer seemed abominable to reproduce and I wanted so so much during the

216

pregnancy for you to look a lot like him that you didn't resemble him at all nor me at all scared to find again in the child my skinniness my perplexities my fears my lack of capacity for real life and when you were finally born and doctors and nuns and nurses came in the room to assure me that it had been months since such a big blond strong beautiful boy had been born impossible to foresee in the baby the skinny ugly ungainly adolescent you now are and I felt content and flattered and a little embarrassed and when the pediatrician commented that such a degree of resemblance to the father was strange and unusual and aunts and cousins took pictures of Jorge as a child out of their purses and wallets and you were indeed so alike in everything when Jorge hugged me tight next to your cradle and told me that now he had done everything he'd wanted to do in life that now he could die peacefully and he said it laughing and I silenced his mouth with kisses because we were fortunate and we weren't thinking at all of death the enemy death relegated to the most remote confines of reality more than ever unlikely and improbable I thought too that everything had been correctly fulfilled and happily carried out but before you there had existed no other form superior to writing to get close to Jorge to love him better and upon meeting him I put my poems my love where before I had raised a defense against death and in this need to interpose barricades or curtains of smoke between us and our death it seems to me that we humans are after all very similar and the most realistic the hardest the harshest the strongest the least propensed and inclined as your father would say to vain literature to vain fantasies the least in appearance worried or fearful share really we all share when we wake up perhaps startled in the night the same basic and elemental fear of dying and we perhaps do nothing throughout life but raise whatever we can erect whatever we can between ourselves and death whatever pretext capable of making us forget we're mortal capable of making us obsessed to such a point to hurt us to such a point as long as the certainty of death is erased and some interpose the desire for money for prestige for fame as if fortune celebrity the respect of everyone could protect them and others interpose more noble and generous and humanitarian ideals and those who commit suicide interpose their suicide between themselves and their horror of dying and believers the lucky ones interpose their provident God their communion of saints their eternal life and there are some who interpose risk and living dangerously risking their lives fearlessly for whatever reason they are likewise conjuring away their terror of death and I first interposed literature because in my indigence I had no other better and more firm barricades at my disposal and then I extracted literature from those shackles and I replaced it with love and since then everything has been resolved for me between these two unique and opposite poles face to face love and death which are distributed in successive avatars in successive advances and retrogressions the battlefield that is my life so that the terrain that love abandons that love doesn't cover is immediately invaded by death and maybe that is one of the reasons why love has always occupied a place in my life that seems excessive to others the reason why everything else has been reduced to being the center of love even you even my poems and you were never for me not even in the first moment I imagined you as possible a recourse as I know children are for other people a barricade against death an attempt to perpetuate themselves and survive in some way as by delegation and achieve that way the deceptive triumph that something of theirs remains alive on the earth when they've died you were never this I didn't imagine you ever as a prolongation of myself maybe as a prolongation of Jorge perhaps the truth is that you were together with my writing the best road to arrive at the man I loved you were together with my writing the most precious thing in this world that I nevertheless reduced to being only the center of my love taking on the risk of losing it along with love as I in fact believed I'd lost it this summer upon losing love untied from everything incapable of writing incapable in a way I'm sorry Daniel incapable of thinking about you as yourself of disassociating my love for you from the love I had felt for Jorge because it's incomprehensible that during this entire summer the possibility of taking you with me when I leave never even once occurred to me gradually more and more sure that I would leave although I didn't know where to because I wasn't capable either of projecting my own image into an unlikely future in which I would be alone and without him expelled this summer from the flow of time ousted from myself suspended above nothingness above not-being above a dreadful void just like death with that strange sensation that the movie had ended for me and it was senseless to keep sitting in the audience like an idiot with that strange calling I suddenly had to become a stone or a lizard a stone polished by the waves until its soul was pulled out and dragged on shore a drowsy lizard that dreams it's a vegetal trunk covered with algae final moldy residue of the last shipwreck and I now know I recognize that the loss of love is always hard bitter sad that its end is always painful for everyone and surely much more so for women so accustomed so tamed and in that I'm not strange or exceptional tamed and constrained and forced from when we're little girls to put our personal experience at the service of another and perhaps it's even worse for the women who are beginning like Eva like me to get old and have shut behind them that magnificent space of life in which one seems capable of doing everything of handling everything of conquering everything of rebuilding everything once again from nothing and who become more and more dependent and perhaps it's even worse even harder for those women who reach thirty thirty-five as we did with the firm certainty of not having to worry ever again about the problems of solitude because at our side was a man who loved us and he would remain there for whatever was left to us of life as a guarantee and endorsement of so many things and it's not true that I can't understand Eva understand other women that I can't in any way realize what it meant for her to discover that Pablo was with that girl how much she feared the peril of losing and which she wanted at all costs to safeguard at any price maintain as she has maintained it finally they've both maintained at a price that I don't know if they'll be able to pay in a mortgaged future because the life of so many years in common the children in common and friends habits security the fear of seeing themselves alone the fear even of playing an unattractive role in the grand farce of being made fools of of figuring forever on the long list of failures of losers of the ones hardly skilled in the job of living was at stake and so so many things it seems were at stake and neither Eva nor Pablo wanted to lose them partly because they believe that if one hasn't lost everything one hasn't lost anything and they knew with certainty that they couldn't have lost everything that at no moment had they risked it and therefore they couldn't have lost but for me the game had been somewhat different more naive more foolish more total also and I don't know at what point I began to tell myself and tell others the beautiful story of a silly and ugly and frightened and grey little girl who had nothing who had never been happy and who found everything including happiness upon finding love the beautiful flattering story that your father and I had invented love on earth the fascinating story that no one had loved each other before as we were loving each other and I don't know either at what point Jorge who had helped pleased and solicitous in fabulating it who had been stubborn in establishing it who had chosen enthusiastically to share it stopped believing in it deep down stopped telling it to himself and telling me he abandoned it for good whereas I on the contrary kept repeating it to myself for too long a time alone and it's grotesque to tell oneself those stories when nobody shares them anymore and it wasn't at the beginning of this summer but long long before at the precise moment when he stopped believing in our beautiful love story fabulated by the two of us sustained by the two of us it was then that he abandoned me although I didn't even realize it I didn't want to or I couldn't realize it stubbornly living my dreams to the end stubbornly denying that this way of mine of loving was suddenly seeming or had gradually been seeming exhausting and excessive to your father and everything was I suppose badly assembled in the air or in dreams from the beginning or perhaps not I don't know it depends what one pursues what one looks for and maybe for what I wanted the story had to be like that because I wanted everything you know I wouldn't settle for less than the moon and whatever the price was later the truth is that I had it I had the moon in my hands and no one will be able to convince me that having it wasn't worth the pain I had it for years and years because Jorge gave it to me in an instant with five words when he said every day our whole lives and he didn't take it away until much later also in an instant and with very few words hasn't it occurred to you that we may have stopped loving each other and no Daniel it hadn't occurred to me that we could stop loving each other because loving each other was a first principle which any subsequent reasoning supported loving each other was the base on which the world and my vision of the world was established loving each other was at the root at the very root of my existence and when this love ceased or my certainty of this love or my blind faith in this love all the complicated scaffolding of my life had necessarily to fall apart and everything did fall apart come crashing down and I repeat that it couldn't have been any other way because if for Eva or for Pablo or for the other poet for Miguel he who hasn't lost everything hasn't lost anything for me on the other hand and for those who live like I do he who has lost a part has irremediably lost everything since everything was united and scrambled and together and there are bids in which bargaining is not conceivable there are wagers which admit no raising or lowering and you either have the moon or you don't and if someone has gone to get it for you at the top of the sky or the last circle of hell and has put it whole into your hands beautiful pale moon of the most radiant full moon and then he comes and takes it away we can't negotiate please leave me a piece you have to open your arms and let the moon escape skidding swiftly dizzyingly once again up to the highest part of the sky and I don't know what I'll do now never as today on this last day of August when I'm going to get you along the coastal highway next to the sea have I been so empty of plans so empty of certain images to project into a future I don't know what I'll do and it's possible that at other moments with other men I too will accept more cautious commitments more prudent wagers but no one must speak then at all of the moon you don't build companies where some contribute the capital and others manage it with calculated risks if what you want is the moon and I wanted the moon and I asked for it and someone brought it to me and then I lost it and there I stood aghast incredulous divested in the middle of the ruins everything in ruins around me a world in ruins betrayed to such a point abandoned to such a point that it couldn't matter in the least whether or not there were other women in Jorge's life what the hell were they talking to me about it didn't even matter whether he had really stopped loving me or whether he had brandished the doubt hasn't it occurred to you et cetera in a fit of exasperation of temper maybe of spite it didn't matter in the least either that as Miguel predicted since my first visit and friends later supported and has been confirmed now with his letter that Jorge would want perhaps in the end to keep living with me or with you or with both of us he would want to save perhaps those realities so valuable so concrete and unrenounceable that couples save from the ruins including the English porcelain coffee service that grandmother gave us as a wedding present those realities those possessions that Pablo and Eva have now saved from their particular disaster good-bye to the redhead who cried so much and had loved him so much but who undoubtedly will remake her life she's so young and so beautiful because at this point of the story Pablo keeps believing in the superior power of very beautiful women who haven't turned twenty yet and who trample it seems harder than anyone and now it's a desire to keep believing Clara returned to her place of origin with some scratches on her soul certain bruises on her body because clumsy to the end stubbornly doing everything wrong she didn't hurl herself in front of a train she only let herself foolishly be run over by a motorcycle not enough to kill her but enough to let herself be led later defenseless and without protesting stupefied by the collision and by the analgesics to her aunt and uncle's house and now Eva and Pablo are collecting and restoring together the remains of the disaster but nothing of that matters in my case not even that I still love him more or less that it's more or less hard to go on without him accept the definitive death of my dreams or of my most beautiful dream drag myself out of the ruins and reconstruct alone with nails and teeth a minimal shelter where I can take refuge and from which I continue and it doesn't matter how long it still takes me to really assume to the end a life without Jorge assume that I'm now entering the final stretch and the crazed steeds gallop around me kicking furiously attacking each other spitting foam from between their teeth neighing impatiently or frightened because we have entered the final stretch and we all suspect now that we've been cruelly cheated that we're competing for nothing that there won't be a winner there won't be a prize at the finish line nobody who crowns us with laurel who makes us sit to the right of the father we all know now that when we arrive at the end we will find only a somewhat higher fence and on the other side the void the tumbling straight down into the void amid desperate neighing and the crunching of teeth and kicking uselessly we all know now that we're running terrified towards death and at our side others like us run aggravated corrupted infuriated and there isn't for them or for yourself or for anyone the most remote possibility of escaping there's no possibility of pausing of asking for a time-out of detaining one single instant that hurled and uncontainable gallop that sweeps us along in a whirlwind of noise and fury all that's left perhaps in the final stretch is the pleasure of running elegantly galloping in the best style for our own satisfaction not in the least because we can no longer do anything else and in this final stretch Daniel which a long time ago I understood as inevitable I always thought that I would run with someone that I would feel your father's warm breath against my skin that we would mix sweat and agony it would have been very beautiful very comforting to run with someone as two jump as two towards the void or simply know that someone was loving you and galloping at your side flank to flank skin to skin and I don't know if this is even possible I don't know if it's ever happened throughout time I've never seen it around me but it would be beautiful it's something in any case that's worth struggling for worth trying to achieve and I made in a way the only wager I consider valid the only honest wager the only sensible wager what else can you ask of love what else can you ask without feeling ashamed of a man in the name of love but this profound solidarity faced with pain and faced with death and I probably played badly and it's true that I lost but I want you to know that my wager was this and that at no moment would I have settled for less because bargains and rebates don't exist for those of us who ask for the moon and now I'm bruised bewildered maybe lame and it's probably because I'm not even a fine-blooded mare a thoroughbred mare and I know that nobody will run at my side after all that nobody will see me fall upon reaching the end and I'm going to run alone and this isn't what I would have wanted nor what I had planned but I'm still alive and I'm going to run I'm going to run in the best way possible without kicking or neighing with the best gallop that my bruised hooves will allow and I think that this was probably inevitable and one always runs alone in the final stretch and I also think that beauty can't trample hard or exercise power it's always gratuitous it's always for nothing it's completed it's fulfilled in itself and I'm going to run a beautiful race for nothing for no one there's no goal there's no prize either there aren't even any spectators but I'm going to run Daniel the best way possible the most beautiful way possible to the end and I want you to know that during the entire summer I was empty hollow exiled from time and from myself incapable of feeling incapable of reacting or of doing incapable even of writing untied from the world because Jorge had been the road by which everything came to me and I had been torn off from the world upon losing him as the road and not even once throughout the summer did I think of being able to take you with me segregated from you as from everything but then you said I want to live with you and it was as if so much blocked love had been excavated in an instant new riverbeds had opened new paths and it was so incredible and so strange so unforeseeable and in that precise instant you stopped being for me someone else's son Jorge's son the little boy I had loved so much and taken care of and pampered and situated in the very center of my life but always as Jorge's son always for Jorge and you turned into a stranger into a skinny and ugly and charming adolescent who laughed at my surprise and at my bewilderment who laughed at me with small eyes that laughter that was born in the depth of your eyes and which was no longer which will never be again your father's laugh but your own laugh an adolescent who seemed to want to protect me this seemed strange to me also that you could protect me when I always had imagined it the opposite way and you are still a boy barely a sketch of an adolescent and in the background was the blue sea as it has now been at my right throughout the entire journey and it pleased me that it should happen on such a beautiful after-noon that you should say it on such a splendid afternoon that the metamorphosis should take place on such a luminous summer afternoon as I'm pleased now that this evening is very beautiful and similar when I'm fulfilling my promise and I'm going to get you and maybe you're waiting for me already next to the fallen trunk because like me you might have a fascina-tion for what is reiterative and ritual the same taste for what is magic and playful and we will both be standing in front of each other laughing from the depth of our eyes and maybe without touching each other like two very close beings unknown to each other whose funereal trails of the Greeks remember those elegant and fine and distant reliefs in which two straightbacked figures look at each other eye to eye and bid farewell or find each other again at the borders of life and death and I will have to learn to know you and we will have to learn to communicate and love each other directly from me to you from you to me without intermediaries and maybe you've been trying to for years maybe you already achieved it a long time ago and I hadn't even realized and I don't know what will become of us what will become of me if I will be able to establish new ties with the world open new roads too if I will find my writing again as I've found you if I will love again sometime nor how a new love will be I don't know anything about anything never in all my life have I known so little have I been so blank so free and floating and available I don't know anything about anything Daniel but I'm alive and I'm running in the race and I'll keep on going alone or accompanied and it's possible that I'll never stop asking for the moon I don't know anything about anything but I'm running towards you I'm going to get you following the line of the same blue sea of all my summers and you know Daniel I'm content really content.

Afterword

Esther Tusquets's *Stranded* (*Varadas tras el último naufragio;* literally, Beached after the Last Shipwreck) is the third novel in a loosely connected trilogy; loosely connected because although the same names reappear (Elia, Jorge, Clara), they do not necessarily refer to the same characters, nor do the stories in one novel continue in the next, as in any conventional trilogy. In fact, Tusquets is not in any way a conventional writer, neither in her style nor in her themes.

The director of a large publishing house (Lumen, in Barcelona) since the 1960s, Tusquets did not publish her own work until 1978, at the age of forty-two. This first novel, *El mismo mar de todos los veranos* (*The Same Sea as Every Summer,* now available in English) could not possibly have appeared during Generalísimo Franco's stifling thirty-six-year dictatorship because of its frank and sympathetic portrayal of a short but happy lesbian relationship between the narrator, a middle-aged woman abandoned by her husband, and Clara, a tender and devoted young woman. Sexuality and eroticism, experienced especially from a female perspective and unmasking the power plays seemingly inherent in a phallic-oriented male desire, also figure at the center of her next novel, *El amor es un juego solitario* (*Love Is a Solitary Game,* also available in English), which appeared in 1979. Elia, again a middle-aged woman of the upper middle class, is bored with her life and seeks amusement in two relationships: one with Ricardo, an initially insecure adolescent she initiates into sex, and the other with Clara, who again in this novel is a devoted young woman in love.

We can see from this brief description of her two earlier novels how important an element eroticism is in Tusquets's work. The post-Franco period in Spain has indeed seen a veritable burgeoning of such previously taboo themes from the pens of women writers. Widely read in Spain and recognized by several Hispanists in this country as the most important woman writer of this period, Tusquets concentrates, in almost all her work, on a profound study of female sexuality in all its aspects from an explicitly female—and feminist—perspective.

Her work, which she herself publishes at Lumen, includes, besides the two novels already mentioned, a collection of short stories, *Siete miradas en un mismo paisaje* (Seven Views of the Same Landscape, 1981), with Sara at different stages of her life the central character; a children's book, *La conejita Marcela* (Marcela the Bunny Rabbit, 1980); a short story called "Las sutiles leyes de la simetría" (The Subtle Laws of Symmetry), which appeared in an anthology of twelve contemporary Spanish women writers (*Doce relatos de mujeres,* Madrid, Alianza Editorial, 1982); and most recently, in 1985, another novel, *Para no volver* (Never to Return), which again has as its protagonist a middle-aged woman of the upper class who narrates her self-exploration through psychoanalysis.

This third novel of the trilogy, *Stranded,* first published in 1980, departs from the previous two in its more optimistic ending as well as in its focus this time on heterosexual eroticism, at least as regards Elia, the main character, and Pablo. It isn't until this novel that Elia will begin to find herself and

228

become a stronger, more self-confident and self-reliant figure. She learns slowly and painfully, during this summer of multicolored pills and peppermint liqueur, not to rely on a man for her identity, nor to resort to a series of casual sexual encounters in order to fill an empty life, as the previous Elias have done. Although sexuality and eroticism are important elements in this novel, most notably in Pablo's narcissistic infatuation with the young redhead he thinks can give him back his own youth and his dream of becoming a writer, as well as in the young Clara's desperate obsession with the unattainable Eva, they do not dominate Elia, and she is thus able to successfully complete her voyage of self-discovery. Pablo and Clara on the other hand will be blinded and overcome by their illicit and omnipotent desires.

The Elia of this novel is more a prisoner of adolescent dreams of love and tales of Prince Charming than of any sexual trammels. And gradually, as she no longer hides from her pain but lets herself experience it fully, she learns to free herself from the seductive clutches of these myths and fairy tales to which women all too often fall victims. A timid, insecure, frightened—and unattractive, she thinks—girl when Jorge came along, she let herself be swept up by him immediately. This Prince Charming and male muse has been her entire world—because it is not easy for her to separate literature from reality—for many years. Only now, middle-aged and with a teenage son, do the myths of eternal love, à la Héloïse and Abelard, loosen their hold on her. No longer encumbered by these self-deluding myths, Elia will begin to accept what we all must accept: our ultimate solitude. And when the book ends, she is ready to face that challenge.

Tusquets's style, as luxuriant and distinctive as her themes, marks her as truly one of the best writers of contemporary Spain. Her language, "a sumptuous, baroque prose rich in suggestive and lyrical images, archetypal metaphors, and literary implications" (as Catherine Bellver described it), captivates the reader with its hypnotic intensity, its unrelenting

229

rhythm. Almost without pauses, her language draws us deeply into the experiences of the four main characters, Elia, Eva, Pablo, and Clara, completely washing away the outer walls of consciousness to reveal the innermost being, the nucleus of the self, in all its raw pain, as when Elia intuits the damage that has been done to her and imagines the terrible wound inflicted, or throes of passion, as when Pablo tries to hold back, then succumbs, to the heaping mountains and over-flowing rivers of the redhead's desire. In the world Tusquets creates, words never lose their magical power. She is indeed a magician, and we are under her spell.

SUSAN E. CLARK

DATE DUE			
APR 2 8 '00			